THE SAVAGE VALLEY

A LOGAN FAMILY WESTERN - BOOK 2

DONALD L. ROBERTSON

Edited by
MELISSA GRAY

Cover Designed by
ELIZABETH MACKEY

CM Publishing

COPYRIGHT

The Savage Valley

CM Publishing

Books@DonaldLRobertson.com

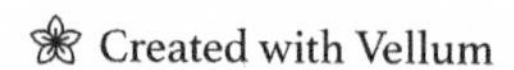

LOGAN FAMILY GENEALOGY

Ethan William Logan, 1779

Married

Rose Isabel Tilman, 1780

CHILDREN

Matthew Christopher Logan, 1797

Mark Adair Logan, 1798

Nathaniel Grant Logan, 1803

Owen Lewis Logan, 1803

Jennifer (Jenny) Isabel Logan, 1812

Floyd Horatio Logan, 1814

Martha Ann Logan, 1816

Matthew Christopher Logan, 1797

Married

Rebecca (Becky) Nicole Doherty, 1810

CHILDREN

William Wallace Logan, 1834

Callum Jeremiah Logan, 1836

Joshua Matthew Logan, 1840

Katherine (Kate) Logan, 1851

Bret Hamilton Logan, 1852

Colin Alexander Logan, 1854

1

Callum Logan heard the scream shortly after the yellow moon climbed above the horizon. Sound traveled far across the plains with only a light wind. It was a woman's scream. Without a second thought, he turned toward the sound.

Upon arriving at the island of trees, he circled the camp and found the wagon tracks. Dismounting, he examined the tracks in the moonlight. They'd been escorted by shod horses, definitely not Indians. The wagon had been traveling alone, which made it easy pickings for Indians or the white scum that preyed on innocent folks just looking for a new chance in life. He'd slipped the leather thong from the hammer of his Colt, loosened the revolver in its holster, and moved the holster to a more comfortable position.

Callum pulled up his horse and sat listening, then eased his .56-56 Spencer from the scabbard and slowly cocked the hammer. He could see the flickering of the fire and could make out several men moving around the flames. The wagon was pulled to one side. He had no idea where the woman was. He felt sure she was not the only innocent, but none were visible. He didn't like the feel of this, but he'd learned from Pa, and experience, that he worked best by pushing. He knew he wasn't an overly smart man, unlike his brother Josh, but what he lacked in smarts, he made up for in action. Most men had to pause and think for a moment. He didn't. He just attacked.

He shouldered the Spencer and put a round into the middle of the campfire. Coals and cinders exploded onto the men. Callum moved his horse a few feet to his left. "You men got a choice. Pull leather and die, or drop your guns. Makes no never mind to me."

"Like hell." The big man next to the wagon grabbed for his Henry rifle that was leaning against the wagon.

Callum put a .56-caliber chunk of lead through the man's belly. The other men froze. The only sound from the camp was the moaning from the man he had shot.

"Ma'am, can you hear me?" Callum called.

"I can."

"Your horses still hitched?"

"Yes, they are."

"Then you best roll that wagon out of there. You boys, stand where you are. I said drop your guns. I'll not be telling you again."

Callum heard a twig break over to his right.

"Get him, boys. There's only one," a voice yelled from the darkness.

Callum, his rifle and reins in his left hand, shucked his Colt with his right and fired three shots in the voice's direction. They came so fast it sounded like a single roar, merging with a yelp and a thump as a body hit the ground. At the same time, Callum wheeled the bay, charging toward the voice. Shots followed him through the night, one clipping his earlobe. He ducked low in the saddle and raced away from the camp in the direction the wagon was pointing. He heard yelling. It sounded like there were only three men remaining. The racket was increased by the wagon racing through the camp and out onto the plains. When he was well out of range, he slipped his Spencer back into the scabbard.

He doubted those boys had the gumption to come riding after them on this moonlit night. His goal now was to get to the wagon and see how badly those folks were hurt. He followed through the night as the wagon raced across the plains. *Sure hope whoever's driving that rig slows down before they hit something.* No sooner had that thought crossed his mind than the wagon started slowing.

He rode closer and called to the woman. "Hello, the wagon. I aim to ride in."

"Come on in," the woman called back.

Callum rode up next to the wagon and could make her out as she peered into the darkness, trying to see him.

"Ma'am, are you all right?"

"Yes, I am, but my husband's hurt. The man you shot by the wagon had been cutting James. He'd threatened to skin him alive."

"I heard you scream," Callum said.

"Yes, that was when the big man hit my son. Jimmy—that's my son—tried to stop him from hurting his pa, but the man just knocked him down and threw him in the wagon."

"They both in the wagon?"

"Yes, they're both here."

"Let's take a quick look at 'em, and then we'll head on outta here. I don't think those fellers will follow us. They've had enough shootin' for tonight, but we still need to chalk up some distance before daylight, just in case."

"I'm fine," came a youthful voice from inside the wagon. Then a boy jumped down from the back. "Pa don't look too good."

Callum nodded at the boy as he climbed into the wagon to check on the man, James. He lit a match to get a quick look. The man was out, probably from the pain. There were several slices across his chest and one across his stomach. Fortunately, it looked like the man who had wielded the knife had known what he was doing. None of the slices were deep—only painful.

"Boy, walk out there a ways and listen for any hoofbeats. If you hear anything, don't yell, just come a runnin' and let me know."

"Yes, sir," Jimmy said, and ran back in the direction they had come.

"Ma'am, looks like your man will be fine. He's got some cuts, but none so deep as to have damaged anything important. If we can keep 'em from getting infected, he'll be fine. I just heard *you* scream, didn't hear him."

"No, you wouldn't. James is a brave man."

"He might be brave, but he led you folks into this predicament. That kinda tells me he don't know what the blue blazes he's doing."

The woman bristled at Callum's comments. "Those men just rode up. How were we to know they had bad intentions? You can't go shooting people indiscriminately. That would be breaking the law."

"Don't see no law around here. Do you?"

"This is a nation of laws, without which we'd be back in the Dark Ages."

"Reckon getting skinned alive rates right up there with the Dark Ages."

The woman sighed. "Maybe you're right. I'm just glad you showed up. Thank you. It was rude of me to argue with you when I should be thanking you."

"Not a problem, ma'am. I'd just suggest you be a mite more careful who you allow near you or your wagon. This ain't St. Louis."

"Yes, well, you're right. It seems to be a different world entirely." She sighed again and said, "My name is Sarah Radcliff. I much prefer Sarah to ma'am."

James moved, a soft moan issuing from him. A moment later,

his eyes opened. He saw Callum above him and then quickly looked around. "Sarah, what's happened? Where are we?"

"Mister, you're alive and out of that camp. You're gonna hurt for a while, but you'll be fine."

"It's fine, James. This man, Mr.—I don't even know your name."

"Name's Callum, Callum Jeremiah Logan."

"Mr. Logan rescued us from those awful men."

"Mr. Logan," James said, wincing as he tried to move, "we're truly grateful for your assistance. I don't know what would've happened if you hadn't come along."

"I'll tell you what would've happened. That man back there, with a slug of lead in his belly, would've skinned you alive while your family watched. Then they'd have had their way with your wife, and no telling what they would have done with your son—"

"Mr. Logan, my wife is present. You don't need to be talking like that in front of her."

"Reckon I do. You folks are greenhorns and too blasted trusting. You've got a lot to learn. If you don't learn it, you'll die. Not just you, but your wife and boy. A lot of folks die out here before they can learn—you almost did. Ma'am, you got something to doctor up those cuts with?"

"Yes, Mr. Logan, I do."

"Then I reckon I'll step outside." Callum turned and jumped down from the covered wagon.

"Boy, you out there?"

"Yes, sir, and I ain't heard a thing."

"Good. Don't reckon those boys had much hankerin' to follow us into the dark. But the wagon'll be easy to follow tomorrow. Soon as your ma gets your pa doctored, we'll head on outta here a ways."

Callum moved over to his horse. He poured some water in his hat and gave the animal a drink. The bay had been cropping some of the short grass. Callum stepped into the saddle and walked him over to the wagon.

"You folks about ready to move out? You need to put some distance behind you before you stop. Boy, give these horses some water before you start out. They've had a pretty good run."

Sarah moved up to the wagon seat.

"Ma?"

"Go ahead, Jimmy. Mr. Logan's right. Grab the bucket, and do what he says."

"Yes, ma'am."

"How old's the boy?" Callum asked.

"He's ten going on twenty," Sarah said. "He's had to grow up fast since the war."

"Reckon that's the case for a lot of younguns. 'Specially those heading west. It's a tough country, but when you're young, you adapt fast."

"Yes, he's really taken to this country. I think he likes these wide open spaces."

"How 'bout you, ma'am? Do you like this country?"

"You know, I felt intimidated at first. It's so big and wide. But it seems to be growing on me. Yes, I do like it."

Jimmy finished watering the horses, tied the bucket back to the wagon, and climbed up on the wagon seat. "All done, Ma."

"Boy, you know how to locate the North Star?" Callum asked.

"Yes, sir, I sure do. You just find the Big Dipper, and aim across the two pointers of the cup. The North Star is right there." Jimmy pointed toward it.

"Good. You keep that star on your right shoulder, and you folks head on west. Keep an eye out for rocks and washes. After about three hours, start looking for a creek with water. Find a place down out of sight. If you're down low, where it can't be seen, you can build a small fire. Understood?"

"Yes, Mr. Logan, we understand," Sarah said. "Will you be joining us?"

Callum could hear the hope in her voice. "Yes, ma'am. I'll be along. Right now, I want to ride back and see if I can tell what those boys are up to."

"Isn't that dangerous, Mr. Logan? Might they be waiting for you?"

"Life's dangerous, ma'am. But I'll be fine. I'm thinkin' those boys have had the steam let out of 'em with two of the five down. You folks do have guns?"

"Yes, Mr. Logan. We have guns, and we know how to use them."

"Then I reckon you ought to have a couple of them up there with you. This is Indian country. Just because you've had one problem today, don't mean you won't have another."

"Jimmy, get the Henry and the Colt," Sarah said to her son. "We'll be ready, Mr. Logan."

"Fine, ma'am. Now you best be gettin' along." Callum touched his hat and turned the bay back toward the outlaws.

CALLUM NEARED the camp in the early morning. The full moon, now hiding behind clouds, gave little light. He could see the fire clearly. The men still sat around the flames. It was obvious they weren't expecting trouble, even in Indian country. A slight breeze had picked up from the southeast. Since he was moving in from the west, his smell and sound would be masked. Their horses would have no idea he was close.

Callum tied his horse to a thick bunch of grass, pulled off his boots, and tied them over the saddle. He pulled a pair of moccasins from his saddlebags and slipped them on, then eased toward the camp on foot. He could see a body draped head to toe with a blanket. His man-skinning days were over. The other was lying next to the fire, his leg bandaged against the bleeding. It looked like one of his three shots had connected. The other three men were passing a bottle around.

Callum shook his head. They were asking to shed their scalps. He'd seen their fire from miles away. Now they were drinking, and had probably been drinking when he jumped them the first time. Plus, they were staring into the fire. When he and Josh were only pups, Pa had taught them, and his other brothers, to resist the temptation to stare into a fire. It ruins night vision. Those boys wouldn't be able to see a durn thing. Course, it probably didn't matter. They appeared to be drunker than the bunch of skunks they were.

He stepped into the circle of brightness from the fire and waited, his Colt drawn and another in his gunbelt. Finally, after almost a minute, one of the men tilted his head back to take a swig from the community bottle and saw Callum.

Callum chuckled at the sight, as the man sputtered and strangled on the liquor. At the sound of his chuckle, the other men whirled around, one falling against the other, both of them sprawling in the dirt. The man with his leg grazed made a move to go for his gun. "Probably not a good move," Callum said. He had the Colt centered on the man. Slowly, Grazed Leg relaxed his hand and moved it away from his holster. The other three men had gained their feet unsteadily and were looking to the wounded man.

"You boys seem to be snake-bit. Why, I saw your fire a mighty fer piece. You do know this is Indian country?"

The men standing looked around with blank gazes. Grazed Leg said, "I reckon that might be the case. But we've got enough firepower to whup any Injun that shows up."

"Like you whipped me? I don't know where you boys come from, but I'm here to tell you, if you keep doing what you're doing, your scalps will be hanging from a Comanche's lance within a week. Course, that's no concern of mine. If you're skunk enough to hijack a family and their wagon out on this here prairie and then torture the man in front of his wife and kid, you ought to get what's coming to you."

One of the drunks said, "Mister, that was Bloody Tom's idea. We wanted no part in what he was doing, but he would've killed us if we'd tried to leave."

"Now that's a sad story, boys. That must be Bloody Tom all covered up with that blanket. Ain't it amazing what a hunk of lead will do? Reckon he's the bloody one now. Here's what I've got for you. Shuck your gunbelts. You, Talky, you pick 'em up. Which horse belongs to Mr. Bloody Tom?"

"That big buckskin was Tom's," Talky said.

"Fine. You saddle up that horse, get his saddlebags, and stick all those gunbelts in the saddlebags."

"See here, Mister," Grazed Leg said, "you can't leave us without our guns."

"Oh, I'm gonna do you one better than that. Talky, what's your name?"

"Jake Shoate's my name, Mister."

"All right, Jake, you pick up all the rifles and bring them over here."

The man on the ground struggled to get up. Once on his feet, he stared hard at Callum.

"Jake, I want you to take . . . what's his name?"

"That's Ben Milam, Mister."

Milam gave Jake a withering look.

"Well, Jake, you just give Mr. Milam his gun. I reckon he's got a big desire to meet his Maker, though I doubt that'll be a pleasant reunion. No, take it out of the holster and hand it to him."

Jake walked over to Milam. He slowly pulled the revolver out of its holster, making sure his fingers didn't get near the trigger. He looked back at Callum.

"That's right, give him his gun. Wait, check it first and make sure it's loaded. I wouldn't want to be accused of killing no unarmed man. Mr. Milam, you can make your move as soon as you get that gun or anytime thereafter. You have such a hankering to die, I'll just help you along."

Jake pulled the Colt out of its holster, opened the loading gate, and checked the loads. "It's loaded, Ben." He held the revolver by the barrel and handed it to Milam.

Callum watched Milam. His kind were all alike. Tough when they had the edge, but when it looked like someone else might call the shots, they weren't so eager.

Milam peered at that six-gun like he was looking at a snake. Then he looked at Callum. "You've got the edge. You're holding your gun on me."

"You're right." Callum lowered his gun to his side. "Anytime, Milam."

Milam looked at the six-gun again. Callum could tell Milam wanted him, bad. He watched the sweat break out on Milam's forehead, even as the cool night breeze drifted through the camp.

Finally, Milam shook his head. "You're too sure of yourself, and I'm weak from that gunshot."

"Okay, Milam, sit down, and keep your mouth shut. You make a move I don't like, you're gonna be a lot weaker. Jake, get his gun and get that horse saddled. Stay where I can see you. You boys can all sit down and enjoy the sights. Why, if you've a mind, you can have another pull on that bottle."

Jake held Milam's gun with thumb and forefinger, dropped it in its holster, and then into the saddlebags. He then saddled the big buckskin. He wrapped the other gunbelts around each of the six-guns and also slid them into the saddlebags.

"Good, Jake, now tie those rifles together with some pigging string and sling them over the saddle."

"Now listen, Mister," Milam said, "you leave us out here like that, you might as well shoot us."

"Don't tempt me, Milam. You boys deserve to be hanging from a tall tree. Here's your deal, and this is the best you get. I'm taking your guns and horses. I'll leave you a rifle and two of your horses. I figure you won't mind doubling up. I recommend you be a mite more careful with your fires and your whiskey. There's plenty of Utes around, and if the Comanches catch up with you, they'll hang you upside down over a fire and roast your head until it pops like a melon—makes a terrible mess.

"When I get to Fort Lyon, I'm going to let them know about you. Men out here don't look kindly on varmints that mess around with the womenfolk. So, if you make it to town, I'd be mighty cautious about advertising who you are."

"What's your name, Mister?" Milam asked.

"Logan. Callum Logan."

Milam gave Callum a hard look. "Logan, I'll see you again. Then it'll be different."

"Why, Mr. Milam, you had your chance tonight. I don't reckon anything will be different next time, except you'll be dead.

"Jake, you loop a rope over each one of those horses and lead them out in that direction." Callum pointed in the direction of his bay. "You boys stay nice and quiet, and if you're lucky, you might make it to where you can have another drink."

Jake walked by with the horses, and Callum backed around so he could watch the others and Jake. He followed him out to his horse. Light was breaking in the east. He'd been here far too long. Callum swung up into his saddle. Jake made no move, except to hand him the ropes.

"You'll find the rest of your horses at Fort Lyon. Except for Bloody Tom's. I figure he owes that family at least his horse and gear."

"Mr. Logan, for truth, we had no idea what Bloody Tom was up to when we approached that wagon."

"Jake, you didn't stop him. That speaks louder than what you're saying. I'd recommend you head back east. This country needs men, and you just don't measure up."

"Reckon I'm stayin'. But I'll sure take part of your advice. I'm gettin' away from this bunch as soon as I can."

Callum watched Jake for a moment, nodded, turned the bay west, and trotted from the camp. He was covered with sweat, and not because it was hot. It was a good thing those boys had been drinking, or he might have had his hands full. Four to one wasn't his favorite odds. Still, he had no use for this kind of vermin. Now he was anxious to get back to the Radcliff family. Hopefully they'd set up camp by now and were fine. He could use a good, hot cup of coffee and some rest.

2

Callum walked his horse slowly across the plains. He was tired, and the big bay was too. He scanned the wide-open miles of blue grama and buffalo grass as he rode. This country was big and open, but it would fool a man. There were hidden draws and shallow canyons where a passel of hostiles might be hiding. He had no desire to run into them at any time. But this morning, with a tired horse, he wouldn't stand a chance.

He'd been riding for several hours. The sun was approaching noon time, when he saw the cottonwoods. It wasn't a big creek, but it was water. Hopefully the Radcliffs had stopped here. He'd know soon enough.

Almost an hour later, following the wagon tracks, he found the family. They'd crossed the creek and located their camp on the other side, well hidden from searching eyes. A small fire sent its tendrils of faint smoke drifting up through the cottonwood's limbs to dissipate and become almost invisible.

"Hello, the camp."

He could see Mrs. Radcliff at the fire. Looked like she was cooking. She looked up, shading her eyes with her hand.

"Come in, Mr. Logan. I suspect you must be hungry."

"Yes, ma'am. I'm so hungry, my stomach thinks my throat's cut." He pulled up at the camp, looked around, and stepped out of the saddle. Callum put both hands to the back of his slim waist and leaned back, stretching his muscles. He felt his back pop. *I'm almighty tired.*

"Mr. Logan, we didn't know if you would come back," she said.

"Why, ma'am, I was hankerin' for some coffee. I wouldn't miss a good cup. Where's your man and boy?" Callum asked as he unsaddled the two horses.

"James is still resting, and Jimmy is just around the bend, catching us some fish."

"How's your man doing?"

"I'm doing fine, Mr. Logan," James Radcliff said, easing out of the back of the wagon. "I'm stiff, slow, and sore, but I'll make it."

"James, you should stay in bed," Sarah scolded. "You don't want those cuts opening up."

"Now, honey, I can't be lying around all day. I'll be fine. Mr. Logan, I see you have an extra horse."

"That I do," Callum said. He watched James walk slowly over to the fire. "Seems those boys wanted to give you folks Bloody Tom's horse and gear, for your troubles."

James looked over the buckskin, and then the gear on the ground. "That's a fine horse. Looks like a Henry in the scabbard. Seems they were quite generous."

Callum stopped wiping down the horses with grass for a moment, and said, "They were at that. Sometimes it's mighty difficult explaining the whims of folks." Then he led both horses to the creek, where they thrust their muzzles into the clear stream. Callum patted the bay on the neck. "Drink up, Red. You've earned it." After they finished drinking, he led them to a grassy area and staked them out where they had plenty of room to graze.

When he turned, Sarah was waiting for him with a cup in her hand. "Coffee, Mr. Callum?"

"Thank you, ma'am." The coffee tasted good. "Mighty fine coffee. While I was riding back, I was sure looking forward to this first cup."

James was sitting on a big cottonwood log that had been pulled close to the fire. "Mr. Logan, can you tell us what happened?"

Sarah had made biscuits. She put several, along with a pile of bacon, on a blue porcelain plate and handed it to Callum.

"Thank you, ma'am," Callum said. He slid half a biscuit in his mouth and chased it with a couple of pieces of bacon. "That, is mighty tasty."

"We've some sorghum for your biscuits, when you finish your bacon."

"Reckon I've just about died and gone to heaven," Callum said around the biscuit and bacon. Then he sat on the log, next to James, and told them about the gang.

James was a good-sized man, pushing six feet, but sitting next to Callum he looked small. Callum slipped his hat off and laid it on the log. Thick, brown, curly hair tumbled around his head as he pulled it off. His eyes, a piercing light blue, missed nothing as he surveyed the camp. "Now, I don't think those boys will be bothering you folks. Don't know where they were from, but they were about as green to this country as you are. They're lucky a party of Utes or Comanches didn't spot that fire. Their scalps would be hanging on some brave's war lance right now."

"I'm glad you didn't harm them," James said. "It looked like those boys, maybe with the exception of that Ben Milam, were just following along, especially that young fellow, Jake. He looked mighty uncomfortable."

"If he's got the gumption to split off from that bunch, he might make it. But I've no use for a man that won't stand up for what's right. Now tell me, how'd it happen that Bloody Tom felt the need to slice you up?"

Sarah walked over to the two men and refilled their coffee cups. "I'll tell you why. That horrible man grabbed me and dragged me off the wagon. James leaped on top of him, before the other men could do anything, and knocked him to the ground. I thought that Bloody, whatever his name is, was going to kill James right there. Then he got this evil look and grinned. It was frightening. I remember exactly what he said, 'Boy, I'm gonna skin you alive, strip by strip. Right here in front of your woman and your boy.' That was when Jimmy came from behind the wagon with the axe handle and hit the man across his back. I'm so proud of my two men." She smiled at James and laid her hand on his shoulder.

Callum looked at James. "Sounds like you and your boy got yourself some gumption. Ma'am, mind if I try some of that sorghum? It's been a while since I've had a taste."

They all turned to see Jimmy walking back from the creek. He had four nice catfish on a stick stringer. His smile lit his face with satisfaction. "Ma, Pa, I've catched a whole slew of catfish."

Sarah smiled. "You've caught, not catched, and please don't use the word slew. They will be a nice change for supper."

"That's a good job, boy, and it looks like a slew to me. Now, if you folks don't mind, I'm plumb tuckered out. Ma'am, I thank you for the meal and the coffee. I'm gonna move over under those trees and catch a little shut-eye. I'd be obliged if you folks would keep a close eye out. This is still Indian country."

Sarah looked at James and he nodded. "Mr. Logan," Sarah said, "feel free to sleep in the wagon."

"No, ma'am, I much prefer the open. Been doing that for most of my life." Logan turned to James. "Mr. Radcliff, I'd suggest you rest up some more. Those cuts weren't deep, but you bled a lot. You'll be needing to build your strength back." With that, he picked up his saddle and bedroll, and moved farther under the trees.

THE COTTONWOOD LEAVES DANCED, flashing green and silver in the late afternoon sun. The moaning of the wind rushing through the limbs woke Callum from a deep sleep. He was usually a light sleeper—sometimes your life depended on it. But his body had needed rest and took it whether he liked it or not.

He looked around and saw Jimmy leading the horses to water. Mrs. Radcliff was frying the catfish, and James was filling the water barrels. It was a homey scene that touched him and reminded him of Ma, Pa, and his brothers and sister. *Wonder where Josh is right now.*

He had split off from his brother in Nashville. Josh had to deliver bad news to the Texas family of his good friend. They'd join up on the land that Floyd Logan, their uncle, had purchased in Colorado. He and Josh planned, together, to build a new home for their folks. Tennessee was a good land, but getting crowded. The Logan clan always had itchy feet and a love of room to stretch.

Callum rolled his bedroll, picked up his saddle, and walked back over to the fire, dropping his saddle opposite the fire from Mrs. Radcliff. "Reckon I slept a little long."

"We didn't want to wake you. You seemed very tired."

"Seems so. Looks like we might have some weather brewing. How long's the wind been up like this?"

James had walked over from filling the water barrels. "The wind only picked up about an hour ago. We thought it best to get supper fixed, so we could put the fire out before the wind gets too high."

"Good thinkin'," Callum said. "You about done there, ma'am? It's gettin' mighty breezy under here."

"I am, Mr. Logan. I fixed another pan of biscuits. They should go well with the catfish. Jimmy pulled some wild onions from along the creek. If you're ready to eat, we can start now."

"That'd be fine, ma'am."

Jimmy had brought the horses back from the water and staked them out in a new spot. "Hi, Mr. Logan. I watered your horse for you."

"Much obliged, boy. I'm sure he appreciated it."

Jimmy had pulled up another log around the fire, while Callum was sleeping. Callum sat down, and Jimmy sat beside him. Sarah passed out plates to everyone. Callum started in on the biscuits.

"Excuse me, Mr. Logan," James said. "We'd like to say grace before eating."

"Pardon me. Been alone for so long, I forget," Callum said, and took his hat off.

"Heavenly Father, we thank thee for bringing us through our trials, and we thank thee for Mr. Logan coming along when he did. We thank thee for our food and ask thee to bless it to the strength and nourishment of our bodies. In the name of thy Son, Jesus Christ. Amen."

"Amen. Dive in," Jimmy said.

"Jimmy!"

"Well, Ma, Pa says it."

"You don't have to do everything your pa does," Sarah said. She gave James the look. He just shrugged and smiled.

"You'll do, boy," Callum said.

"Mr. Logan, don't encourage him."

"No, ma'am," Callum said and winked at Jimmy. Jimmy beamed.

"Mighty good food. I surely forget what good cookin' is after eatin' mine for so long. Now, what are you folks planning? Where're you headed?"

"We're trying to make it to Salt Lake City, but we got a late start. I'm concerned about getting over the Rocky Mountains."

"You folks Mormon?"

James said, "No, Mr. Logan, we're not, but my brother is. He and his family are in the Salt Lake area. He wrote me, asking us to join them, and we decided to go."

Callum took a last sip from his cup. "Any coffee left in that pot?"

Sarah refilled Callum's cup.

"Now," Logan said, "from what my Uncle Floyd's told me, you folks don't stand a snowball's chance of getting through those mountains to Salt Lake this year. Considering that, what's your plan?"

"We will probably stay in Denver until the spring, and move on then," James said.

"You're a mite south for that, ain't you?"

A low rumble was heard in the west. Everyone turned to look in that direction. The southeast wind had picked up even more. The fire's flames whipped in the wind.

"Reckon we best get this fire out," Callum said, tossing dirt over the fire.

Sarah poured the remainder of the coffee over the flames. "Jimmy," she said, "get the shovel, and cover the remaining coals with dirt."

"Yes, ma'am." Jimmy ran to the wagon, grabbed the shovel, and started sifting dirt over the coals.

"Folks, we best get ready to take off if need be. As strong as this here southeast wind is, we're liable to have a big storm moving this way," Callum said.

A closer rumble of thunder sounded, and in the darkening sky, lightning skittered across the clouds. The setting sun had disappeared behind the bank of clouds. A gold ribbon outlined the towering tops of the clouds as they pushed the sun from view.

James started hooking up the horses to the wagon. Callum saddled Red. He tied the bay to a big limb, picked up Bloody Tom's gear, and led the buckskin to the back of the wagon. He tossed the saddle and gear into the wagon, and tied the buckskin to the gate.

"Pull your wagon a little deeper into the trees," Callum yelled to James.

James hesitated and yelled back, his voice almost lost in the wind. "Shouldn't we get out from under these trees? That's a lightning storm coming."

"Mister, we're between the devil and the prairie. You want to pull out there and be the highest thing around you? Yeah, this ain't ideal, but I'd rather take my chances here than on that open prairie. But it's your family. You do what you think best."

Callum pulled the bay's reins loose from the limb and walked deeper into the cottonwoods. He pulled out his slicker and slipped it on. Lightning slammed into the prairie, the thunder crashing against their ears. The lightning was almost continuous, racing across the sky from cloud to cloud, while jagged shafts smashed into the ground.

James yanked the team over and into a thicker part of the trees near Callum. Sarah and Jimmy huddled in the back of the wagon. The wind died for a few minutes, and all there was in the early night was lightning and thunder.

"Hang on, here comes the rain," Callum shouted over the thunder.

Now the wind shifted to the northwest and blew with a vengeance. The cottonwood trees bent and groaned from the stress. The rain came in sheets. Callum mounted and rode over to the wagon. "Keep an eye on the creek. If it starts rising, we may need to get out of here, in spite of the lightning." He held the bay on the lee side of the wagon, got off, and crawled back up against the same side—and waited.

Down the creek, a big cottonwood gave up. The top broke and ripped away in the wind. Other limbs were breaking. Some fell close to the wagon, but none hit it. Lightning hit the top of the cottonwood that had broken. It split down one side and burst into flames. In the light, Callum could see the creek rising. "Get those horses moving," he yelled, as he mounted Red. He rode up to the lead horse and slapped him across the rump with his reins. The horse threw himself into the harness, and the others followed.

The terrain was steep, and as the horses labored, water roared down the creek, only now it was no longer shallow. It had surged out of its banks. Their campfire was completely under water. Water lapped at the back wheels of the wagon. James laid the whip across the horses. They had never felt the sting before and leaped forward, pulling the wagon up the last rise.

"Keep 'em moving," Callum yelled. The small creek that had been only ten feet across and no more than ankle deep in most spots, and four or five feet deep in its deepest holes, was now at least fifty feet across and threatening to surge out onto the prairie. Callum watched for a moment more and, with his slicker pulled around him, followed the wagon into the driving rain. His horse tried a couple of times to turn away from the wind, but Callum held him moving west. When the lightning flashed, he could make out the wagon ahead.

The prairie turned from hard-packed to foot-sucking mud, but Red continued moving forward. Callum patted him on the neck. "I'm sure glad you had some good victuals, water, and rest." Callum had always liked working with horses. *I may not be as good as Josh with 'em, but I get by. Of course, Pa gave Chancy to Josh. That's a special horse. He got Josh through the war.*

Up ahead, the wagon had stopped. The wind and lightning had let up some, but the rain was still pouring. Callum rode up next to the wagon and could see the reason for stopping. It was a small wash. Normally it would be no problem to cross, but, now, it was roaring with water. They'd have to wait until the rain moved on east. It was pitch-black. Moon and stars were hidden by heavy rain clouds that continued to dump water on the thirsty prairie.

Callum swung up onto the wagon seat next to James. "That

was a good job, parking your wagon on the bank side in the direction you're headed. You folks are more savvy than I gave you credit for."

James chuckled and then said, "Credit where credit's due. It was Sarah who thought of that. She said it just seemed like good common sense."

"It danged sure was. You may not've seen it, but that little creek is a mighty big river right now. It was spreading out on the prairie when we left it. Why, it's probably fifteen, maybe twenty feet deep. You should've seen the logs come rolling down that thing. They had to've come for miles, 'cause there ain't no other trees near that I could see as I rode in."

"Glad we were able to get out when we did. Thank you for your assistance. I'm not sure we would have made it without you. That's twice you have saved my family. I'm in your debt, Mr. Logan."

"You folks already settled up with me. Those biscuits and bacon your missus fixed were mighty good. You just forget about who's got debt for who. Why don't you stop calling me Mr. Logan. My friends call me Callum."

"Thank you, Callum. I'm James."

They sat for a while longer in silence. The rain had relented and now was a slow, steady shower. The wind, out of the northwest, brought a chill to the air, cold for early August.

"We can't cross this wash right now. I'd say you folks oughta get some rest. You've done a lot this evening. I'm bettin', what with getting those horses wheeled around and out of that wash, you've broken those cuts open. You best go back and let your missus get you doctored up again. I got plenty of sleep, so I'll just sit here and watch the horses."

Callum noticed that James started to object, but then common sense took over.

"Thank you," he said, and disappeared into the wagon.

Mighty nice folks, with grit, Callum thought. He looked across the prairie. Here and there, the moon was breaking through the clouds and painting spots of shimmering silver across the prairie. The rain died down to an occasional sprinkle. Wet and chilled, Callum rested his boot against the brake. *Uncle Floyd was right. This is a big country, fit for a man, or a woman.*

3

The morning broke clear and cool for an August day on the Colorado Plains. Callum wrapped the reins around the brake and stepped down from the wagon seat. He had dozed a little. His body was chilled. He walked over to the wash. There was only a trickle of water flowing. It would be dry enough to cross in a few hours. In the scrubbed-clean morning air, he could see the faint outline of the Rocky Mountains jutting up from the horizon. He'd be meeting Floyd Logan, his uncle, in five or six more days, in Pueblo. Then they'd be on to the ranch.

Mrs. Radcliff stepped from the back of the wagon and walked through the drying mud. "Good morning, Mr. Logan."

"Morning, ma'am. Reckon we survived the night all right, though I had a wonder or two back at that creek."

"As did I. I thank God we are safe. Do you think it would be all right if we lit a fire?"

"Ma'am, I think it'd be mighty fine. Fire won't show up much more than this big wagon."

Callum moved back to pull some wood off the sheet hung beneath the wagon. "Who told you folks to collect wood and buffalo chips? Can't imagine you thinking of that by yourself."

"The gentleman at the store in Topeka was kind enough to share that piece of information. He told us we'd be running out of burnable material out on the plains. He was so right. I can't believe how far we've gone at a time with nothing to burn except buffalo chips. I am so grateful for his help."

Callum started the fire as Jimmy came jumping out of the wagon. "Look, Ma. You can see the mountains. We're almost to Denver."

"Depends on what you call almost, boy," Callum said. "Those mountains you're looking at are roughly a hundred miles from us. That'll be a solid five days' travel, maybe six."

"That far, Mr. Logan?"

"Yep. Out here in this clear air, things seem a lot closer than they are. Now, why don't you grab some more wood for the fire?"

James stepped down from the back of the wagon and slowly straightened up. "Morning."

Sarah moved quickly to his side to help him.

"That's all right, Sarah. I'm just a little stiff. All I need is to move around some, and the sun feels good."

"You must take it easy today, James. You opened up several of those cuts, and now they'll have to start healing all over again."

James glanced over at Callum, who was cleaning his Colt, and grinned. "Yes, ma'am. Callum, how long you think it'll be before we can get across this wash?"

Callum continued to wipe down the revolver. "Reckon by the time we eat and get the stock taken care of we'll be able to be on our way." He recharged the revolver, then pulled his Spencer out of the scabbard and started cleaning it.

"We'll have some breakfast in no time," Sarah said. "Jimmy, get me the skillet and coffeepot. I think we all need some food in our stomachs."

"Looks like we might have some company, Mrs. Radcliff. You might plan on a few more stomachs."

"I don't see anything," Jimmy said.

"Boy, if you'd close your mouth and open your eyes, you'd see those soldier boys coming up from the south."

Jimmy looked to the south. After a few more minutes, he said, "Pa, I see 'em out there. It looks like they're coming this way."

Callum pulled the saddle off the bay and laid it in the back of the wagon, along with his cleaned and loaded Spencer. He took the bay and the buckskin over to the wash and let them drink. He had staked the horses out to feed when the soldiers rode up. The ten troopers were commanded by a first lieutenant and a sergeant.

The lieutenant doffed his hat and said, "Morning, ma'am." He then addressed James. "Sir, are you aware of the Indian activity in this area?"

"No, Lieutenant, I am not."

"Sir, if you don't mind my saying, you should not be here with only one wagon."

"We are well aware of that, Lieutenant. Mr. Logan, here, saved us from some very unsavory characters."

The sergeant turned to Callum. "You any kin to Floyd Logan?"

"Yep," Callum said.

"Lieutenant, you know Floyd Logan. He's the gent that scouted some for Colonel Moonlight of the 11th Kansas Calvary, during the '64-'65 campaign, " the sergeant said. "Last I heard, he was in Pueblo, stocking up to head out west of there."

"Are you folks headed for Pueblo?" the lieutenant asked.

"We are. We were hoping to make it over the mountains to Salt Lake City. Mr. Logan said that it would be prudent of us to wait in Denver, and head out next spring."

"Lieutenant, we forget our manners," Sarah said. "Won't you and your men step down and have some coffee?"

"Thank you, ma'am, we'd like that. Dismount the men, Sergeant."

"Dismount. See to your mounts and have a cup," the sergeant said.

The men dismounted and gathered around the fire. Sarah looked embarrassed. "I'm sorry, but we don't have enough cups for everyone. Some of you will have to wait."

A young trooper spoke up, "Not to worry, ma'am. It's well worth waiting to have a good cup of coffee with a nice lady." He nodded at James as he spoke. "We don't see many folks on these patrols. This is most welcome."

"Have you seen any Indian sign?" Callum asked the sergeant.

"No, sir, we haven't, and that is the worst sign of all. When you don't see these red devils is when they be the most dangerous. Word is that a party of Arapaho were moving south. That's why we're scoutin' around, though I don't much like being out here with only twelve men and no scout. 'Tis askin' for trouble, if you ask me." With the last comment, the sergeant looked over to the lieutenant.

"We're following orders, Sergeant," the lieutenant said.

"Aye, sir, that we are."

The soldiers had all finished their coffee and watered the horses. James told the lieutenant about their capture, and the subsequent rescue by Logan.

Callum chimed in, "Lieutenant, I've got the horses and gear belonging to the remainder of that crew. Would you mind taking them off our hands? You might be able to use them on your patrol, and if any of them show up, you can give them their gear."

"You say there were five of them?" asked the lieutenant.

"Yes, sir, but when I left, there were only four. The man called Bloody Tom suffered from lead poisoning. Don't reckon he'll be along. Another by the name of Ben Milam will have a mighty sore leg."

"Lieutenant, when I was in Missouri, I heard of this Bloody Tom," the sergeant said. "He's supposed to have a brother. They're known as the Wister brothers. They're both bad medicine. My understanding is that they rode with Quantrill. Now, Elwood Wister is said to have a gang of men that are up to no good." The sergeant turned to Logan. "Were I you, I'd be keeping my eye out for this Elwood Wister. He'll not be taking this lightly."

"Thanks, Sergeant. I'll be keeping an eye out. If you ever find yourself in the valley just west of the Greenhorn Mountains, look me up. My brother and uncle will be starting a ranch there. You'd be welcome. You too, Lieutenant. Any of you boys want a cup, feel free to swing by."

"Thank you, Mr. Logan. Have the men mount up, Sergeant."

The sergeant turned to the men. "You heard the lieutenant, mount up."

The lieutenant doffed his hat to Sarah. "Thank you, ma'am, for your hospitality. This was a pleasant break. Mr. Logan, I'd suggest you get these folks to Fort Lyon as quickly as you can. This is dangerous country."

Logan nodded to the lieutenant and the sergeant. "We'll be movin' out right quick, Lieutenant. See you around."

"Move them out, Sergeant," the lieutenant said.

"Aye, sir." The sergeant nodded at Logan. "Move out, boys."

The patrol trotted north from the wagon. The young trooper turned and waved to Sarah. "Thank you, ma'am."

She waved back and said, "James, that boy is so young. He needs to be home with his mother, not out here on these plains as a soldier."

Callum spoke up. "Ma'am, this is hard country. Boys turn into men early.

"Now we need to get moving. This ground will turn dry fast, and those soldier boys will be kicking up dust in no time. We want to be well west of here before that happens."

With the team hitched and Callum saddled up, they crossed the wash and moved west. Callum rode a ways alongside the wagon.

"James, you made up your mind what you're going to do? Do you want to go to Fort Lyon, or direct to Pueblo?"

"Callum, I think you're right. I don't want my family caught in those mountains in the winter. I've heard stories. I guess we'll go to Pueblo, and maybe up to Denver."

Sarah sat up front with James as the wagon rolled west.

"Folks, I've got a proposition for you. Might serve you well, for your winterin'. I'm meeting my Uncle Floyd in Pueblo. We've got some land west of there in what he says is a fertile valley. We'll be starting a ranch out there. My brother Josh will be joining us later this year. We'll be needing some help to get the house and shelter for the stock built before the snow flies. James, if you've a mind, you can sign on for the winter. When it thaws out in the spring, you can find a wagon train going to Salt Lake and join up. Pay'll be thirty a month.

"Mrs. Logan, if you'd be a mind to cooking, that'd be another thirty a month for you. Now, I'm not trying to twist an arm here, and the work won't be easy. It'll be rough until we get the ranch house built, but if you're willing to lend a hand, I'd be much obliged."

James looked over to Sarah. Tears were coursing down her cheeks. "We've been praying for an answer, James. I know you didn't want to chance those mountains in the winter. I believe this is our answer."

"Can we, Pa? I'll work real hard," Jimmy said.

"We'd be obliged to you, Mr. Logan. As Sarah has said, it is an answer to our prayers."

"I don't know about that, but I know Floyd and Josh will be glad to have you, as will I, for sure. We'll consider it a deal."

"WE'VE GOT A HEAP OF TROUBLE," Floyd said. "Somebody's claimed our land."

Callum and the Radcliff family had just rode into Pueblo. It had been five long days since meeting up with the cavalry. They had watched the mountains slowly grow, until the distinct crags could be seen thrusting up to the clear, blue sky. The sun, though it was barely past ten in the morning, blazed down on the little town.

Located near the junction of the Arkansas River and Fountain Creek, Pueblo was small and dusty. It had originally been established for trade with the Indians.

Callum had stopped in front of the general store that also doubled as a post office, hoping to have word of his Uncle Floyd. Floyd was there on the same mission.

Callum gave some money to James. "Get the stock put up, and find rooms for us at the hotel. We'll spend the night here. Floyd and I'll be along later."

James nodded and drove the wagon down the street to the livery. Callum could see Jimmy hanging out the back, taking in all of the Pueblo activity.

"That's no problem. You've got a bill of sale. Did you show it to them in the land office?" Callum said, appraising his Uncle Floyd.

He didn't look much different, maybe a little grayer, a few more of those long distance wrinkles around his eyes, but still much of a man. Those blue eyes could laugh one minute and pierce like a dagger the next. He sure looked like a Logan. All the Logan men, and women, went to height.

"Yep, I surely did. The land-man looked it over and said it looked legitimate. I paid him to make a copy and file it. Then he said, 'Possession is nine-tenths of the law.' I reckon it's time we went out there and did some unpossessin'!"

"Did the land-man tell you how long they've been out there?"

"He did. Been there nigh on to a year. I should've come back sooner, but with the war and your pa healin', I shore hated to leave."

"You did fine. We'll just have to ride out there and let those folks know they've settled on owned land, and hope they'll be reasonable. Don't know how you feel, but I'd be glad to pay them for whatever development they've done."

"I'll tell you, boy, I don't know what kinda folks they are. But if tables were turned, I'd be hard pressed to leave that land. It's fine country, plenty of grass and water, and mighty perty. Don't reckon they'll be too anxious to move on."

Callum nodded. "You may be right, but we should at least try. I've been through enough war to last me my whole life. I'm not hankerin' to start another one."

"Fine. First, let's talk to this storekeeper," Floyd said. "Mr. Storekeeper, you got a moment?"

"Name's John Thatcher. Most folks just call me John. What can I do for you boys?"

"This here is Callum, and I'm Floyd Logan. My other nephew'll be arriving shortly. His name is Josh," Floyd said, pulling out the bill of sale and land title. "You know this area?"

John read over it for a moment. He looked up at Floyd and then Callum, then looked back down at the papers lying on the counter. "I do know that country. Spent a parcel of time prospecting over that way. Mighty fine land for cattle."

He looked closer at Floyd. "You wouldn't be *the* Floyd Logan, would you?"

"Don't know about *the* Floyd Logan. Can't say as I know you."

"You wouldn't. I just recognized you from a description of you I heard in Denver City. You tackled the Barrett boys there. Am I right?"

"Yessir, I did have a run-in with those boys. I felt mighty bad about the youngun—couldn't have been no more'n seventeen or eighteen."

"Mister, they were all bad. Don't know how many people they'd killed, but they weren't worth the lead you used on 'em. It was said you killed all three of them. Dropped in the street."

"That was some years back. Tell me now, what about this land I'm talking about?"

"Mr. Logan, looks like you've got legal right to that land, by these papers you're showing me, but there's a young married couple over there that has moved in on it. Seem like pretty nice folks."

Floyd scratched his beard for a moment. "You reckon they'd move off if we paid 'em for their improvements?"

"Well, sir, they strike me as stayers. I don't see them up and moving, just on somebody's say-so."

Callum spoke up. "There's no say-so here. There's legal, binding paper that shows my uncle is the owner of that land."

John thought for a moment. "Yes, I see that. Unfortunately, they're on the land. Don't see a way around that."

"Much obliged, John," Floyd said. He picked up the papers and put them in his pocket. "We'll be needing supplies. See you later."

Callum and Floyd walked out of the store and turned up the street toward the hotel. They were both quiet as they walked through Pueblo. It was Callum's first time west, but he was no greenhorn. Growing up in the Tennessee hills had sharpened his instincts.

Callum stepped onto the boardwalk in front of the bank.

A young Mexican boy was bodily tossed through the open bank door into the dusty street, followed by a big man wearing a white shirt, garters on his sleeves, and a green visor. "I told you once, Mex, you don't have any money in this bank. Now I'm gonna teach you a lesson you'll remember, so you won't be showing up here again. You can tell your pa, if he shows up here, I've got the same thing for him."

The boy had jumped up and was facing the man. He pulled a knife from his belt and crouched, ready to defend himself. The big man laughed. "Boy, I'm gonna take that little pig sticker away from you and carve my initials on your Mexican face."

Callum stepped forward and, with one easy motion, grabbed

the man's arm and spun him around. "Reckon that boy's a tad small for you, Mister. Think I'll do?"

The banker stood a good two inches taller than Callum, with shoulders that strained his white shirt.

"You best mind your own business, Cowboy. You'll find I don't brook interference. Now step back, or when I finish with this boy, I'll take care of you."

"Oh, you're finished with this boy," Callum said. Pa had taught them that there was no sense talking when a fight was brewing, so Callum just hauled off and slapped the big man with the back of his left hand, and buried his right hand in his belly.

The man grunted and stepped back, reappraising Callum, a slight smile on his face. "You shouldn't have done that, Cowboy."

Callum stood ready. He was surprised at the hardness of the belly he had just hit. He fully expected the banker to hit the ground. There was more to this man than appeared through the green visor and white shirt.

The banker threw a short left jab that caught Callum above his right eye. A knot popped up on his forehead and his ears started ringing. He took one step back, and the banker hit him with the same jab again, right on top of the knot, then he crossed a right that slammed into Callum's left jaw. The next thing he knew, his mind was foggy and he was on the ground. The banker was swinging his boot straight for his head.

Without thinking, he grabbed the big boot and twisted. Using the man's momentum, he carried the leg through and lifted, tossing the banker to the ground.

The word of the fight spread quickly. The saloon emptied, and the townspeople poured out onto the street.

Both men were on their feet. Callum had recovered from the banker's right and stepped into him, throwing a left to the jaw and another right to his belly. The banker chopped down on Callum's ear with a short left and tried to connect again with his powerful right. This time, Callum shoved the right out of the way and hit him with another right to the belly.

The banker doubled over with the third right to the belly, and Callum grabbed the back of his head and drove the man's face into his rising knee. Blood spurted all over Callum as he shoved the banker back and stepped into him. The man came up with both forearms to protect his face, and Callum hit him again in his exposed belly.

"Here, stop this. Stop this, I say." A man with a badge stepped in between Callum and the banker. Floyd moved up to Callum's side and stood there, saying nothing.

"Mr. Jessup, what's going on here?" the town marshal asked the banker.

"This cowboy attacked me. I had to defend myself."

"Reckon it's harder to defend yourself against a man than a boy, ain't it?" Floyd said.

"Who are you?" the marshal asked.

"My name's Floyd Horatio Logan, and this young man with a bump on his head is my nephew, Callum Jeremiah Logan. Who might you be?"

"I'm the marshal in this town, and I aim to keep the peace."

"You got a name?" Floyd asked.

The marshal glared at Floyd. "My name is Nester. Marshal Nester to you."

"Well, Marshal Nester, are you going to arrest this man?" Floyd indicated the banker.

"Arrest Mr. Jessup? Now, why would I do that? Seems to me your nephew started it. A few days in jail should have him cooled down a little."

"You got it wrong, Marshal. This here banker fella threw that boy out into the street and was about to beat him and carve up his face when my nephew here walloped him. I'd say he walloped him pretty good, too."

"That's right, Marshal. I saw it all," John, the storekeeper, said.

"I followed these boys out of my store and was sweeping up in front when Jessup threw that Lopez boy out into the street. He was going after him too, when that Callum fellow slapped him good. Jessup's to blame. I'm thinking a few days in jail would allow *him* to cool off some."

From several of the bystanders, there was "That's right," and "Arrest Jessup. He's the guilty one. He's nothing but a bully anyway."

Callum could see the marshal was in a quandary. He obviously did not want to arrest Jessup, and there were enough witnesses that he couldn't get by with arresting Callum. The marshal turned to Callum. "You move along. I want you out of this town, now, and don't start any more fights before you leave, or I'll throw you in jail."

The crowd booed the marshal, with many of the men shaking their heads.

"Marshal, I'll be leaving tomorrow, but not before then. I've got no problem with the law, but you're not running me out of town. If that don't work for you, then you can look me up. I'll be at the hotel."

"I'm telling you to leave now."

"Marshal," John said, "this fellow's uncle here is Floyd Logan. The Floyd Logan of Denver City. You might have heard of him."

The marshal looked around at the crowd. "You folks move along. The show's over." Sweat was breaking out on his brow. "All right, but you leave in the morning. You hear me?"

"I'll be glad to, Marshal." Logan turned his back to the marshal and addressed the crowd. "Thanks, folks. I'm obliged for your support."

The men nodded as they walked away.

Callum looked for the Mexican boy. He still stood his ground in the street. He had put his knife away. "Come on over here, boy. What's your name?"

"My name is Lopez, *Señor.* I wish to thank you for your help."

"You're mighty fast with that knife, boy," Floyd said.

"Mr. Jessup laid his hands upon me. I do not allow another man to do that. Had I my gun, I would have killed him."

"Son, you got to rein in that temper, and let your mind work for you," Callum said.

"Like you, Señor?"

Floyd coughed and looked at Callum. "I reckon he's got you."

"But I must thank you, Señor. I am not so young I do not know that even if I cut the Mr. Jessup, he could have hurt me bad." The boy bowed in a most regal way.

"Not necessary," Callum said. "I'm Callum Logan, and this here fella is my uncle, Floyd Logan. Now what'd you say your full name was?"

"I did not, but it is Alesandro Felipe Lopez Carmona, but you may call me Alesandro or Alex."

"Alex it is, then," Callum said. He looked the boy over. His clothing looked expensive.

"I must go back into the bank," Alex said.

"Why, that's stirring up a hornet's nest, boy," Floyd said.

"My sombrero is still in the bank. It is mine." With that, Alex marched back into the bank. He emerged after only a moment, slipping on his sombrero and dusting off his pants.

"Reckon that's a determined lad," Floyd said. "Give him a few more years to fill out, he'll be a tough hombre."

"I'd say he's pretty tough right now," Callum said.

The two men joined the boy on the boardwalk in front of the bank. Jessup had disappeared inside, and the crowd had dispersed.

"Alex, you going to be all right?" Callum asked.

"Si, Señor, my father and mother are at the hotel. I will be fine. When I tell my father what has happened, I am afraid he might kill Mr. Jessup. We still have money in the bank, even though Mr. Jessup claims we do not. I think killing him would not be good, at least until we get our money."

"No, boy, I figger that would not go over well with the marshal, at all," Floyd said. "We're headed to the hotel. If it's all right with you, we'll fill him in?"

The two big men, one wearing confederate trousers with chaps over them and a brown leather vest, the other dressed in buckskins, who looked alike in so many ways, walked on each side of the boy, up the street to the hotel.

4

The Pueblo hotel looked much like any western hotel. The boardwalk stretched the length of the hotel front. The false front, made of cedar planking, had weathered to a dingy gray. Care had to be taken when leaning against the dried cedar, for fear of picking up a splinter.

Callum stepped into the hotel lobby. Floyd and Alex followed. To their right, there were two large leather chairs and a matching couch that were showing their age. The eating area, to Callum's left, had five or six tables with once-white tablecloths spread over them, clean but now stained and dingy. Stairs ran up to the right, leading to the rooms.

"Hello," the desk clerk said. "You eating or staying?" Then he smiled at Alex. "Hi, Alex, your folks are upstairs in their regular room."

"*Gracias,* Señor Nathan."

"Stayin' first, eatin' later," Callum said. He strode up to the counter, where the desk clerk spun the register around to him. He could see the Radcliffs had already checked in, and had gotten a room for him. "I'm Callum Logan. This is my uncle, Floyd Logan. We'll be needing a room with two beds."

"Upstairs, last door to the right. The Radcliffs are across the hall. I believe they put your things in the room. You folks will be staying only one night?"

"That's the plan for now," Callum said.

Callum slipped his hat to the back of his head, and the hotel clerk saw his forehead.

"Mister, we've got a doctor in town, if you need one. His office is right next door. First door on the left."

"I'm fine."

"Reckon it might be too crowded, what with Jessup in there getting his nose fixed up," Floyd said, and then chuckled.

The clerk looked closer at Callum. "You were the one in the fight with Mr. Jessup? Looks like you came off pretty light. He beat a cowboy nigh on to death a couple of weeks ago. He's a pretty tough man."

Callum turned and headed up the stairs, with Floyd following. Alex started, then stopped and turned to the desk clerk. "Señor Nathan, Mr. Jessup is no longer looking tough. Señor Callum beat him very nicely."

"Come on, Alex. You need to introduce us to your folks," Callum said from the top of the stairs.

Alex raced up the stairs two at a time, and led them to his parents' room. Reaching a door, Alex said, "Wait a moment, *por favor*."

He slipped through the door and closed it. Callum could hear him speaking to his parents in Spanish.

"He's telling them that we are fine gentlemen, who saved him from Jessup," Floyd said. "Pays to pick up the lingo, if you're gonna live in this part of the country."

The door opened, and a sharped-faced man stood in the doorway. His eyes were the first feature Callum noticed. They were black, intense, and angry. The full mustache, touched with gray, reached just past the corners of his lips. His thick, graying hair was pulled back in a short stub at the back of his head.

"Please, come in. I must apologize for my son leaving you in the hallway. I am Rodrigo Saburo Marcas Lopez. I am indebted to you both for saving my son from the jackal, Jessup."

"I'm Callum Logan, and this here is my uncle, Floyd Logan. It was our pleasure, Señor Lopez," Callum said, as he and Floyd took turns shaking Lopez's hand. "Although, it looked to us like Alex here"—Callum nodded toward Alex—"was about to take on Jessup when we walked up."

Lopez smiled. "Yes, unfortunately, it seems my son has inherited his father's temper. Now, let me introduce you to my wife and daughter."

Callum and Floyd stepped into the room. *This must be the biggest room in the whole hotel*, Callum thought. In fact, it was two rooms. There was a sitting area, where they were standing, and then a door leading to what he thought must be the bedroom.

"May I present my wife, *Doña* Isabella Valentina Carmona Ruiz de Lopez and my daughter, Gabriella Renata Lopez Carmona."

Callum was struck by the regal beauty of Doña Lopez. She was almost as tall as her husband. Her black hair was arranged on top of her head, exposing a long, attractive neck that disappeared into a lace collar on top of her gray dress, which did nothing to hide her shapely figure. Her hand, with long, tapered fingers extended to them as she stepped confidently across the room to shake their hands.

"Thank you for defending my son. It would devastate his father if anything happened to him. We are deeply in your debt."

Callum took notice of her firm handshake. He looked at their daughter as she stepped forward.

"I too am grateful, Señor Logan," she said. Her smile lit the room.

Why, she's the spittin' image of her mother, Callum thought, *only younger*. He couldn't help notice her trim waist and how she filled out her tan dress in all the right places.

Callum smiled back, seeing the same dark eyes of her father nestled in a soft, olive skin. "Why, ma'am, it weren't nothing I wouldn't do for anyone. Like I said, Alex was standing his ground. He just needed a mite of help. A couple of years and your brother won't need anybody to step in."

"Just the same, Señor Logan, we are grateful." She turned to Floyd. "To you also, Señor Logan. I feel your nephew is very fortunate to have you."

"Well, ma'am, don't know about that, but we're just glad to help."

"Gentlemen, I would be honored if you would join us for lunch. The hotel offers a filling meal, even if it does lack refinement. It will give us some time to get acquainted," the don said.

Callum glanced at Floyd, who nodded. "That would be pleasurable to us," Callum said. "We have a family—husband, wife, and son—traveling with us. Would it be all right with you if they also joined us?"

Doña Lopez crossed the room to her husband. She smiled at her husband, who nodded, and turned to Callum. "Mr. Logan, that would be most wonderful. We would love to meet them."

"Thank you, ma'am. Now, we need to get this trail dust off. Be all right if we meet you folks in about an hour?"

"Yes," the don said. "We will see you then." He escorted Callum and Logan from the room, and closed the door behind them.

"Fine folks," Callum said to Floyd. The two men walked down the dark hallway to the Radcliffs' room, across from their own.

"Yep," Floyd said. "But I'm betting you don't want to get the don riled. Looks to me like he'd be a heap o' trouble. Think I'll go on over to the room and get cleaned up a little. Might be nice to not smell too bad, sitting down with such pretty women," Floyd said. His eyes danced with mischief as he looked at Callum.

Callum, ignoring the look from his uncle, said, "I'll be along shortly," and knocked on the Radcliffs' door. It opened quickly.

Jimmy looked up at Callum. "Hi, Mr. Logan."

James stepped to the door, right behind Jimmy. Callum noted that the family had cleaned up. "Horses and wagon are all settled at the livery," James said.

"Hi, Jimmy, Callum said to the boy, before addressing James. "I'm glad you folks are cleaned up a bit. We've got a lunch invite from Señor Lopez. That includes everybody, Jimmy too."

Sarah Radcliff stepped around the door. "What happened to you, Mr. Logan?" she said, looking at his swollen face.

"Had a disagreement with a banker," Callum said. "We need to meet downstairs, in the hotel dining room, in one hour. Okay with you folks?"

James looked at his wife. When she nodded, he said, "That'll be fine."

"See you then," Callum said and turned to his room.

When he stepped inside, Floyd was wearing his boots and buttoning up a clean pair of red long johns. "You better get yourself ready, boy. Those Mexican folks will be expectin' you all nice and shined up."

Callum laughed. "Looks like you're gonna take a pile of shining, Uncle."

"Boy, I'm gonna trim up this beard some, and then I'll probably have to beat the ladies off with a stick."

"I reckon you might, Uncle."

"Now, you can stop calling me uncle, boy, and get yourself all nice and spiffy. Time's gonna be here and you'll still be jawin'."

Callum peeled his shirt off over his head, grabbed the water basin, tossed it out the window, and poured in some fresh water. He washed up, pulled a clean shirt out of his saddlebags, and slipped it on. *I sure need some new clothes*, he thought. He grabbed the towel and wiped down his black trousers. Then he wiped off his boots. He looked in the mirror, and, using his hands, combed his thick brown hair back. A few wrinkles were developing across his forehead.

The war had taken its toll on everyone. He'd been fortunate, and hadn't collected any souvenirs in the way of visible scars. Everyone brought back scars from that war, though, whether they were wounded or not.

He pulled out his razor, stropped it a couple of times on his boot, and commenced removing the black stubble on his face. He was careful of the dimple in his square chin. He'd sliced into it on more than one occasion. Shaved, cleaned somewhat, though he hadn't time for a bath, he now felt at least presentable. He swung his gunbelt back on and checked the bowie knife inside his right boot. That knife had saved him in the war when he'd fired his last shot, and those Yankees kept coming. He was almighty glad he'd never looked at Josh or any other family member over a gun barrel. He knew he wouldn't have pulled the trigger.

"You 'bout ready, boy?"

"Yep, let's head on down."

THE LOPEZ FAMILY was waiting in the restaurant when Callum and Floyd arrived. Moments later, he could hear the Radcliffs coming down the stairs. Introductions were made, and the two families and the Logans sat down to lunch.

Callum found out that the Lopez rancho was southwest of the Sangre de Cristo range. Señor Lopez knew exactly where Floyd's land was located. He also knew the previous owner, who had sold the property to Floyd.

Several times, Callum had trouble concentrating on what Señor Lopez was saying. His eyes kept drifting over to the *señorita. She's a mighty good-looking young woman, but I've got a lot of country I'm hankerin' to see before I settle down.* Yet, his eyes drifted back to her, again, and he caught her looking at him. She gave him a direct smile, her eyes laughing. *Keep your head, boy. Keep your head.*

They were almost finished with lunch when Jessup walked

into the eating establishment. His head was down, and he was well into the room before he realized they were there. He looked up and stopped, his eyes shifting from Callum and Floyd to the Lopezes. His nose, swollen to twice its size, was covered with a stark white bandage, making his face almost comical. Both eyes were already starting to blacken.

Before anyone could say anything, Señor Lopez stood. He wore a short black Spanish jacket and a red sash. In the sash rested a very businesslike Colt .44. "Are you ready to die, Jessup?"

"I have no gun, Señor Lopez. I was just coming in here for a cup of coffee and piece of pie."

"My family is here," Lopez said. "Otherwise, I would be tempted to shoot you right here. I will be patient. Perhaps another time." Lopez smiled, showing even white teeth, but there was no friendliness in the smile. It reminded Callum of a panther just before it leaped.

"Now I will tell you what is going to happen. My son is going to your bank. He will be given the amount of money remaining in my account, in gold. He will have no problem, will he?"

"I'm not sure we have that much on hand."

"Then I suggest that you locate it, for he will be there within the hour. We are closing our account. Yours is not the only bank in this country. Is that agreeable to you? There is no question as to our having an account in your bank?"

Callum watched the big man closely. This was going much too easily. Jessup was almost being nice. If there had been the problem indicated when he threw Alex from the bank, why would he accept this withdrawal so willingly now? Certainly, Lopez presented a sizable threat, but that was no different than three hours ago.

"No, Señor Lopez, that was just an unfortunate misunderstanding. The money, in gold, will be waiting when you're ready."

"Good. You may go." Lopez dismissed Jessup as if he were a lackey, and sat back down at the table.

Callum kept an eye on the big man as he walked from the room. He could see the anger in the man's eyes before he turned, yet he left without another word. *There is definitely something going on here that I'm missing.*

"Mrs. Radcliff, should you like to visit us, I would consider it a privilege," Señora Lopez said. Lunch was almost over.

"Why, thank you. I'd love to, if we have time." Sarah looked at her employer.

"I'm thinking that could be worked out," Callum said. "We've got a lot to get done on the ranch before snow flies, but later, maybe."

"You would all be welcome, Señor Logan," Don Lopez said. "We are in your debt, and if you should need any help, at any time, let us know."

"Thank you, Señor Lopez. If you are departing for your ranch today or tomorrow, I was thinking Floyd and I might accompany you as far as our ranch."

"We are leaving as soon as my son returns from the bank with our money. We would most appreciate the two of you accompanying us. The more guns, the better."

"Just what I was thinking," Callum said. "We'll be ready."

The lunch broke up, and the Lopez family headed upstairs.

"You folks mind waiting around here until we get back or send word?" Callum asked. "I've a mind to straighten out the problem we have with the ranch, before you move out there. I'm hoping this can be settled peaceably."

"Why don't I go with you?" James Radcliff said. "Better three than two."

"Reckon that's true. What do you think, Floyd?"

"If it's all right with Mrs. Radcliff, sounds good to me."

All eyes turned to Sarah. "We'll be fine here, and if you men will give me a list, Jimmy and I will have everything purchased and loaded when you get back."

"Fine, let's get the horses ready and loaded."

"I was shore likin' the idea of spending one more night in a nice, soft bed," Floyd said, and winked at Jimmy.

"Uncle, I know you're just raring to get outta town. You've spent too much of your life outside to stay cooped up in a hotel for long."

"You might be right, boy. You just might be right."

ALEX HAD PICKED up the gold without a hitch, while Callum was ensuring, that the room for Sarah and Jimmy was taken care of for as long as they needed it. The Radcliffs said their goodbyes, and everyone was mounted and ready to leave. Callum bought a gray mustang at the livery and contracted with the owner to stable all of their stock. James was riding the late Bloody Tom's big buckskin. Floyd was on a calm, intelligent-looking bay, while his pack horse was a big dun. The ladies relaxed in a plush black coach, with a wagon of supplies following.

Callum counted four vaqueros accompanying the caravan, plus the coach and wagon drivers. "Didn't realize we'd be riding with so many men," Callum said to the don.

"These days, I must protect my family. They are good men. I want you to meet my *Segundo*. Ricardo Valdez. Ricardo!" Lopez called.

A slim hipped, wide-shouldered man wearing a huge sombrero looked up from checking the shoes of his horse, rubbed the horse's foreleg, and let it softly down to the ground. He turned and walked over to Lopez and Callum. "*Si, Jefe.*"

"Ricardo, I would like you to meet Señor Logan. He is the one who persuaded Jessup to leave Alesandro alone."

"Ah, it is a pleasure to meet you, Señor. I understand you were very persuasive indeed."

Callum liked the tall Mexican. It looked like the don had surrounded himself with good men. "Pleased to meet you. I reckon you'd have done the same if you'd been there."

Ricardo smiled and said, "No, Señor. I am afraid I would have been forced to open up Mr. Jessup like a ripe watermelon. Alesandro is a special boy. No man will lay a hand on him in my presence."

Callum felt sure there was no brag in what Ricardo had said. The man was just stating fact.

"Let us be on our way," the don said. "Ride with me for a ways, please," he addressed Logan.

"*Listo, vaqueros,*" Ricardo called, leading the procession out of Pueblo, with the vaqueros surrounding the coach that Doña Lopez and the Señorita Lopez were riding in.

People lined the streets, as if for a parade, some waving and speaking to the individual riders as they left town.

Don Lopez and Callum rode together behind Ricardo. "Mr. Logan, I have been meaning to ask you. Your uncle, do you know if he has ever been in Denver City?"

"You speaking of the gunfight?"

"Ah, si."

"From what I understand, that was him. He hasn't said much to me about it."

"No, a man like him, I think, would not speak of such things. That fight involved my younger brother. He was only passing through Denver City on his way back to our *rancho*. You would have to know my brother. He has, how do you say, a short fuse?"

Callum nodded, and the don continued. "It is my understanding that your uncle had words with one of the older Barretts. He had backed down and they were looking for trouble. Evidently, they did not like our kind. The three of them saw my brother in the stable. Your uncle was there also, but they did not see him. I imagine they felt a lone Mexican was easy prey—they did not know my brother. They were on him before he had an opportunity to shoot. Though he did get his knife into one of them, he would have still taken a severe beating, had not your uncle stepped in. It was over quickly. They backed off. One Barrett sported a stiff leg from the knife. It was later that they tried, unsuccessfully, to kill your uncle.

"I had been wondering if he was the Floyd of Denver City. Now, I know. We are doubly indebted to your family. If you need help with your land," the don said as he turned to look directly at Callum, "in any way, call on us."

"Thank you," Callum said. "I'm hoping this will go peaceably. We Logans don't shy from a fight, but I prefer those folks be willing to abide by the law."

Floyd trotted up to Callum. "Pretty country, ain't it?"

"It sure is," Callum said.

Señor Lopez scanned the mountains from their left front, to the right. "You will find, as we move west, it will be even more pleasing to the eye. Your uncle made an excellent choice of the land east of the Greenhorn Mountains. It is rich with grass, and you will find all the timber necessary to build your home. Unfortunately, you may have to fight to claim your land.

"The banker Jessup sold it to the family who is living there now. They have worked the land, moved in a few cattle, and, the last time I saw it, they were building a home. I am afraid it will be difficult to move them off the land. They believe they own it."

Floyd looked over at Lopez. "It's our land, Señor, and we aim to have it. We're hoping to be moving our whole family out from Tennessee come next spring."

"Ah, so you have a wife in Tennessee?"

"No, sir. Neither one of us do. I'm talking about my brother, his wife, and kids. Callum's folks. Also, another of my nephews will be coming up from Texas—Josh Logan. So, we'll have quite a crew when everyone gets here. I reckon you can see we need to take our ranch back as soon as we can."

"Yes, I can see that." Lopez looked at Callum. "You are not married, Mr. Callum?"

A faraway look momentarily clouded Callum's eyes. "No. I reckon my feet don't let me stay still long enough to get thrown and hog-tied. I've got too much country to see. Figger I'll stay here until we get everything settled. Reckon, then, I'll move on. I've a hankerin' to see some of the country Floyd here has talked about."

"Yes, I understand. Before I married my wife, I, traveled a great deal. But when I met her I no longer wanted to travel. One day, you will meet someone and it will change for you."

"Maybe," Callum said. "Do you know how Jessup came to selling land he don't own?"

Lopez thought for a few moments. "I do not. Yours is not the only land that he has sold. He has some bad men working for him, who have persuaded a few owners to sell their land for pennies on the dollar. He then resells it for a significant profit. It is my understanding he wants to become a big man in Colorado."

Callum thought about what he had just heard. *So, there were others who had lost their land.* "Do you know if he has sold land that he did not have title to?"

"I do not, Señor. I know he is not a good man. I made the mistake of putting money in his bank when he first came to Pueblo. I was in hopes of building a stronger relationship with your people. Unfortunately, that has not worked out."

Callum could see the worry that settled on Lopez's face. "Is he after your ranch?"

"I believe so. No one has yet approached me, but it would seem he has a desire for our *rancho*."

5

Daylight slipped in front of the stars, their fading light giving way to the early dawn. Floyd was up, fixing a pot of coffee, and James was checking the stock. Callum slipped out of his bedroll, slapped his hat on, and shook out his boots, having no desire to upset a scorpion or tarantula that might have homesteaded in them. He stomped them on and slung his gunbelt.

"Smells mighty fine," Callum said, pouring a cup of steaming coffee into his cup.

"Uh." Floyd had less use for conversation in the morning than he did throughout the day, which wasn't much then.

"Morning," James said.

Callum noticed James was getting around better. He'd have some scars, but it appeared his cuts were healing well.

Shafts of red punctured the early dawn, leading the gold that would follow across the scattered clouds. The Sangre de Cristos thrust their jagged peaks toward the growing light. Vaqueros ginned around, saddling horses and hitching teams to the rolling stock for the day's journey. An early start covered distance while the day was still cool. Later, the heat would settle over them like a blanket, along with the suffocating dust.

"*Buenos Dias.*" Don Lopez walked up to the fire.

"Morning, Don Lopez. Care for a cup of coffee?"

"No, thank you, Señor Callum. I feel you will be leaving us today?"

"Yessir, that's a fact. Floyd here says we'll be heading out to our valley mighty soon. We're thinking of building the ranch house off the Sangre de Cristos."

"That is a good idea, Señor. You will find the northwest winds chilling in the winter. The mountain will help block some of it. I want you to know, as I have said before, I am in your debt. My rancho is open to you at anytime. Please come see us when you have time."

"We'll sure do that. We've got a slew of work ahead of us before winter sets in. But when we git 'er done we'll head down to see you."

"Good." The don turned and headed back to his coach.

Floyd had pulled out some side meat and was frying it in the skillet. "Might as well eat somethin' 'fore we head out. There's some biscuits in that tow sack."

Callum grabbed a couple of biscuits for each of them. They chased the meat and biscuits with coffee. "How far you reckon we are to turnin' off?"

"Not far. Those mountains to the north of us are the Greenhorns. A couple of hours more and we'll be leaving these folks and headin' north." The three men finished eating and poured the remaining coffee over the fire. Then they covered it with dirt. By the time they had loaded the pack horses and saddled their mounts, the coaches were on the move. Alesandro rode back to them as they mounted their horses. "*Mi Padre* said you will be leaving soon."

"That's right," Callum said. "We've a lot to get done before the snow flies. But understand, you'll be welcome anytime. We can always use another man's help."

"Thank you, Señors. I would like that." The young man swung his horse around and raced to the front of the cavalcade.

"Reckon you made that boy's day. Why, it looked like he was goin' to bust those fancy buttons on his vest."

"He's a fine lad, Floyd, and not far from being a man. Another year or so on him, he'll start filling out. My guess is, he'll be someone to reckon with."

The three men brought up the rear. They pulled their bandanas up over their noses to keep out the heavy dust. Callum took in the Sangre de Cristos rising in the distance. It looked like all of this country had been turned on end. What he used to consider as mountains in Tennessee would be mighty small hills out here. These mountains reached up like they wanted to grab the very heavens. *Almighty pretty country*. He could feel the excitement building. He wanted to find the canyon that Floyd had talked about and get the ranch house started. If they could get that built and throw up a barn and corral for the stock, then all they'd need to do would be put some meat in the larder—a lot to do and not much time to do it in.

His mind drifted to the señorita. Mighty lovely girl—almost a woman. She had a quick mind and was filling out in all the right places. She'd make some man a fine wife. But not him. He wasn't yet ready to consider another woman. It was too soon. His thoughts, momentarily, slipped back to Tennessee and Charlotte. He could see her leaning against the big old oak, rays of sun slipping through the branches, glistening in her golden hair. They had been engaged, prior to the war. But while he was away, cholera swept, like an evil cloud, across that isolated part of Tennessee and took his Charlotte away from him.

Two hours passed quickly. The coaches had pulled to a stop. Callum and Floyd rode up to the family's coach. "We'll be heading north now," Callum said. "Much obliged for allowing us to ride along with you."

"It is our pleasure," Don Lopez said. He stepped down from the coach. "Keep an eye out for the Indians . . . and others. There has been raiding going on."

Callum leaned down and shook the don's hand. "Take care."

Floyd and James tipped their hats as they swung their palouses north.

"Goodbye, Señor Logan."

Callum turned in the saddle. There, next to her father, stood the señorita smiling up at him. "Bye, ma'am." He doffed his hat to her and then to the señora, who was watching them, with twinkling eyes, from inside the coach. He nudged his horse with his spurs, heading to their new ranch.

THE THREE MEN rode along the creek that ran near the eastern slopes of the Greenhorn Mountains.

James couldn't take his gaze off the range of peaks that jutted into the western sky. "Those are some tall mountains."

"Yep," Floyd said. "You're looking at some of the highest mountains in this part of the country. They rise up t'ward the sky like they ain't gonna stop. I've been up around some of those peaks. Gets mighty cold up there. Wind seems to blow all the time. You don't want to get caught up there in a storm, 'cause you're liable to get fried by lightnin'."

While he was talking, Floyd was constantly watching the timberline. "Keep your eyes peeled and your rifles handy. Utes like this valley. They might be a sight upset to see us here."

Callum said nothing, but continued to read the countryside. Aspen groves, intermingled with douglas fir and lodgepole pine along the slopes above the creek gave way to cottonwood, alder, and willow along the rushing creek. A family of mule deer calmly fed on the western slope no more than a hundred yards away occasionally glancing up at the unwelcome intruders.

The men continued to ride for three more hours. Floyd pulled his horse to a stop. Callum and James rode up alongside him and stopped. The valley floor spread out in front of them. As far as they could see, the valley was covered with grass, waist-high to a tall man. It was several miles wide and no telling how long, with the tall grass washing like the ocean against the mountains in the distance.

Callum said, “I had a picture in my mind from all your descriptions, but nowhere this impressive. Ma and Pa are going to like it here. They never had this much land.”

“I knew it was the place, first time I saw it. There’s feed and water here for many a head of cattle and horses. It’ll be a fine ranch.”

Callum glanced down to the creek. “How ’bout some coffee? We’ll give the horses a break and eat a bite.”

The three men rode down next to the creek and dismounted.

“I’ll water them,” James said. He took the reins from Callum and Floyd, and waited while Callum pulled some supplies from the saddlebags, then he led the horses to the creek.

Floyd gathered some dried alder branches and started the fire. Here, under the cottonwoods, the faint smoke of the alders would disappear quickly.

Callum set the coffeepot next to the fire, stood, placed his hands on his hips, and leaned back. “My body ain’t as young as it used to be.”

Floyd chuckled. “Son, just wait a while. It gets even better.”

The faint scrape of rocks up the creek caused both men to disappear into the timber.

“Hello, the camp,” came softly through the trees.

“Come in with your hands empty,” Floyd answered.

“Floyd Logan, is that you?” answered back, followed by a deep, hacking cough.

A grizzled, stooped-shouldered old man, no more than five feet seven inches tall, staggered into the camp leading a mule loaded down with prospecting gear. Piercing green eyes, now red from strain, were recessed into a face covered with a shaggy gray beard. A dirty slouch hat covered his head. He turned loose the lead rope and dropped next to the fire. "That coffee's smelling mighty good."

Floyd moved quickly out from behind the cottonwood and strode over to the fire. "Shorty, what the blazes happened to you?" He dropped down next to the old prospector, spotting the blood seeping through the man's jacket from his left shoulder.

"Jumped by a couple of Utes just south of the Arkansas where it turns northwest. Darned near got me, too. Reckon they figgered an old geezer like me was easy meat. Their scalps be hanging on Lucy's pack. She ain't much fond of 'em. They managed to get a slug into my shoulder 'fore I plugged 'em."

James had returned with the horses and staked them out to graze. "I have some medical experience, if you don't mind me looking at your shoulder?"

"Have at," Shorty said. "I patched it up best I could. You fellers have any whiskey?"

Callum poured a cup of coffee and handed it to Shorty. "This'll have to do for right now."

Shorty took it in his right hand and took a couple of swallows of the hot coffee. "Mighty good." He looked up and winked at Callum. "Be a might sweeter with a touch of whiskey."

James had pulled a bottle from his saddlebags, along with a small medical kit. When he saw Callum's frown, he said, "For medicinal purposes. I don't drink, but it can come in handy for cuts and scrapes, even bullet wounds."

He knelt down next to Shorty and poured a little in his cup.

Shorty took a long slurp. "Now that's just what a man needs to chase the ague away." He held out his cup to James.

James poured a little more in it and stuffed the cork back into the bottle. "That'll have to do you. Now let's take a look at the wound." He pulled the man's jacket off, being careful not to spill the spiked coffee, and then started to unbutton the man's shirt.

"Ain't no cripple. I can get it."

Callum watched as Shorty set the cup down carefully and, with one hand, unbuttoned his shirt. Once his shirt was off, he tried to pull his red long johns off his shoulder, but couldn't do it.

James grasped the long johns and pulled them down off the man's shoulder and arm. Shorty couldn't repress a groan with the movement of his shoulder.

Callum watched James at work. The bullet wound was red, with red streaks running across to his neck. It was puffed out on the front, and there were visible pieces of dirty cloth that the bullet had driven into the wound. James looked up and saw Callum watching. He made an almost imperceptible shake of his head and poured more whiskey into Shorty's cup.

"This is going to hurt."

Shorty took another swig from the cup, now almost pure whiskey. "Well, get with it, boy."

James took a long instrument from the case, poured whiskey on it and the wound, and began probing. Shorty grimaced, his body shaking. Floyd grabbed the man's good shoulder and held him upright. James extracted three pieces of cloth from the wound. The stench was almost overpowering. Shorty had finally passed out. James picked up another instrument, put a clean patch on the end, doused it with alcohol, and pushed it through the wound, extracting the patch from the man's back. He then wrapped the wound as best he could. Shorty was still out.

"He gonna make it?" Callum asked James.

"I don't think so. You can see it has become infected. He needs a doctor with more skill than I have, but even then, I don't think he'd make it. You see the red lines going up to his neck? Odds are that the infection has made it to his heart. If that's the case, he'll be dead before morning."

Callum nodded. "We'll make camp here until we know for sure." He walked over to the bay and started stripping the gear from the horse's back. Once finished, he stripped the pack from the mule, and after watering her, staked her out with the horses.

Floyd and James followed suit. The men settled their saddles around the fire.

"So, how do you know Shorty?" Callum asked Floyd.

"Met him late in '42. We wuz doing some trapping not far from here. He was one salty character. He seemed old then. Can't imagine him surviving this long."

"I'm liable to see dirt thrown in your face." Shorty roused from his sleep and coughed. "Floyd, who're these younguns you're ridin' with?"

Floyd nodded toward Callum. "The big fella is my nephew. Goes by Callum or Cal. The gent that cleaned you up is James. Now, what the blue blazes are you doing out in this country at your age?"

"Gold, Floyd, gold. You know I've been searching for that miserable mistress my whole durned life, but she stayed hidden from me. Anyway, what am I supposed to do? Sit in a blasted rocking chair with a blanket over my knobby knees for the rest of my life? No, sir. That's not for me! Anyway, ain't you fellers gonna offer a poor old man something to eat?"

"I'll get something started," James said, and started rummaging through his saddlebags. He pulled out some bacon, and Floyd tossed over the sack of biscuits.

"I'm taking a look around," Callum said. He stood and walked north along the creek. They were close to where the valley opened up. The stream swung to the west, taking the cottonwoods with it. He stopped at the edge of the trees, where there were several large boulders. Easing up beside one, he used it to rest the binoculars he had taken from his saddlebags. Slowly, he scanned the valley. Even with the binoculars, he couldn't see the north end of the valley. What he could see blended with the mountains in the distance. He stayed in place for several hours, mapping the valley in his mind. He studied the western slope as it reached the lower mountain meadows, the canyons that ran off each side of the valley. Callum picked out several ridgelines falling into the valley that formed side canyons—possible building sites for the ranch house.

Through all of his searching, he saw no humans. But that didn't mean the valley didn't teem with life. Deer, elk, and buffalo were scattered within his view. None seemed skittish. As the sun started to slip behind the western peaks, he eased back toward camp.

"See anything?" Floyd asked.

"Not what I saw, but what I didn't see. I didn't see one head of cattle out there, not one. No riders around either. No ranch house. No smoke. I understand it could be up one of those side canyons, but no smoke? Where's this ranch that's supposed to be here?"

"Ain't no ranch in this valley," Shorty roused up and said, then dropped back against his pack. He was breathing hard from the exertion of talking.

"How're you feelin', Shorty?" Callum asked.

"Reckon I won't be breaking any broncs today."

Callum looked to James, who solemnly shook his head. Callum could see the rapid rise and fall of Shorty's chest. Floyd had moved his saddle next to his old pardner, and was leaning against it, long legs pointed toward the fire. His hat tilted over his eyes.

Without moving his hat, Floyd said, "Shorty, you may not make it this time."

For a moment there was no response, then Shorty opened his eyes. They were bright, in a feverish face. "Had to happen sometime, old hoss, but I'm suspectin' you might be right."

"Anybody you'd like us to tell?"

"Got a niece, brother's daughter, lives in Denver City, sweet little gal. Always gave me a place to stay when I was in town. Works in the dry goods store there. Name's Naomi, Naomi Gwendiver. Right proud of her. If'n you'd let her know, I'd sure be obliged." Shorty's body was racked with a coughing attack. When it was done, James offered him a cup of water. Shorty took a sip and frowned. "Ain't you got any of that whiskey left?"

Floyd nodded to James. He pulled the bottle of whiskey from his saddlebags, splashed some into the cup, and handed to Shorty.

Shorty took it, looked into the cup, and pushed it back to James. "More."

Floyd nodded again, and James poured the cup half-full.

Shorty put it to his lips, sipping at the liquor. "Sure am glad you boys were here. I couldn't have lasted much longer, and to die without one last sip of whiskey would be a shame."

The sun had set, and the evening was cooling quickly. A breeze was flowing down the mountains, chilling the air. Callum tossed more wood on the fire and watched the sky lose its golden cast and turn a deep purple. A single star braved the remaining daylight, a faint sparkle, growing stronger as the sky darkened. A couple of extra blankets had been tossed over Shorty, in hopes of keeping him warm.

"I might as well tell you, Floyd." Shorty's coarse voice had dropped to a whisper. "I think I found it. I've got a few bags in the pack on Lucy." He stopped to catch his breath. "I gathered it before those danged Utes came along. It's right up there where they hit me. Found a chute that runs right into that little creek. Don't think it'll last long, but it's mighty rich. You take it and split it with Naomi."

"I'll take care of it, Shorty." Floyd had sat up and was leaning close to his old friend.

"You be careful. I've seen a slew of tracks on the outlaw trail—all from shoed horses. There's a bunch of bad hombres hanging around here, but there ain't no other ranch in this valley. None!"

The darkness had taken the valley. A pack of coyotes lifted their voices to the starlit sky. Shorty suddenly reached out for Floyd's hand. "Promise! Promise me you'll split with my niece."

"I'll see she gets it all, Shorty. I don't need your gold."

Shorty relaxed. His breathing became slow and almost relaxed. "You take Lucy, Floyd. You always was a good mule man." He leaned back and gave one last shuddering breath. Shorty's face relaxed in the firelight, and he almost looked like he was smiling.

Floyd looked at his friend for a moment, then put his hand down. "He was quite a character. Never stopped searching for gold. He always believed he'd find it—and I guess he finally did."

6

Callum's breath drifted white in the pale dawn light. Clouds covered the mountain peaks. He threw some sticks on the remaining coals, to chase the mountain chill away, and watched as the dry wood smoldered and then flamed. Floyd and James roused from their beds and both looked over at the covered body of Shorty.

"We've got to figger what we're gonna do about Shorty's niece," Floyd said. "With her working in a store, I reckon she'll be needin' that gold Shorty said he has."

"Cold this morning," James said.

"It's like that up here," Floyd said. "This time of year, nights are might chilly. We get into winter, it can get downright frigid.

"What's your take on Shorty, Callum?"

Callum, on his way to the creek to fill the coffeepot, stopped, slid his hat to the back of his head, and turned to Floyd. "First thing is to get some coffee. Then we should take care of Shorty. Might want to bury him a little higher up, so's there's no chance of the creek washing him away."

"Good idea, but what about the niece? What'd he say her name was, Naomi?"

"One of us needs to take her the gold and tell her about her uncle. I'm some concerned about spending time looking for his strike. We've got to get buildings up, feed cut, and shelter for the horses, or we'll be in big trouble soon." Callum turned and continued to the creek, filled the pot, and returned. He squatted down and put the pot on the edge of the fire, shifting his holster to a more comfortable position.

"Well, boy, there's three of us. Who do you think should go?"

Callum glanced at James and then looked over at his uncle. "If it's all right with the two of you, I'm thinking you should go."

James spoke up. "I was thinking maybe I should go. Then, after seeing his niece, I can drop down to Pueblo, and pick up Sarah and Jimmy."

Callum stared at James for a moment. "How'd you figure on gettin' to Denver City?"

"Well, uh, I'd . . . I see what you're getting at. Guess that's not the best idea."

Callum nodded. "The part about picking up your wife and boy on the way back is, but I think Floyd here should be the one to do it. He knows this country and can get there and back a lot quicker than either one of us."

Floyd reached for the pot and poured himself a cup. "I'd prefer to stay. We've much to do and not a lot of time to do it in, but you're probably right. Let's fill our stomachs and get Shorty in the ground. We wanta make sure those scalps are buried with him. Last thing we need is for a bunch of Utes to come up on us with those scalps hangin' off Lucy's pack. Once that's done, I'll show you where I had in mind for the ranch house. There's plenty of timber and a couple of creeks close by."

Without another word, James grabbed the skillet, sliced up bacon and started cooking. As soon as it was cooked, the men ate the bacon with cold biscuits and hot coffee.

. . .

THE THREE MEN stood around the covered grave. "Lord, Shorty weren't the best, but he sure weren't the worst. He was just a man that loved these mountains," Floyd said. Then he put his hat back on, followed by Callum and James.

The men mounted up, crossed the creek, and, with Floyd leading the way, moved out toward the west side of the valley. They crossed another creek, and trout flashed in the knee-deep water as the horses waded across. Several long-eared mule deer watched them pass by, then went back to feeding.

Callum, riding up to Floyd, said, "Where do you reckon that couple who bought land here might be?"

Floyd looked around. "It's a mighty big valley. They could have built up any of these side canyons or on t'other side of the valley up against those Greenhorn Mountains. Interesting thing being, like you mentioned earlier, I ain't seen no cattle. Don't think we'd miss 'em, even in this tall grass."

After the brief conversation, the men rode in silence, rifles resting across their saddles.

Cuts, ridges, and small valleys or canyons ran off both sides of the main valley. Creeks plunged out of the high mountains to course into the main valley.

They had ridden for four or five miles, crossing numerous streams while riding northwest up the valley. Large pines, interspersed with aspen, covered the ridge fingers that thrust down from the mountains. One prominent ridge cut deeper into the main valley.

"There 'tis," Floyd said. "Notice how that ridgeline runs deep into the valley. 'Bout a mile up that little canyon is the prettiest place I ever did see. That ridge gets almighty steep. Way too steep for anyone to come down it. Be a perfect place for a ranch house."

Callum admired the little canyon. *Reckon this is even prettier than back home in Tennessee. Ma will like it here.*

The spot Floyd had chosen was obvious to Callum when it came into view. The canyon had narrowed, with the steep ridge dominant. Building the ranch house with the back up against the wall of rock would provide them with a secure advantage. There would be little opportunity for anyone to approach the house from the rear. The front of the house would look out on a park of grass and flowers with tall pine and aspen on the southern ridge. It would catch the morning sun, providing warmth on cold mornings. Best of all, it was an easily defensible position.

"Floyd, this is a mighty fine spot," Callum said. "Reckon Ma and Pa will be mighty pleased." He swung his leg over his horse and stepped to the ground, his Spencer gripped in his left hand. James dismounted.

Callum walked back to the pack horse and started unfastening the packs. "We've got plenty of work ahead of us, James. We ought to get started."

"I'll be heading out to Denver City," Floyd said. "Be back as fast as I can. Be looking for me in a week, maybe two."

"You take care, Uncle."

"I'll do it. You boys keep an eye out. I'm thinkin' them Utes may not be too happy with our arrival. Don't happen often, but both Comanches and Apaches range up through here. Any of 'em would love to have a couple of new scalps to brag about."

Callum watched his uncle for a moment, and then turned to James. "Let's get to work. I'd like to get up a lean-to and a corral as quick as we can. Then we'll get started cutting timber for the house. Keep your rifle handy, and don't be too trusting. The majority of folks out here ain't itching to be our friends. Like Floyd said, they're more apt to lift our scalp than not, but don't shoot until I do, unless you have to."

"I'm learning. If I'd been less trusting, those men wouldn't have taken my family. They won't do it again."

Callum nodded. "A man has to expect the worst out here. It's nice when you're wrong, but it don't happen often."

The two men swung their axes over their shoulders, and

James followed Callum to a patch of Aspen, where the uniform trunks provided the perfect size for the corral.

THE SUN DISAPPEARED behind the peaks of the Sangre de Cristo mountains. The two men sat in their lean-to, admiring the results of their efforts. The ring of axes had been echoing across the valley for the past four days. The corral was finished. It had been built near the stream. The lean-to opened out to the east, giving them a panoramic view of the valley and the Greenhorn Mountains. Callum had killed an elk on the second day. The back strap made a fine dinner, and they had strips of meat hanging, drying into jerky. He wanted to kill more game for the winter, but that would have to wait until Floyd returned. For now, it was important to get the house built.

When he rode into the valley, he'd had a plan in mind for the house. He had laid it out and he and James had cut the grass and leveled the site. Then they dug a trench along the perimeter of the house. They had built a sled from the aspens and hauled rock to fill the trench. Tomorrow, they would start cutting the pines to build the house.

Callum was thinking how smoothly everything was going. They had seen no sign of Indians. Even with the noise created by their axes and handling the rocks, there had been no visitors.

His thoughts turned to his brother Josh. They had separated in Nashville. In the war, Josh had promised his dying friend that he would go to Texas and tell the man's family of his death. Hopefully, there would be no delays and he would be arriving soon. Josh was the thinker. Callum, well, he thought, *I usually jump in with both feet*. The two brothers had always made a good team. James was a hard worker, and he was learning, but he was no Josh.

The lean-to was situated behind the corral, where he could

see the horses. He glanced toward the corral, just in time to see his horse jerk his head up and stare down the valley.

"James. Get your rifle! Something or someone is coming up the valley."

James grabbed his rifle, and the two men slipped into the trees. Four horsemen rode slowly up the valley. The big man in the lead sat tall in the saddle. Callum figured he was a couple of inches taller than he was.

The four men rode into the camp and looked around. They all had their rifles in hand. "Come on out. I ain't gonna hurt ya," the big man called.

Callum motioned for James to stay hidden and stepped out from behind the pine, his Spencer covering the big man. "Well, I'm glad of that. You sure enough had me shaking in my boots."

The big man laughed and started to step to the ground.

"Whoa up there, big fella," Callum said. "I reckon you ain't heard an invite." At the same time, he eared the hammer back on his rifle. The harsh metallic click echoed in the camp.

The man froze with his leg lifted over the back of his horse, then slowly lowered his foot back into the stirrup. Even in the fading light, Callum could see the man's face flush with anger.

"That's him, Wister! I thought I recognized that voice. That's Callum Logan, the feller that ambushed Tom and put a bullet in my leg."

Callum moved around to the front of the four men, where he could make out the speaker. His rifle remained trained on the man called Wister. "We meet again, Milam. Been ambushing any innocent travelers lately?"

"I told you I'd get my chance, Logan."

Milam was right-handed. The muzzle of his rifle needed to move only inches to cover Callum. He slowly started to ease it over.

"Milam, you move that rifle one more inch, and this time, it won't be your leg," Callum said.

Milam stopped the swing of the rifle and glared at Callum.

"You sure this is the man?" Wister asked.

"Dead certain."

"Mister, I'm gonna leave you to rot, right here in these mountains. You done killed the wrong man, when you killed my brother." Wister made a motion with his head, and the other two riders started spreading out.

"That's far enough," Callum said. "Wister, or whatever your name is, I don't much care who opens the ball, but I know this 330-grain slug is gonna give you a bad case of indigestion."

The riders held their position, but Callum knew he was in a tough spot. "James, take Milam with your first shot, then we'll work on the other two."

"My pleasure, Callum. With this Henry, I imagine I can get at least one more, before he hits the ground."

The four riders' heads snapped around in unison, looking through the gloom, trying to locate the voice.

Wister thought for a moment, then relaxed, allowing his rifle to rest across his saddle. "There'll be another day, Logan. If you've got any sense, you'll pack up and git, 'cause the next time I see you, I'll kill you."

While Wister had been talking, Callum saw the man with the buckskin vest, who was partially hidden by Wister, go for his handgun. The man was fast, but not fast enough to beat a cocked and ready rifle. The Spencer roared in the evening quiet. The sound bounced off the mountains and echoed through the canyon. The slug struck the buckskin vest just above the left pocket and drove through the rider. He bounced back in the saddle, then collapsed forward over the pommel. He was dead before his head hit his horse's neck. The three other men sat frozen.

Callum worked the lever of the Spencer, throwing another round into the breech, and cocked the rifle. No one had moved.

"Stupid kid thought he was fast," Wister said.

"Take your men and get off my land," Callum said. "Just so you know, I own all of this valley. I don't want to see you or your men anywhere near it. Now, like I said, git!"

Wister eyed Callum for a moment longer, then wheeled his horse and galloped out of the canyon. His men followed, with one of the riders holding the dead man in his saddle.

"Come on out, James."

"That was too close for comfort," James said as he walked back into camp.

"Yep, sure makes it tougher. We'll need to keep a watch all the time. With just the two of us, it's going to be hard to watch and build."

"Do you think they'll return?" James said.

"Sure as shootin'. That Wister wants my hide. He'll get it too, if I'm not careful. I don't think that's all of 'em. Back after I shot Milam, he was talking like this Wister had a big gang, so we'll have to keep a sharp lookout.

"There'll be no fire tonight, and we'll have to split the night watch. If it's all right with you, you can take the first watch until midnight, and I'll take it until daylight."

James nodded. "Fine with me. It'll make it tough with only two of us."

"You're right there. I'll be glad when Floyd makes it back."

7

The sun had just passed its zenith when Floyd rode into Denver City. "Whoa, horse," Floyd said, pulling his mount and Lucy to the side of the street. "These people look like a bunch of bees, rushing from one place to the other. If we're not careful, we'll get run over."

There was only a light breeze, and the dust rested heavy on the town. Freight wagons passed him en route to Colorado City and Pueblo. The rattling of the wagons and the shouts of the mule skinners added to the cacophony. Lucy brayed and pulled on her lead rope. "I'm with you, girl. I'd like to turn around and head back to the mountains myself. This place is way too loud for me."

Floyd had pulled the horse and mule over near the boardwalk. A well-dressed man wearing a black derby and puff tie hurried down the boardwalk toward him. "Howdy," Floyd said.

The man stopped in his rush and looked up at Floyd. "I'm pretty busy, Mister, what can I do for you?"

"I'm looking for the general store and a place where a man can cut the dust in his throat."

"We've two general stores, and more saloons than you can

shake a stick at. You just keep heading the way you're going and you'll run into all of them." With that, the man turned and continued his rush down the boardwalk.

"Much obliged," Floyd yelled after him. "So, horse, which do we do first, look for Miss Naomi or wet our throats?"

The horse shook its head.

"I thought you'd go for that. Let's go find a place to settle this dust."

He rode down Main Street until he came to the first saloon with a watering trough. He let Lucy and his horse drink their fill and then tied them in front of the saloon. Floyd unfastened the hammer thong on his Colt and strolled into the bar. He paused when he stepped through the door. Coming from the bright noonday sun into the dark interior of the saloon left him momentarily blinded. He stood for a few moments letting his eyes adjust, then moved to the bar on his right. To his left were six or seven round tables. A couple of them were occupied.

"I'll take a beer."

"Warm or cold?"

"Cold? I ain't never heard of a cold beer, 'cepting during the winter."

The bartender laughed and then said, "I've got a deep cellar where I keep several kegs. It keeps 'em nice and cold. A regular beer is a nickel and a cold beer is ten cents."

"Why, Mister, I'll have a cold beer." With that Floyd tossed ten cents on the counter.

The bartender disappeared for a couple of minutes and returned with a beer. "Try that."

Floyd picked up the mug and put it to his lips. The cold brew felt soothing as it ran down his parched throat. "Now that there is mighty fine tastin'," he said, and smacked his lips. "Reckon I'll take another one of those." He slapped another ten cents on the bar.

"Comin' up," the bartender said, taking his mug and heading to the back.

As soon as he disappeared, a young cowboy with a tied-down holster, who had been sitting at one of the tables, jumped up and hurried behind the bar, turned the spigot on, and got himself a free beer. He glanced up at Floyd. "Keep your mouth shut, old man." He then turned and rejoined his friends at the table, just reaching it before the bartender returned with Floyd's beer.

Floyd hadn't moved, but using the mirror behind the bar, he kept his eyes on the table where the kid sat. He watched as the three laughed and the cowboy winked at him in the mirror.

"You sell a lot of this cold beer?" he asked the bartender.

"Quite a bit, 'specially when it's a hot day. Sales are mighty tall during the heat of the summer."

"Ever notice if your keg up here gets light before you expect it to?"

"Sometimes I've had to change it out before I expected to, but I just figgered it wasn't filled all the way."

Floyd nodded. "Don't reckon any law-abiding man would stoop to stealing a beer, just to save a nickel, while you were in the back, do you?"

The bartender looked hard at Floyd. "Did somebody steal a beer?"

"You better keep that trap of yours shut, old man," the young cowboy yelled across the room.

The bartender looked at Floyd and then at the cowboy. Floyd turned and walked over to the table where the three cowboys sat. "Son, I don't usually butt in, but I don't much like a smart mouth, and I danged sure don't like a thief. So why don't you just stand up, walk over to the bar, and pay the man for the beer you took. I reckon you can afford a nickel."

The cowboy jumped to his feet and grabbed for his six-gun, but he couldn't draw it. Floyd locked his big, calloused hand around the boy's fingers and crushed them to the revolver. With his left hand, he shucked his Arkansas Toothpick from its scabbard, riding on his left hip, and pressed the point against the cowboy's throat. The other two cowboys jumped to their feet and started reaching for their guns.

"You boys might want to rethink that," Floyd said. "All I've got to do is twitch, like this." The point of the blade disappeared into the boy's neck, replaced with a trickle of blood. "Now you don't want your friend to die over a nickel, do you? Why don't you take your guns out of those holsters, toss 'em across the room, and sit down."

"Do it! Do it, now," the young cowboy said, barely able to get a word out while standing on his tiptoes.

The other two pulled their six-guns, tossed them on the floor, and sat back down.

Floyd looked at both of them. "Now that's right nice. What's your name, boy?"

"It's Luke, Luke Justis. Don't cut me, Mister."

"Well, that's up to you, Luke Justis. Now, we'll just mosey back to the bartender and pay him his due. How does that sound to you?"

"Sounds real good, Mister," the cowboy said in a high, strained voice.

Floyd guided him back to the bar with the point of the knife.

"Now reach in your pocket and pull out that nickel. Better yet, let's make it a dime. I figger you've done this afore. Is that all right with you?"

"Yes, sir. I'm real good with that."

The cowboy slipped his hand into his vest pocket, careful not to move his head, and pulled out ten cents. He laid it on the bar and gingerly slid it across to the bartender.

"Now, Luke, that's right nice. You reckon you can be a mite more polite to your elders?"

"Yes, sir. I sure can."

"Fine," Floyd said. He pulled the knife from the cowboy's

throat, wiped it on his sleeve, and slid it back into the scabbard. "Now shuck that hogleg outta that holster and put it in on the bar, real gentle like."

Justis eased the revolver from his holster with his thumb and forefinger. He laid it on the bar.

"That's just fine. Now, git. I want to finish my beer. You boys leave those guns where they lie. You can come back and get 'em from the bartender after I've gone."

The three young cowboys hurried from the saloon.

"You're Floyd Logan, aren't you?" the bartender said.

"Reckon I am."

"I thought so. I mostly don't forget a face. Comes from the business. I was here in Denver City, when the Barrett boys jumped you. I was standing right on the boardwalk when it all happened. Ain't never seen the like."

Floyd took another sip of his beer and wiped his mouth with his sleeve. "Mighty fine beer, Mister. That was a while back."

The bartender walked from behind the bar and picked up the two six-guns the cowboys had left and laid them with the third one on the bar. "When they come back in to get these, I'll be sure and tell them who they messed with."

"Well, it don't mean much. I just can't abide a thief, 'specially one that lets his mouth run."

"I appreciate what you did. How about another cold beer on the house?"

"Much obliged, but two's my limit." Floyd chuckled and said, "My brother, back in Tennessee, he don't hold with drinkin', but there ain't nothin' like a beer to wash away the trail dust.

"Mr. Bartender, you might be able to help me."

"Name's Clyde."

"Well, Clyde, I'm lookin' for a girl."

"Sorry, I don't run that kinda place."

"Not that kinda girl. Her name's Naomi Gwendiver. Works in a general store here in Denver City."

"Why, sure. I know her. Right nice lady. Her ma and pa passed a while back. Don't think she has anyone but her uncle. An old prospector who goes by the name of Shorty. Mighty pretty woman. She's seeing a banker from down Pueblo way."

Floyd tilted the beer mug and finished the last of his beer, placing the mug back on the bar. "Can you tell me where I could find her?"

"Just go on down the street a ways. You'll see the store on the other side of the street. Can't miss it. It's a busy place."

"Thanks. Be seein' you." Floyd turned and headed out the swinging doors. *Clyde couldn't be talking about the same banker, could he?*

FLOYD WALKED into the general store and looked around. The place was busy. An older man and woman were helping customers at the main counter. A ladder, on rollers, extended to the bottom of the top shelf along a side wall. Dry goods were stacked on the five shelves below it. The shelves covered all of the north wall. A young woman stood on the ladder, stocking the top shelf.

Her brown hair was pulled back in a bun, and the cream-colored lace collar of her blouse complemented a long white neck. A soft brown skirt was snug around her slim waist and flowed smoothly over her hips.

Floyd walked down the nearest aisle to reach her. He took off his hat, looked up, and said, "Ma'am, are you Mrs. Gwendiver?"

The young lady looked down at the big man questioning her, smiled, and said, "Why, yes. May I help you?"

Floyd felt a pang of sadness that he was about to ruin that lovely smile. "Ma'am, I'm Floyd Logan. I'm a friend of your uncle."

She climbed down from the ladder and extended a dainty hand. "I'm Naomi Gwendiver, Mr. Logan. Nice to meet you."

"You too, ma'am. Is there anywhere we can talk?"

Naomi looked around the store. "Mr. Logan, we're pretty busy right now. Can it wait until later today?"

"Mrs. Gwendiver, it's mighty important. If you could see your way clear to take off for a bit, I'd be mighty grateful."

A small frown creased her brow, and, making a decision, she said, "Wait here a moment. I'll be right back." She turned and marched over to the couple behind the counter.

Floyd couldn't hear the conversation, but it was evident the man was not happy with her leaving. The woman patted the man's arm, and said something. He nodded and responded to Naomi. She smiled at the two of them, then turned, motioning Floyd to meet her at the door. He slipped past two ladies admiring a bolt of material and made it to the door, just in time to open it for Naomi.

"I have a few minutes now. We can go to The Steakhouse. If you haven't eaten, they have an excellent lunch for twenty-five cents."

"That's fine, ma'am."

They crossed the street in silence as Naomi guided them to The Steakhouse. Floyd towered over her. His buckskin shirt pulled tight across his broad shoulders. Her heels clicked on the floorboards as she led the way inside the establishment and over to a corner table covered in a red-and-white checkered table-cloth. Several men sat at the other tables. Admiring eyes followed her as she moved past. She left the corner chair facing the door for Floyd. He held her chair for her as she seated herself. Then he moved around to the corner.

A middle-aged lady came from the back with a pot of coffee and two cups. A loose strand of graying hair hung down from near her temple. She put the cups on the table and pushed the strand of hair back in place. "Coffee, Naomi? Who's this big galoot you have with you?"

"Yes, please. Pearl, this is a friend of Uncle Dave."

"You a coffee drinker, Mister?"

"I've been known to drink a cup or ten," he said as he moved the cup toward the pot.

"Best coffee in town, if I do say so myself," Pearl said. "You got a name?"

"Yes'm. Floyd Logan."

Pearl had started to pour his coffee. There was an almost imperceptible pause at the mention of his name, then she continued.

"Thank you," Floyd said.

"You folks eating?"

Naomi leaned back and turned her head to look up at Pearl. "I've already had lunch, but I'd love a piece of your delicious cherry pie."

"I'll fix you right up. How 'bout you, Floyd?"

Floyd looked at Naomi. "You might want to hold off on the pie for a few minutes."

Naomi's face was a silent question. "Nothing but coffee, for now, Pearl. We'll order later."

"Just give me a shout when you're ready." Pearl turned to the other tables with the coffeepot.

"Now, Floyd—may I call you Floyd? I feel like I know you from listening to my Uncle Dave talk about you."

"Yes, ma'am. Floyd's just fine."

"Good. Please call me Naomi. So what is this important news you have for me?"

"Ma'am, Naomi, there ain't no easy way for me to say this, so I'll just say it outright. Your Uncle Dave is dead."

Naomi's slim right hand rushed to momentarily cover her mouth, then dropped back into her lap and clasp her left hand. Her brown eyes grew big, and tears edged to the corners of her eyes. She sat still for a moment and then took a deep breath.

She fixed Floyd with an inquiring gaze, and with a steady but soft voice, she said, "How did it happen?"

"He was attacked by Utes near the Sangre de Cristos, not far from the Arkansas. He killed them both, but they got a bullet in him. He made it to our camp a couple of days later. Till he showed up, I never knowed he was anywhere around. He died that night with us."

"Uncle Dave was so tough. I know we all shall die, but he seemed almost immortal. I can't believe he's dead. So a bullet wound killed him?"

"Surely did. That ole bullet took a bunch of his shirt and long johns into his shoulder. Reckon it'd been a long time since he or his clothes had seen any water. The wound got infected somethin' fierce. We tried to doctor him the best we could, but he died anyway. I'm mighty sorry."

Naomi laid her hand on Floyd's arm and said, "Floyd, it isn't your fault. I'm just glad he found your camp and didn't die alone. I'm sure he was surprised to find it was you. What are the odds?"

Floyd ran his hand through his thick hair, pushing it back from his forehead. "It was good to see him. We had some good times together. I just wish it could have been under different conditions."

"Thank you for bringing me the news. If he hadn't found your camp, I would have never known. I am deeply in your debt. He was my last living relative. My mother and father died five years ago." She sat silent for a moment, then gave a deep sigh and smiled at Floyd. "But life must go on, mustn't it, Floyd?"

"Yes, ma'am. Reckon it must, but that's not all the news. I've got Lucy tied out in front of the general store. She's yours."

"Well, thank you. I don't know what I'll do with a mule, but Lucy is a sweet thing. I'll be glad to take care of her."

"She's not just a pack mule, ma'am. She's a good riding mule, too. If you wanted to sell her, I'd be pleased to buy her from you. But there's still more."

This time Naomi's smile was broader. "My goodness, Floyd, you're just full of news. What else do you have to tell me?"

Floyd leaned forward and spoke in a low, conspiratorial tone. "Gold."

Naomi's eyes widened again. Keeping her voice low, she said, "Gold?"

"Yep. There's three bags out there on Lucy. Each one'll weigh a little more than ten pounds. Last I heard, gold was going for twenty-seven, twenty-eight dollars an ounce. I reckon those bags are worth well over *ten thousand dollars.*"

8

Floyd watched Naomi try to digest his news. He knew what it was like for a single woman with no relatives in this country. If she had no money she might find a job in a store—if she was lucky. Worst case, she might end up in a saloon as a soiled dove. Watching her, he could see the realization dawn that her money worries might be over.

"You need to take part of that gold, Floyd. I know my uncle would want you to have it."

"No, ma'am. That won't be happening. I know what this kind of money means to a woman in this country. It's all yours. You just need to be careful."

He watched the last patrons of The Steakhouse leave. "There's more," he continued, before she could say anything. "Before he died, Shorty described where he made the discovery. I moseyed over to where he was talking about. He and I were all over this country, and I had a pretty good idea about its location. You ready for that piece of pie?"

Naomi let out the breath she had been holding. She was sad about the loss of her uncle, but the excitement of finding gold had pushed the sadness down. "Yes. Pearl," she called.

Pearl came out of the kitchen, wiping her hands on her apron. "Well, you folks made up your mind?"

Naomi nodded. "I'll have that cherry pie, now."

Pearl looked over at Floyd. "You hungry, big fella?"

"My stomach thinks my throat's cut. What do you recommend?"

"The name of this place is The Steakhouse. I guarantee my steaks will stick to your ribs and you'll be dreamin' about them for weeks to come."

"Sounds good to me. Toss in a piece of that cherry pie, and I'd take a warmup to the coffee."

"You won't regret it," Pearl said as she headed for the kitchen.

"Tell me more," Naomi said.

"I found his claim, and it looks rich. I don't know how long it'll last, but I'm sure you can get enough out of it to keep you from worrying about money for the rest of your life."

Naomi leaned back. Floyd felt he could almost read her mind. It felt good to be able to give a person freedom. He had always been free, but he could see her realize this was not just about a few dollars now, but possibly the rest of her life. He grinned at her. "Feels good, don't it?"

"You have no idea. I have a good job, but one never knows when a job might disappear or when illness might strike. I've never felt this kind of freedom. So, what do I do?"

"First thing you do is keep this to yourself. You've got to get this claim filed, and then we'll find someone to work it."

She thought for a moment, then said, "I'll work it."

It was Floyd's turn to be surprised. "No, ma'am. Naomi, you can't do that. We're talking about hard work for a man. Plus, you'll be smack dab in the middle of Indian country, and those Utes have a dim view of folks traipsing across their country. Look what happened to your uncle. Nope, you just cain't do that."

Pearl walked out with the pie and Floyd's steak. "Think this might curb your appetite, big boy?"

Floyd grinned as he looked at the big, thick, sizzling t-bone with a huge helping of mashed potatoes, along with a couple of roasted ears of corn, slathered in butter. "This should sure take the edge off."

He sliced a sizable chunk of steak, shoved it in his mouth, and followed it with a forkful of mashed potatoes. "Now that's good," he said around the steak. "Callum and James are sure missin' out."

Naomi sliced a small piece of pie while watching Floyd attack his steak. "I love to see a hungry man eat. Who's Callum and James?" she asked as she lifted the pie to her mouth.

"Callum, he's my nephew. Just came west from Tennessee. He and his brother Josh are planning on building a ranch on property I own west of the Greenhorns. They both fought in the war. They were on different sides, but they're brothers, and the war's over."

Naomi became pensive. "My husband was killed in the war."

Floyd stopped eating. "I'm right sorry, ma'am."

"Thank you, but many people lost loved ones in the war. We just have to move on, but you were saying about your plans?"

"Yes'm." Floyd continued eating. "James is working for Callum. Callum rescued James and his family from marauders that were about to kill him and his family. Then Callum hired 'em both, James to work the ranch and his wife to cook. After I leave you, I'll be heading down to Pueblo to pick up Sarah, that's James's wife, and their son and take 'em out to the ranch."

"So Sarah is going to be out there, in the Indian country?"

Floyd could see where this was going. "Yes, ma'am. She sure is. But she'll have some men around her for protection. What you're talking about is being out there, alone, doing a man's work. It just ain't fittin'. And it's dangerous."

"Mr. Logan, I can assure you that I am not afraid of hard work. We had a farm in Virginia, and I had to take care of it while my husband was away at the war. Work is something I am familiar with. Furthermore, I have made up my mind. I intend to go work this claim—with or without you."

Floyd leaned back from the table, exasperated. He locked Naomi with a stare from his hard blue eyes. "You could be killed, or worse."

Naomi softened her voice. "Floyd, I'm not a fragile flower. I have taken care of myself for a long time. We all die, and I assure you, the Indians will *not* capture me. You must understand, I am going and you can't stop me. I'd prefer to go with you, but . . ."

Floyd knew when he had lost. "Let's plan on pulling out in the morning. That'll give the stock some time to rest up. It's a fairly long haul back to the ranch by way of Pueblo. By the way, can you shoot?"

Naomi smiled again. "My father taught me to shoot when I was a very little girl. I can usually hit what I aim at."

"You ever used a handgun?"

"Yes, I have. In fact, I have a .36 Remington Navy in my room, with three extra cylinders. I know guns, Floyd."

He looked her over in a new light. Here was this little woman, no more than five feet, three inches tall, with more sand than a lot of men he knew. "All right, do you know any man you can totally trust who can work the claim with you? Now, just wait, I'm not saying you can't do it, but it's always better if there are two people working. The work goes faster, and there's another set of eyes to keep a lookout."

"Uncle Dave had another friend. You might know him, Asa Brooks?"

"I know him, but I don't much like him. He's a crusty old codger in my book."

"Do you trust him?"

"Oh, yeah. The man's word is his bond. I just don't like to be around him. Never heard anybody complain as much as he does."

"Do you think he would work out?"

"I hate to say it, but he's a hard worker and honest. He's just a pain in the—I mean, he's hard to deal with."

The corners of Naomi's eyes crinkled as she tried to keep from smiling at Floyd's near slip. She was not a hothouse flower. She had grown up around rough men and knew how many of them talked. But she appreciated Floyd. "He's always been nice to me."

Floyd frowned and shook his head. "Yeah, he's just a real nice feller."

Naomi took the last bite of her pie as Floyd was finishing his. "Floyd, what do we do next?"

"First, I need to pay for this and we need to get moving. Hey, Pearl?"

Pearl appeared from the kitchen. "More coffee?"

"Nope, that was mighty good. How much do we owe you?"

"A nickel for the pie and twenty-five cents for the steak."

"I'll pay for my pie," Naomi said.

"Nope, another nickel won't break me." Floyd gave Pearl fifty cents. "Keep the change, Pearl. I might need a free meal sometime."

Pearl laughed a deep belly laugh and said, "You come around anytime, big boy."

"I just might," Floyd said.

"Bye, Pearl," Naomi said.

"You take care of yourself, girl."

The two of them stood, Floyd slapped his hat back on, and they walked out the door.

Once outside, Floyd looked around to make sure no one was close enough to overhear them. "You need to file on Shorty's claim. That concerns me a little. If word gets out of a new find, we could have another gold rush, and the vein just didn't look that big. Then you need to cash in some of the gold. No more'n five or six hundred dollars. Any more and people'll start askin' questions. We've got to find a place to stash the rest of it, where no one can find it, and you need to buy some additional equipment, since there'll be two of you. Also, you're going to have to talk to Asa. And that's all got to be done this afternoon."

FLOYD LOOKED up and down the street. He could tell that Naomi was a bit flustered with all she had to do. He had to admit, her plate was full for the afternoon. "Naomi, why don't you go quit your job? I'll take my horse and Lucy to the stable, get them fed, and make sure they get a good rubdown. Should have done that first thing. Then I'll meet you at the land office."

She looked relieved to have a direction. "Thanks, Floyd. I'll meet you there in a few minutes."

They crossed the street together. Naomi went inside the store, and Floyd untied the horse and mule and led them up the street to the livery. He led them to the trough. While they drank, the stable owner, a big, red-faced man, with a plug of chewing tobacco in his jaw, came out of the wide double doors.

"Can I help you?"

"Yep. Need to stable and feed these animals for the night. How much for a good bait of corn and oats?"

"Name's Otis. That mule looks familiar."

"She belongs to Shorty. How much?"

"Fifty cents for the two of them, and I'll throw in a rubdown for both. So where's Shorty?"

"I appreciate the rubdowns. Normally I'd do it, but I'm a little busy today." Floyd handed Otis a fifty-cent piece. "I'll be needing them early in the morning."

Otis took the half dollar and dropped it into the front patch pocket of his homespun overalls. "I'm here all the time. Didn't hear where you said Shorty was?"

If I tell him or not, the fact that Lucy is here without Shorty will be all over town in no time. "Shorty's dead. Utes killed him."

Otis scuffed his boot in the dirt and shook his head. "Durned idjit. I told him time and again to stay out of those mountains. Those danged Injuns finally got him. Does his niece know?"

"Yeah, I already told her. Take good care of these animals, and I'll see you in the morning." Floyd turned away from Otis before he could ask more questions.

He saw Naomi coming from the store. They met at the land office, and he gave her the piece of paper with the claim boundaries on it. "How'd they take you quitting?"

"Not well. Mr. Spivey was very upset, but he'll cool down. Mrs. Spivey was just worried about me. I'll miss them both. They've been very decent to me." She turned and entered the building. Floyd followed.

"Hello, Mr. Duggan."

"Why, how are you, Mrs. Gwendiver? I'm a little surprised to see you here."

"Yes, Mr. Duggan. As am I. This is Floyd. A friend of my late uncle Dave Harrison."

"Do you mean Shorty? Shorty's dead?"

Naomi stepped up to the counter and laid the piece of paper out. "Yes. Killed by Ute Indians. Mr. Duggan, I'd like to file a claim on this land. My Uncle Dave gave it to me."

"Well, I can sure do that, Mrs. Gwendiver. It'll take me just a moment."

Duggan pulled a ledger from behind the counter, picked up the piece of paper and logged the boundaries. He then turned the ledger to face Naomi. "I'll need you to sign right here, Mrs. Gwendiver."

Naomi took the pen and signed where he indicated.

Duggan blotted her signature, examined it, and looked up at her. "You have yourself a claim." He filled out an official-looking form and handed it to her. "Of course, you understand that to be given a patent on the claim, you must show improvement or effort equal to one thousand dollars."

"Thank you, Mr. Duggan." Naomi turned to go.

"If you have anything for me to assay, I would be glad to take care of it for you."

She turned back to him. "I don't, Mr. Duggan. This was something Uncle Dave wanted."

Duggan gave her a condescending smile and said, "I understand. He filed many a claim, but I don't think one of them panned out."

"Have a good day, Mr. Duggan."

Floyd held the door for Naomi, and she exited the office and turned toward the hotel.

"I know it's not Christian of me, but I cannot stand that little man. He is so pompous."

Floyd grinned and then said, "Yeah, but did you catch what he said about your uncle and all the claims he filed? That's good. That means if he does say anything about it, he'll be laughing. I don't expect there'll be any interest in your claim. At least not until you get it working and show up with gold. Now, I recommend we round up Asa."

"That's where we're going. He stays at the hotel. There's a small restaurant and bar that he hangs out in when he's in town. We can check there first."

"Good," Floyd said, his brow wrinkled with concern. "Callum and James are by themselves. We need to get back as soon as possible. Lot of work to do before winter sets in."

9

Callum had stripped off his coat, vest, and shirt, exposing the outline of rippling muscles through his tight, red long johns that were stretched across his shoulders and biceps, almost to the point of ripping. He swung the axe into the soft wood of the tall lodgepole pine. The blade bit deep into the tree, sending bark and wood chips flying. The ring of the axe connecting with the tree reverberated across the valley.

He paused for a moment and scanned the entrance to the homeplace, where tall pine and aspen gave way to open valley. Mule deer fed in the flat, no more than two hundred yards from where he and James were working. Occasionally, the deer would look up, watch them for a moment, and go back to feeding. The animals had quickly become used to the sound of the men and their axes.

Callum surveyed James and his axe at work. *I'm glad I hired him. He's a mighty hard worker.*

The two men had been hard at it for the past five days. They were fortunate to have the stand of lodgepole pine so close to their building site. The lodgepole grew tall and straight, with limbs only near the top third of the tree, making it perfect for the barn and house. His plan was to finish the barn first. If necessary, they could live in the barn with the animals if the snow moved in before they finished the house.

Callum had fully expected a raid from the Wister Gang, but it had not yet materialized. The men kept their weapons handy, in anticipation of an attack. He walked over to the bucket of water, picked up the tin dipper resting in it, and took a long drink of the cold water, then dropped the dipper back into the bucket. He had rested his axe against an adjacent pine. He picked up the axe and checked the blade, still sharp from his work on it last night. He took one more glance down the flat, just in time to see the small herd of mule deer start flashing their tails.

They stood for a moment, started walking toward the aspen, and then broke into a run.

"James," Callum called, "get your rifle and get over to the logs. Looks like we've got company."

James looked up just in time to see a large group of riders round the end of the ridge in the valley. He grabbed his Henry and, with his axe in his other hand, trotted to the stack of logs.

"Good thing we built this breastwork," James said. He slid his rifle forward over the top log.

Callum watched the riders close the distance. "Figgered it might come in handy. It was right nice of them to wait until we got it built." He checked his Spencer and his loading box, containing ten reloading tubes of seven rounds each. He laid out four pre-loaded cylinders for his two .44 Colt New Army revolvers.

The riders were now where the mule deer had been, and all of them had rifles across their saddles. Callum eased the Spencer over the top log and took aim, then brought it back down. "Reckon we want 'em closer."

"I count fourteen," James said. "We don't want them too close, do we?"

The riders were passing one hundred yards. "They've come to

kill us," Callum said. "I aim to kill as many of them as we can. Don't let 'em get past us."

The gang was riding up a slight grade to the homeplace, which put Callum and James looking down at them.

"Get ready, and pick your targets." Callum brought the Spencer back to his shoulder. He was mad clean through. These men were riding in to destroy him and his plans for the Logan clan. It was time they were stopped, for good. He nestled the rifle into his shoulder, like he had done many times before. The front sight settled into the notch of the rear sight, with Wister's chest balanced on top. He started to squeeze the trigger, when he was suddenly slammed into the logs. He lost his grip on the Spencer, and it tumbled across the top log, falling into the dirt on the other side. He could see the horses had slowed and were walking toward them.

He heard another shot. It must be James firing. No, James was bleeding from a wound in his shoulder. Callum tried to stand. His legs were weak. He had to help James and stop the Wister Gang. He felt another crushing blow to his back, and his legs collapsed. James had his hand on his arm, trying to pull himself toward him. James's head exploded, blowing blood and gore over Callum, followed by the echo of the shot.

I can't move my legs. I can't breathe. I'm sorry, Ma . . .

"Boss," Milam said, "looks like your plan worked like a charm."

"You're right, Ben. I had an idea these yahoos would never spot Blue. That boy is half-Injun. All he had to do was slip over that ridge, and he'd have a perfect shot. Course, it must be nigh on to seven hundred yards, but he's a shooter."

Wister stood in the saddle and waved his hat toward the ridgeline. Barely visible, a man stood on the top of the ridge and waved his hat back, then disappeared.

"Ain't this a mess?" Wister said, then laughed. He had ridden his horse up to the breastworks and looked at the carnage on the other side. "Looks like that feller just lost his head." He broke out in laughter as he stared down at the remains of James. "And look over here at Mr. Tough Guy. Looks like Blue drilled him twice. Got a hole in his shoulder and one smack dab through his back."

The gang had encircled the two prostrate men. They dismounted and walked up to the two bodies. Milam turned to one of the gang members. "Get their guns." He then looked up at Wister, still sitting on his dapple gray. "Looks like they were ready for a war." He pointed toward the four laid out cylinders and the magazine block for the Spencer.

Wister laughed again. "Tweren't ready enough, I'd say."

Milam walked over to Callum and kicked him in the side. "Told you I'd see you dead. Not so big, now, are you?" He kicked Callum again. Callum moaned and opened his eyes.

"Looka here, Boss. The big man ain't dead."

Wister swung down from his horse and handed the reins to a short man standing next to him. "Let me see." He walked over and knelt beside Callum. "Didn't go like you planned, did it, Tough Guy?"

Callum pushed up on his elbows for a moment and tried to move his legs. Nothing happened. He dropped back and muttered, "My legs."

"What's a matter, Tough Guy, your legs not working?" Wister roared with laughter, spittle running down his chin. "Might have something to do with that hole in your back."

"We ought to finish him, Boss," Milam said. He drew his .44 Remington and stepped next to Callum, the muzzle pointed at his forehead.

Wister knocked the revolver aside.

"Why, no, we ain't. I can't think of nothing better than letting this big fella lay here and die. Fact is, coyotes or wolves, maybe even a bear, can find them a nice meal. Might give him time to think on killing my brother." Wister leaned down in Callum's face. His breath smelled worse than a week-dead cow. "That a good idea, Tough Guy?" He spit into Callum's face, straightened up, and kicked him in the side.

"Gather up everything. Guns, tools, all the supplies, and the horses. I don't want anything left here that he might be able to use. Course, I reckon he'll be dead 'fore we round the end of that ridge yonder."

The men quickly picked up all the equipment and supplies, then saddled and packed everything on the horses.

Callum's eyes were still open. They followed the men as they moved about the camp.

When the gang was ready, Wister rode his horse over to Callum. "This is what happens when you buck Elwood Wister. Enjoy your last minutes." He yanked the reins of his horse and galloped from the homeplace, his gang following.

CALLUM TRIED to move his legs. He couldn't. They felt like tree stumps attached to his body. His upper body was numb from the gunshots, but he knew the intense pain wasn't far away. He tried to pull himself over to James, but had no strength. *I'm sorry, James. I brought you out here, away from your family, and now you're dead. I reckon life ain't fair. Sometimes the bad guys win.*

He lay back down. Death was so close. He gazed up through the lodgepole pine at the brilliant blue sky. Dying in a place like this wasn't so bad—the smell of the pines, the cool breeze wafting up the valley and softly caressing his cheek. Not a bad place for his life to end. Callum closed his eyes. His chest rose, then fell, rose again. He released a long sigh. He was still.

Where am I? He looked around the valley. He was standing, and he felt no pain. *Wait. Who is that on the ground next to James? Is that me?* There was a cloud. A low cloud, almost on the ground. It was a cloud, yet it wasn't. There was movement in the cloud, then a woman stepped out. *It can't be!*

She came toward him, her hands reaching out to him. The sun glinted on her long blonde hair. "Hello, Callum."

"Charlotte? Am I dreaming? You're dead."

"No, Callum, you're not dreaming. You're dying."

"I've really missed you," Callum said.

Charlotte smiled. "I know, Callum. It was my time."

Callum grasped her hands and pulled her to him, wrapping his arms around her. He could smell the light, sweet scent of lilacs. "I've missed you so much."

She leaned back in his arms and looked into his eyes. "I've missed you. But, Callum, you stopped living."

He looked into her soft green eyes. "I'm ready to start again. We can be together."

She gently pushed him away. "No, we can't. You need to go on living. Your time is not now. You still have much to do." She reached up and caressed his cheek. "I want you to enjoy life. Live it to its fullest."

Charlotte smiled again, then gently extracted herself from his arms. "Now, you must go back. It's going to be hard, hard and painful. But I know you. You can do it."

He watched her turn and reenter the cloud. Then he glided closer to his body.

Callum gasped in a deep breath. His chest expanded, and blood ran from both bullet holes. Pain slammed into his chest like another bullet. A groan slipped from his lips as his eyes opened. *Water. I've got to get to the water. If I can lay in the creek, it will at least rinse through these wounds. Shorty died of an infection. If I don't get them cleaned out, so will I.*

He tried to move his legs again. Nothing. The muscles in his chest and arms flexed, bringing excruciating pain, as he gripped the ground in his fists. Straining every muscle, he pulled and moved a few inches. He was at least fifty yards from the stream.

His jaw clenched, and again, he pulled himself forward to the stream. This time he moved over a foot. With each effort, the pain intensified. *Charlotte, I'd danged sure rather be with you right now.* He pulled again.

After several tries he had moved no more than six feet, but he had moved. *Pa always said, don't be a quitter.* The blood flow had slowed. He pulled again. Slowly, through the afternoon, Callum pulled himself across the rock-strewn forest floor. He could feel the pine needles packing inside his long johns and into the top of his pants. He kept pulling.

He was only a few feet away from the stream. He needed to get the top of his long johns down so the water flow could get to the wounds. Callum, lying on his back, unbuttoned them down to his pants. He rolled on his side and, after working through the pain, managed to get his right arm out of the sleeve. He lay on his back for a few minutes, then slowly worked his left arm out of its sleeve.

His biceps stood rigid as he pulled his body into the fast-flowing current of the stream. The cold water shocked his body, and within moments his teeth were chattering and his body was shaking. Now he needed to turn over so that the exit wounds in his chest could wash. He attempted to roll over, but with no help from his legs, he couldn't make it. He knew his strength was slipping away. If he was going to get turned over, it had to be now. He lifted himself with his left arm and grasped the pants leg of his right leg with his right hand. Mustering all of his strength, he threw his right leg over his left and twisted his torso.

The pain was overwhelming. He collapsed facedown in the stream. He managed to get his hands under him. Coughing and sputtering, he pushed his head up enough to get his nose and mouth out of the water. *I've got to hold this long enough to rinse these wounds.* Now his body was shaking uncontrollably from the cold and shock.

This has to be good enough. I can't stay in this water any longer.

He grasped the rocks and gravel in the bottom of the shallow stream and gradually pulled his body out of the water. The sun was about to disappear behind him as it neared the peaks of the Sangre de Cristo.

His clothes were soaked. His red long john top was down around his waist, and his back and chest were bare. He collapsed on the pine needle-covered ground near the lean-to, and the shadows walked slowly toward him.

10

Callum moaned in pain. His eyes fluttered open, and he raised his head, peering into the darkness. From the breastworks came the sound of scuffling and occasional growls. He felt the ground around him, searching for rocks or limbs. His hand closed on a rock a little larger than his fist. When the wolves were through with James, they would be coming for him.

He was near the lean-to. If he could drag himself inside it, he would have some protection. He tried again to move his legs. No success. His chest hurt something fierce, but he had to get into the lean-to. When he started crawling, the growls stopped. He could hear the soft padding of several four-footed creatures moving toward him. Then, from no more than six feet away, came a low growl.

Callum had made it to the tree that provided one of the front braces for the lean-to. He pulled himself up into a sitting position against the tree, facing the advancing animals, his only weapon the rock in his right hand. Sliding himself upright against the tree trunk had started his wounds bleeding again.

Wolves. At least two, maybe three. He could just make out the outline as the big one jumped. He had one chance. If he could muster the strength, and if he timed the blow just right, he might kill his attacker. He needed to kill him. He swung the rock with all of the power in his upper body and felt the rock smash into the wolf's head. With his other hand, he grabbed the fur around the animal's neck and hung on, while the rock crashed against the furry head again and again, until it was still.

The other wolf had backed off and was sitting on his haunches, watching. The stench of the wolf was strong, but Callum hugged him close. The warmth was welcome to his freezing body. His clothes were soggy from the stream, and he had yet to pull the top of the long johns back up over his body. Working through the pain and cold, he managed to get his arms in the sleeves of the long johns and, after a few minutes, had successfully secured the buttons. The wool, though it was wet, would keep him warmer.

Dragging himself with one hand and pulling the wolf with the other, he worked himself back into a corner of the lean-to. The strong man smell kept the other wolf outside. Callum again pulled the dead wolf up close to him, his body savoring the warmth. He knew that the warmth from the wolf would be gone soon, but the fur would help him retain some of his own body heat. He lay propped up inside the lean-to, clutching the dead wolf to him.

How fast life changes. When the sun came up, we were both strong, facing the day with optimism. Now James is dead and I'm . . . No! I'm going to live. I don't know how, but I'm going to live and hunt down Wister, if it's the last thing I ever do. With that thought, Callum passed out again.

The bright morning rays of the sun, as it climbed over the Greenhorn Mountains, warmed the feverish face of Callum. He blinked at the brilliance stabbing his eyes and turned his head. Slowly, the lean-to came into focus. Puzzled, he looked at the dead wolf that lay beside him, then the memories of yesterday and last night came flooding back into his consciousness—along with the intense pain in his chest and shoulder.

He needed water, but the thought of dragging his pain-racked body back to the stream and then back to the lean-to again exhausted him. *How am I going to survive? I'm shot through the chest. I should already be dead. I have no food. Wait! Did they get my knife?* With both hands, he grasped his right leg and pulled it up until he could reach the top of his boots. He slid his hand inside his boot and felt the haft of his knife. Relief flooded through his body as he pulled the big knife from his boot. *A weapon. I at least have a weapon.*

A laugh burst from his mouth. He immediately regretted the laugh, as it was followed with a crushing pain from his chest. *I had my knife last night, and I killed the wolf with a rock. I must have been out of my mind.* He looked at the wolf again. *Food. I have food.* Callum started skinning the wolf carcass. It was slow going. He had to skin a portion and then pull the wolf along so that he could get to the next section. He skinned one side and laid the hide back so that he could get to the meat without the flesh touching the ground. He sliced along the backbone, taking out small strips of the backstrap. He shoved the bloody meat into his mouth.

"Thanks, wolf. You just might have saved my life," Callum said between chews. The backstrap was tender. He had eaten raw meat before. It wasn't his favorite, but it danged sure beat nothing. He ate several pieces and made up his mind he had to go for water. Callum pushed against the wall of the lean-to, fell to his face, and started crawling toward the stream.

The sun was high overhead when he awoke again. His body was angled toward the stream, his face at the water's edge. He moved his head over the water and drank deeply. He lay there for a moment, drank more water, and passed out again.

His chest burned like liquid fire. He opened his eyes to see a man kneeling over him, pouring whiskey into his chest wound.

The man wore a buckskin shirt and a fur hat that had seen better days. He had a full beard that was going to gray, a hawkish nose, and serious light blue eyes. Callum looked around and saw two horses in the corral.

"You're in mighty bad shape, young feller," the man said. "This is gonna hurt a bit." He poured more whiskey into the shoulder wound. "I already cleaned out the bullet holes in your back. I'll be danged if I can see how you're still alive. Don't have any idea how that bullet made it through your chest without blowing up everything of importance. But it did."

Callum opened his mouth to talk, but nothing came out.

"You relax, young feller. Ole Jeb's here. I'm gonna take good care of you. Don't know how you managed to kill that lobo in your condition, and with a rock. Boy, you must be a real catamount."

Callum whispered, "James?"

"You must be talking about your friend, or what's left of him. I've buried him behind your corral and what looks like a barn you were building. Now you just relax and get some rest. Only one knows whether you'll make it or not's the Lord. But I've got my money on you. Now, rest."

Callum slipped in and out of consciousness. He could remember the man giving him some kind of drink that tasted worse than what Ma used to give him when he was sick. He dreamed of red-eyed wolves riding up on fire-breathing horses and ripping flesh from his body. The dreams came and went. One, he wanted to come back, but it wouldn't return. It was Charlotte, and they were together before he rode off to the war. She was so young and pretty. Her face always lit with a smile. A secret promise in her sparkling green eyes.

HE AWOKE TO VOICES. Men's and women's voices. Where was he? He felt like he was in a bed, but that couldn't be. He took a deep breath and felt the pain in his chest. His left shoulder was stiff and sore. He tried to use his legs to sit up, but they wouldn't move. Callum opened his eyes. He was in the back of a wagon. He tried to speak, but his throat was dry. He tried again. "Hello?"

The voices stopped. Almost immediately, Sarah Radcliff climbed into the back of the wagon, followed by Floyd. There were tears in Sarah's eyes as she felt his forehead. She turned to Floyd. "His fever's broken."

Callum looked into her sad brown eyes. "I'm sorry," he said.

She picked up his hand. "It isn't your fault. It looks like the two of you never had a chance."

"I can't move my legs."

She nodded her head. "I know. In your delirium, you spoke about your legs often. But, Callum, there's hope. The bullet didn't hit your spine, so you may regain the use of your legs, in time. Your job now is to get well."

"That's right, boy," Floyd said. "You get yourself well. When you do, we've got some business to take care of."

"What happened?"

"They set you up. You were ready for them. I reckon you woulda wiped them out, 'cepting they pulled a fast one on you. There weren't no way anybody could get to you from behind, but they had a sharpshooter up on the ridge. It must be a solid eight hundred yards. I found where he set up. There was just one little opening for him to shoot through. He laid out with his rifle 'cross a log. Most men couldn't make that kinda shot, but for him, you and James were sittin' ducks."

"I shoulda known better."

"No, boy. No one woulda thought of that. It's way too far. They just happened to have them a backshooter that was good. But I've got his number. He's a small-built man that wears square-toed boots with a gash in his left boot heel. We'll get him.

"Course he could show up there again, anytime. So, I left a few little presents for him. If he comes back to try again, he'll have a nice surprise waiting for him. Now you get some more rest."

"Josh?"

"No sign of him yet, but he'll be along. Now, rest."

Callum lay back on the bed and closed his eyes.

HE WOKE THE NEXT MORNING. The pain was still there in his chest, but it wasn't quite as bad. He raised both arms and stretched them the width of the wagon. His left shoulder was sore, but better. His legs were hurting some, and that bothered him. He reached down and rubbed his thighs. He could feel it! He tried moving his left and then his right. They both moved, but they hurt like crazy. Callum didn't care how bad they hurt. They were moving! *Maybe, just maybe, I'll be able to walk again.*

The wagon jostled, and Jimmy was looking in on him.

"Ma, Mr. Logan's awake."

"All right, Jimmy, you don't have to wake the dead."

Callum looked at the boy and motioned him into the wagon. "How are you doing, Jimmy?"

"I'm okay, Mr. Logan."

"Jimmy, I'm right sorry about your pa. He was a brave man."

Jimmy's brown eyes brimmed with tears. "Yes, sir, he sure was. I really miss him."

Callum felt something cold and icy flow down over him. "I know you do. But I promise you, Son, the men that did this will burn in hell soon." He gripped Jimmy's hand. "I promise you."

"Mr. Logan! Don't talk to my son like that."

"Ma'am, I'm just telling him the truth. Your husband was a fine man that didn't deserve to die from a backshooter. Those that did it are going to pay for it, and that's a promise."

"Jimmy, go on back outside and help Mr. Floyd."

Jimmy turned to leave. When he reached the back of the wagon, he turned to Callum. "I believe you, Mr. Logan. I just wish

I was old enough, I'd send them there myself." Then he quickly jumped down before his ma could say anything.

"See what you've done, Mr. Logan? I don't want my son to grow up to be a cold-blooded killer, like—"

"Like me, ma'am?" Callum pushed himself up on his elbows and locked her in his steely gaze. "Ma'am, you elected to come out west. This is a hard country. A man has to defend what's his, whether it's property or family. Sometimes that means being judge, jury, and executioner because there's little law available. If your son doesn't learn that, then he'll just be an innocent victim. I'm sure you don't want that for him."

Callum dropped back to the mattress. His breathing was hard and rapid. Sarah placed her hand on his forehead to check his temperature. "Thank goodness you aren't running a fever, but you can't get yourself worked up like that. You still need to rest."

"How long have I been out?"

"Today makes almost two weeks, but the rest is what you needed."

"Two weeks. I've got to get out of here. Ma'am, I need to get dressed and get out of your wagon. You and the boy need to be in here."

"Mr. Logan, I want you to stay here and rest."

Callum turned his head and yelled, "Floyd!"

A moment later, his uncle stuck his head in the back. "What can I do you for, boy?"

"Uncle, can you get me out of this wagon? I know I'm a handful, but I can't lay around here all day. I've got to be out. I've just moved my legs, so I need to be where I can work 'em."

Floyd's head bobbed up and down. "I'm glad to hear that. We'll get you out of there in no time. Mrs. Radcliff, if you wouldn't mind stepping out of your wagon, it'd be a mite easier getting him out."

"He needs to rest, Mr. Floyd."

"He can rest out here."

Sarah Radcliff gave up and left the wagon.

Floyd hopped up into the wagon, belying his age. "Got you some new clothes. Stocked up on supplies in Denver City and Pueblo. Figgered we would be out here for a while. Good thing I did."

Callum noticed the clean long johns he was wearing. "How'd I get in these?"

Floyd chuckled, and then said, "Well, boy, you're a big feller and you were mighty dirty, especially those bullet wounds. Mrs. Radcliff cleaned you good and helped me get these long handles on you."

Callum shook his head. "Help me get dressed, Uncle. I swear, a man ain't got any privacy."

11

Jeb helped Floyd lift Callum from the back of the wagon. They guided him, as he made tentative steps, to a chair made from split aspen and sat him in it.

"This here," Floyd said, "is Jeb Campbell. I knowed him from way back. He made this chair for you, Son. He's mighty handy with an axe."

Callum looked up at Jeb and extended his hand. "Mr. Campbell, this chair's sure fine. Hopefully, I won't be spending too much more time in it. I reckon I owe you thanks for more than just this chair. If you hadn't showed up, I don't think I woulda made it."

Jeb scratched his beard. "Don't sell yourself short, boy. I never seen any man in your condition do the things you done. You saved your own life when you killed that wolf. But I'm proud to help, and call me Jeb. Mr. Campbell is way too highfalutin."

Callum looked around. There were two more new faces in the group. An attractive woman was talking to a man around Floyd's age. Floyd waved them over.

"This here is Mrs. Naomi Gwendiver, and this old reprobate with her is Asa Collins."

Naomi smiled. "Nice to meet you, Mr. Logan. I'm sorry about what happened, but I could hear the good news. Hopefully you'll recuperate quickly."

Callum slid his hat back so he could get a good luck at Naomi. Her brown eyes were alive with light. He could feel the warmth and strength of her handshake. "Nice to meet you, ma'am. I'm like Jeb. I don't much care for mister. I'd be obliged if you'd just call me Callum."

"Thank you, Callum. Please call me Naomi."

Callum nodded to her and shook Asa's hand. "Nice to meet you."

Asa turned his head and spit a stream of tobacco juice. "Likewise." He gave Floyd an icy look and went back to what he was doing.

Callum shot a questioning look at Floyd.

"He's just a cranky old geezer," Floyd said.

"To hear you tell it," Asa shot back. "Mrs. Gwendiver, how much longer we gonna hang around here? We've got work to git done."

"Asa," Floyd said, frustration clearly evident in his voice, "you've got to realize it ain't safe for you and Naomi to be out working that claim by yourself. You know this country. Utes could come up on you anytime. Now we've got bandits to contend with on top of that."

"Ain't never seen a Ute I couldn't deal with, and bandits of any kind don't scare me none."

Floyd shook his head. "It's not just about you. What about Naomi? You're going to take a woman out there with what's happening in this valley? That's crazy!"

Asa spun around, his hand close to his six-gun. "You callin' me crazy, Logan? I'm just about tired out of puttin' up with your guff all these years."

Everyone stopped what they were doing. Callum couldn't

believe this old guy was bracing Floyd. Jeb leaned against the side of the lean-to, picking his teeth with his bowie knife.

"Asa," Floyd said, "you don't stand a chance with that hogleg against me, and you know it. So just cool down. You know I'm right."

"Well, you just understand, you ain't tellin' me what to do. Not now, not ever." He turned back to the pack he was working on.

Callum motioned Floyd over to him. "What's going on? What is Mrs. Gwendiver doing out here?"

Floyd explained her desire to work her own claim, and her hiring of Asa.

"You let her come out here?"

"Callum, Mr. Logan, I can hear you," Naomi said. "Nobody let's me do anything. I do what I feel is necessary."

"That's fine, ma'am," Callum replied, "but you can see what happened here. It would be foolhardy to try to find and work your claim with only the two of you, at least until Wister's gang is taken care of."

"So, your uncle calls Mr. Collins crazy, and you call me a fool. With those kind of attitudes, do you really expect us to stay here?"

"No, ma'am, I don't expect you to stay here. I expect you to go back to Denver City until this gang is brought to justice."

Sarah stepped up to Callum and put her hand on his shoulder. "Callum, don't overdo it. This argument will tax your strength. You need to relax and heal your body."

Callum wanted to brush her hand away. He didn't need to be mothered by anyone, and he definitely didn't need the complication her move created, but he remained calm and said, "Thank you." He noticed that Naomi didn't miss Sarah's proprietary movement.

"Asa," Naomi said, "get the animals loaded. We're leaving."

"About time," Asa grumbled, and started loading the pack animals.

"Now, Naomi," Floyd said, "this ain't the right move. Stay here. You and Asa have been a great help the past few days. Just a couple more days, we'll have the barn finished and a place for everyone when the snows hit. You and Asa are welcome here. Once we get the house built, we'll go with you and help you work your claim. This can work out good for all of us."

"We're leaving, Floyd. We have a claim that is rich enough to provide a new life for both Asa and myself. We need to be working it before the winter snow sets in. I appreciate your help and hospitality, but we have worn out our welcome here and must get to work."

Floyd shook his bear-like head. "This is the wrong decision. I know Shorty would want you to stay and wait."

Naomi's face softened. She walked over to Floyd and grasped his hands in hers. "I know you're just trying to help, and, yes, I know it is dangerous." She turned and looked at Callum, to make her point. "But I've got to do this. If we stay until the house is built, we could be snowed out of the claim until spring. I'm determined to work the claim." She smiled up at him. "Thank you so much for all of your help."

She released Floyd's hands and walked over to Callum. "Mr. Logan, I sincerely hope the next time you see me, it will be from horseback."

Callum frowned. "You're making a big mistake, lady. The next time I see you, you could be pushing up daisies."

"You don't give an inch, do you?"

"Not when I'm right."

Naomi whirled, marched to her horse, and swung up into the saddle. "Let's go, Asa."

The older man mounted up. The two of them rode away from the encampment, with Asa leading the two pack mules. Naomi sat tall, erect in the saddle, never deigning to look back.

Floyd watched Naomi and Asa ride toward the center of the big valley. "Mighty feisty woman."

Callum shook his head. "She'll get herself killed. If the Indians don't get her, the Wister Gang will. It's only common sense to stay together until we get finished here, then we can help her."

"I'm some worried about her," Floyd continued. "You'll never guess who her man-friend is."

Callum had also been watching them ride off. At Floyd's statement, his head jerked around. "Someone we know?"

"You could say that. Reckon you know him better than most."

Callum, puzzled, said, "Well?"

"That banker what throwed the boy into the street. Name of Richard Jessup."

Callum's face registered shock. "You're kidding."

"Nope. Not a bit. I tried to tell her what he is, and she got plain uppity with me. She wouldn't hear of it. In fact, she told him all about the claim and left the gold in his bank in Pueblo."

"Women," Callum said, then realized Sarah was standing close. "Sorry, ma'am. I meant no offense."

"None taken, Mr. Logan. We're just like men, in that we can be fooled. Love does strange things to people."

"Yes, ma'am. I reckon it does." He turned back to Floyd.

"I don't like it, Floyd. I don't trust that man. But, as long as he stays in the cities, I guess he can't bother her or us."

Floyd nodded. "We're keeping our eyes open anyway, what with Wister and his gang around, so Jessup shouldn't make much difference."

"Looks like they're gone," Jeb said, motioning down the valley. "Least she's got Asa with her. He ain't pleasant to be around, but he's a good man to have with you when the goin' gets tough."

Floyd nodded and turned to Jeb. "What's your plans?"

"Ain't got none, other than to do a bit of trapping and hole up for the winter."

Floyd shot Callum a questioning look.

"Jeb," Callum said, "looks like these mountains have plenty of streams for trapping. There'd be a job for you here, if you've a mind. We need to get a house built before the winter hits, and Josh should be showing up any time. It'd pay you thirty a month and all of Mrs. Radcliff's fine cooking you could eat. 'Course there's the Wister Gang. I'll be settling up with them, so we'll have some fighting to do, for sure."

Jeb looked over the corral and the nearly completed barn. He turned and looked up the canyon that climbed into the high country of the Sangre de Cristos. "I reckon there's worse places to winter." He looked at Sarah Radcliff. "And I'm gettin' mighty fond of a good meal. Haven't had many of those since I was a button. I'll hang around, at least till spring."

"Good. We're glad to have you here." Callum turned to Sarah. "Ma'am, I know this is a hard thing to lose James. But if you and Jimmy still want the job, it's here for you. When the winter's over, we'll get you lined up with a wagon train going to Salt Lake, but you'd be welcome here, and we could sure use your help."

Jimmy was standing next to Sarah. He looked up at his ma. "Can we, Ma?"

"Thank you, Mr. Logan. Jimmy and I would like that."

"Good, then that's settled.

"Floyd, until I get back on my feet, it looks like you and Jeb are stuck with the building. What do you think about getting the barn finished first? Once it's finished, we'll move into it and get started on the house."

Floyd looked at the barn. "We'll finish with the roof, and we'll be done. It could use some spiffing up a little, but I reckon once it's wind and snow tight, it'll be fine for now.

"How are you feelin'?"

"That's what I was coming to next." Callum looked over to Jimmy and Sarah. "If it's all right with you, ma'am, I'd like for Jimmy to help me keep an eye out for Wister and his bunch. If they get wind of us building, they'll be back. I'd like for Jimmy, when he's not doing chores, to head down to that aspen thicket. It gives us a little better angle to see them before they turn up the valley, and it's close enough so he'll be back long before they get here."

"If you think he'll be safe, that's fine, Mr. Logan. Just don't harm my boy."

"Ma, I can take care of myself," Jimmy said, embarrassed by his mother's concern.

"He'll be fine, ma'am. He could run back long before they got here, but we're going to send him down there on a horse. That'll give him a big edge."

Callum turned to Jimmy. "When you see anything, Indians or the gang, you just start waving your hat, get on that horse, and hightail it back. Be sure to keep those aspen between you and the mouth of the valley—they'll never see you. You don't wait. As soon as you see something, get yourself back here. Understand?"

Jimmy, his eyes bright, said, "Yes, sir. That's just what I'll do."

"Good, we'll be counting on you." Callum turned back to Floyd. "Now, let's get to me. I'm not going to be much good around here until I get to walking. I can feel my legs now, and I have some use of them, but that's not walking. I need you to set me under that limber pine and swing a loop over the lower limb. That'll give me a way to pull myself up and get used to walking again."

Floyd shook his head. "Callum, you been shot in the chest and shoulder. You go pulling yourself up by a rope, and you're liable to open up those bullet holes. It's only been a couple of weeks. You need to let them wounds heal for at least another week or two."

"It ain't happening, Floyd. There's only two of you to cut timber and build the house. The sooner I can pitch in, the faster it'll get done."

"Boy, you're pushing too hard. Jeb and I ain't newcomers at this. We built many a log house. We'll get it done a lot faster than you think. You just rest for now."

"Floyd," Callum said, frustration coloring his voice, "I need you to do this. I'll take it easy, at first, but I need it done!"

Floyd shook his head. "Well, I want you to know I'm agin it. But I'll do it."

"Thanks. Now, we've got a bigger problem. I'm without a gun. As I'm sure you saw when you rode up, Wister took everything. I don't have guns, horses, possibles, nothing. Do you have any extra weapons I could use, until we get back to Pueblo and I can get a new outfit?"

Floyd grinned, and then said, "We're in luck there. I figured we'd be out here for a few months, so whilst in Denver, I bought some additional supplies, including hammers, picks, nails, lead and powder. You know I've always been a sucker for guns. So I was in that store, and I saw a matched pair of 1858 Remington Beals. They'd been worked over by a gunsmith that knew his business. They both were perfectly balanced with smooth trigger pulls. They included four additional cylinders, bullet mold and powder measure. I couldn't walk away from 'em."

Floyd walked over to his saddlebags and pulled out the two Beals, nestled in a two-gun rig. He pulled out a leather bag containing the cylinders resting in leather pouches that would fasten to the gunbelt, the bullet mold, and powder measure. He carried the rig and the bag back to Callum and laid it in his lap. "Reckon that'll work for you?"

Callum pulled one of the revolvers out of the holster, feeling the balance. "Excellent balance. Never had a two-gun rig."

"Always a first time," Floyd said.

"Not much good with my left hand."

Jeb piped up, "You're a young feller. Plenty of time to learn."

Callum looked back up to Floyd. "Let me pay you now. Fortunately, Wister didn't find where I buried our stake."

"Least of my worries," Floyd said. "Reckon you need to get used to 'em, and we need to get to work. We're burnin' daylight. Come on, Jeb, let's finish up that barn."

"Before you do, how about moving me under that pine and facing me down the valley. I can at least keep watch. Swing the rope over that limb and tie it off. I'll be fine there."

After getting Callum set up, the two men headed for the barn. Within minutes, the sound of a saw and hammer rang throughout the trees. Callum worked with the Remingtons, getting used to them. Then he hung them on the armrest and reached up for the rope.

"Can I help, Mr. Callum?" Sarah called.

"No, ma'am. This here is something I need to do for myself."

He pulled himself into a standing position, his chest and shoulder gripped with a deep ache. He took one step forward, his leg dragging in the pine needles. He pulled his right leg even with the left. Callum worked, moving first his left and then his right. Moving forward and then stepping back, until he was situated again in front of his chair. He eased himself back into the chair, his breath coming in gasps. *I've got a long way to go before I sit a horse again. I have to be ready for Wister's next attack.*

12

Wister leaned back in the chair and put his feet on the table. He looked around at the men seated at the table and throughout the small kitchen and living area. His eyes settled on Milam. "Took you long enough. What'd Jessup have to say?"

Milam took a sip of the cup of coffee he had just poured before he sat down. He savored it for a moment, then turned to Wister. "Getting cold out there."

Wister's feet dropped to the floor as he slammed the front legs of the chair down. "I ain't askin' for a weather report. I'm askin' what did Jessup have to say?"

The hum of voices in the room halted. Wister had a violent temper, and none of his men wanted to give him a reason to turn on them. All eyes focused on Milam.

Ben Milam was a gunfighter. He had killed ten men in gunfights and ambushed many more. He knew he was faster than Wister. He also knew that Wister was much better at planning and running the gang than he was. He turned his head toward Wister, waited for a moment till not a sound was heard in the room, and said, "Jessup said to tell you howdy."

Wister's face turned red. His frown brought his eyebrows together over his bulbous, red nose. Joined together, they looked like a big black wooly worm crawling across his forehead. He held the frown for a moment, then he relaxed and pointed a beefy index finger at Milam. "One of these days you're gonna push too hard, and we'll find out who's the fastest."

Milam laughed, his cold eyes remaining on Wister. "Elwood, I'm hoping that never happens. Jessup wasn't too happy that you took your part of the gold before sending the rest to him. I think he planned on a fifty-fifty split."

"He'll take what he gets and be happy. We took all the risk. He ought to figger himself lucky he got what was left. Anyway, he's got a great deal. We do all the dirty work and live out in these mountains, and he gets to live in the city and be Mr. High and Mighty. He didn't impress me in Missouri and he don't impress me here. One day, he'll get too big for his britches, and I'll have to cut him down a peg or two. What took you so long?"

"It's a long way into Pueblo, Elwood."

"Ain't that long. Next time, don't dally, and stay away from the liquor. I know what you were doing. You were drinkin' and playin' cards. When you start drinkin', you talk too much. If this is the best you can do, I'll have to send somebody else instead of you. Reckon I'd get plenty of volunteers." He looked around the table and then at the men standing. They were all nodding, everyone thinking about the chance to hit the saloons.

Milam chuckled. "Why, I don't think they'd care to go once I had a conversation with them."

The smiles left the men. Each one made it a point to look somewhere other than at Milam. As rough as these men were, no one wanted to go up against him in a gun or knife fight, not with his reputation.

Wister waved his hand. "No matter. Did Jessup have anything else to say?"

"Yeah, he was mighty concerned that some of Lopez's bunch

might have survived the ambush. He doesn't want any witnesses. I think he has the governor's office in his sights."

Wister started to respond, but Milam held up his hand. "I assured him that they're all dead, that no one survived the ambush. I think that calmed him down. He also wanted to let you know that there is a woman and an old mountain man coming into the mountains. Seems she thinks she has a gold mine and plans on working it before winter sets in. He wants us to leave her alone. Looks like he's planning on marrying her. That's about it."

"Coming into our mountains?"

Milam took another long sip of his steaming coffee, waited a moment, and said, "That's what he said. He appears to be mighty fond of her."

Wister was silent for a moment. *I'll leave her alone for now, but she might come in handy in the future.* "Well, ain't that nice. He wants us to leave her alone. We might just ride around and see if we can locate her, so we can keep an eye on her—for Jessup." He leered at Milam, his grin showing yellowed and broken teeth. "I'd do just about anything to help Jessup. Yessir—"

The sound of a horse galloping up to the cabin grabbed all of the men's attention. Guns were drawn as the door was yanked open, and a breathless man rushed in.

"Boss, there's someone working Logan's place."

"What?"

"Yep, I was ridin' the timberline, and I heard axes. Somebody's definitely down there."

Wister looked around the room until his eyes came to rest on a man of slight build. He wore a dirty gray slouch hat pushed back and resting on a head of hair that appeared it hadn't been washed since before the war. His right cheek had a blue birthmark extending from his ear to his nose, down to the corner of his mouth.

"Blue."

"Yeah, Boss."

"Get on that nag of yours and ride over to your lookout. Find out how many are there. If you can, kill 'em. If not, get back here and let me know what's going on. I don't know how more people could wind up in the same place, unless they knew this here Logan."

Blue wiped the snot from his nose with his thumb and forefinger, slinging it on the floor. The man's voice was an irritating, high-pitched whine. "It's afternoon, Boss. There ain't no moon, so I couldn't ride back tonight. How 'bout I leave early in the morning?"

"You'll leave now and like it. You think I care if you have to spend the night out? You men are gettin' too danged spoiled livin' in this here fancy house. Now git and bring me back some answers."

Wister watched Blue walk out the door, then shook his head. "I swear, if he couldn't shoot a gnat off an elk's rear, I'd kill him right now. Anybody else have a complaint to make?" He gazed around the room, stopping at each man.

A chorus of "No, Boss," echoed around the room.

"All right. Milam, did you notice anything around Logan's place when you came back from Pueblo?"

"I didn't come right by there, but no, I didn't notice anything unusual. Any idea who it could be?"

"I ain't got nary a thought. But I danged sure don't want any squatters getting settled in this here valley. This is too nice a deal for us. 'Course, we got that fine young couple to thank for this setup. Sure sorry we had to kill 'em, but they did right by us. This cabin is far enough into the mountains where no one can find us and close enough so we can raid when we want. But if we let squatters move in, we're done for."

Milam nodded. "Blue will find out. If there's too many of them for him to take care of, we'll know something tomorrow. I suspect it'll be necessary for us to make another ride down there." He rubbed his leg, where Callum had shot him. "Hope this works out as good as the last time."

The men listened as Blue rode away from the cabin. The wind was picking up. It brought the promise of a cold night.

JESSUP relaxed in front of the roaring fireplace in the Pueblo Hotel lobby, with a whiskey cradled in his hand. Life was going well. Callum Logan was dead. That was the best news he'd had in a while, if you didn't count his future fiancée's gold claim. That old uncle of hers was a useless old geezer, always in the mountains searching for gold. Served him right to get himself killed by Utes.

When Naomi told him about her claim, he had initially passed it off as another of Shorty's pie-in-the-sky deals. But then she deposited the gold in his bank. That was some of the richest he had seen. Even if it played out, there were thousands of dollars just in the bags she had given him to store in the vault, which he was happy to do, assuring her he would keep her secret. Of course he would keep her secret. He wanted her and all of her gold to himself.

He took a sip of his whiskey and smiled. Life was working out very well. Life had turned for him when he left St. Louis. He had gotten out of there just ahead of a necktie party. There wasn't enough evidence to convict him for murder, but the vigilantes didn't need evidence, they just needed a suspect. Now he was in high cotton. He had his three banks, Wister and his gang was working for him, Naomi's gold was in his safe, along with a copy of the map to the claim, and Lopez's gold had been returned. Although, that was a sore point. Wister had taken two-thirds of it. He'd have to be careful with Wister. The man was useful but dangerous. He'd have to be taken care of when he wore out his usefulness. It wouldn't do for a governor to be connected to a man like Wister, even though he could be useful.

"Mind if I join you?"

Jessup glanced up to see the town marshal standing next to his chair. "Not at all, Marshal Nester. Have a seat." He indicated the chair to his left. "What are you drinking?"

"A whiskey'll be fine."

Jessup waved to the restaurant waitress, pointed to his glass, and held up two fingers. "What brings you out on a night like this?"

"Deputy's sick, so I'm makin' the rounds. The wind's pickin' up. Gettin' mighty chilly."

The waitress came in from the restaurant with two whiskeys. She handed the marshal one and traded out one for Jessup's empty glass. Jessup dropped two dollars on the tray and winked at her. She gave him a brazen smile, then whirled back toward the restaurant, her exaggerated hip movements meant for him. He smiled. It was wonderful to be rich.

The marshal broke into his thoughts. "Glad I found you. Feller rode into town today, a bounty hunter."

Jessup was just barely listening, his mind on the waitress.

"Said he had come all the way from St. Louis."

At the mention of St. Louis, Jessup's interest switched from the waitress to Nester's words.

Jessup took a sip of his whiskey, gratified to see his hand was steady. As unconcerned as he could manage, he turned to the marshal. "What's a bounty hunter doing here, all the way from St. Louis?"

"What all bounty hunters do, Mr. Jessup. He's lookin' for a man. He didn't have a poster, but he did have a description."

Jessup started to take another drink of his whiskey but thought better of it. He noticed a slight tremor in his hands and felt his pulse elevate. The fireplace was no longer interesting. In fact, he found it hot and stifling here in the hotel. He needed fresh air. He needed outside, away from the marshal. But he couldn't leave. He had to find out. "He had a description? Did it fit anyone around here?"

"Yes, sir. It sure did." The marshal took a long drink from his whiskey glass and set it down on the arm of his chair. "Mr. Jessup, you don't happen to have one of those fine cigars you're known for carrying, do you?"

Jessup felt the anger rising. This two-bit marshal was needling him. The man better watch his step, or he'd be out of a job, or worse. "I sure do, Marshal. Would you care for one?"

"That'd be mighty nice of you, sir. Mighty nice."

Jessup pulled out one of his expensive cigars and handed it to the marshal.

The man bit off one end, spit it on the floor, then rolled the stogie in his mouth. After a moment, he reached for a match. Speaking around the cigar, he said, "Aren't you going to have one, Mr. Jessup?" This time he emphasized mister.

Jessup felt both fear and anger. He knew he couldn't smoke a cigar. His hands were shaking too much. He couldn't let Nester see his fear. He'd love to have the marshal in a dark alley. He'd break him in two. "No, Marshal, not tonight. I've had a long day. It's getting close to my bedtime."

"Too bad," the marshal said. He leaned back in the leather chair, struck the match on the wooden armrest, and puffed contentedly on the cigar. Once it was lit, he shook out the match and tossed it into the fireplace. He took another long draw on the cigar, and slowly blew the smoke up, then turned to Jessup. "Mr. Jessup, he described you!"

Jessup could feel the blood leaving his face. For a moment, he felt weak, afraid he would pass out. He took a couple of deep breaths and turned to the marshal. "That's absurd. Where's this bounty hunter now?"

"In my jail. Nobody's seen him. He thinks I've got him locked up because I don't like bounty hunters, and, actually, I got no use for 'em."

Jessup looked around to make sure no one was near. "All right, Marshal. What do you want?"

The marshal looked around the empty room and then leaned forward to Jessup, speaking in a low, conspiratorial tone. "Well, life's been pretty tough on a man like me. I've had some ups and downs, mostly downs. I'm tired of walking around with a target on my back, just waiting for some drunk cowboy to hit a bullseye. I'd like to be able to get a little place and enjoy my last days. Is that too much to ask?"

The old codger's blackmailing me. But I've got to pay him. It's that or kiss the governor's mansion goodbye. "Let's say you found that pot of gold. What could be expected for it?"

Marshal Nester smiled. He took another draw on the cigar, blew smoke rings up toward the hotel ceiling, and said, "I just imagine that bounty hunter would disappear, and, as old as I am, I have a terrible memory. I probably couldn't even remember this conversation."

"How much?"

The marshal stared at the cigar for a moment, rubbed his chin, then looked directly at Jessup. "Twenty thousand dollars."

Jessup couldn't prevent himself from gasping at the amount. "Twenty thousand? Man, are you crazy? I don't have that kind of money."

Marshal Nester chuckled. The sound was cold and harsh. He flicked the ashes off the cigar, sat for a moment longer, then stood erect. "Too bad." He turned and started for the door.

"Wait."

Jessup watched the marshal slowly turn and walk back. "I'll pay you, but the bounty hunter has to disappear tonight."

"I can do that."

Jessup's brain raced. "You have to continue to work for

another month or so. You can't leave right on the tail end of the bounty hunter's disappearance, understand?"

"I can do that too. When do I get the money?"

"You'll get it tonight."

"It'll have to be before I take care of the bounty hunter."

Jessup stood up. "Let's go to the bank right now."

The marshal smiled. "You first."

Jessup walked along the boardwalk toward the bank. He could feel Marshal Nester behind him, but out of his reach. They reached the bank. He unlocked the door and moved to his office. The bank was dark, but he knew every chair and desk. He stepped into his office and said, "Close the door."

He reached for the lamp and lit it. For once, he was thankful he didn't have a window in his office. The lamp cast its glow around the room, somehow lending no warmth as light usually did, but bringing out the stark angles of the room. He knelt down in front of the safe, entered the combination, and unlocked it. There the money was. Much more than twenty thousand dollars. Also, next to the money, was a Colt five-shot pocket revolver. He looked at it only for a moment. He didn't need a gun. He didn't want the noise.

Jessup counted out twenty thousand and took the money from the safe, setting it on the table. To this point, the marshal had been cautious and ready for anything Jessup might try. But when the money was placed on the desk, his vision narrowed until all he saw was the money. He stepped forward against the desk, and his hands reached out for the money. His fingers caressed the bills. He looked up at Jessup with a smile. His eyes widened as he realized the man was too close. He started to go for his gun, but Jessup's big hand clamped over his right hand and crushed it. His scream was muffled behind Jessup's other hand, which was covering his mouth and nose. Jessup watched the marshal's eyes as he struggled. They grew large as his body convulsed, his lungs demanding the air that they could not draw in. He fought with all of his might, but Jessup was too strong for such a small man. Finally, his convulsions stopped, and he lay limp in Jessup's arms.

Jessup dropped the marshal to the floor and put the money back in the safe, locking it. He had to think. He still needed to get rid of the marshal's body, and the bounty hunter. How could he do this without implicating himself? Could he get them out of town? Too many complications, but he had to get it done.

He blew the lamp out and tossed the man over his shoulder. The marshal was so light. He moved through the dark to the bank door, looked up and down the street, carefully looking for any signs of company. It was quiet. Fortunately, no cowboys were passing through. He pulled the bank door closed, locked it, and hurried to the marshal's office. Just before he stepped through the door, he thought, *What if he has someone else in jail with the bounty hunter?* His heart stopped. But the only one in the jail was the bounty hunter.

The man jumped to his feet when Jessup entered. "Who are you? Is that the marshal? What's wrong with him?"

Jessup found the bounty hunter's gun. The jail keys were lying on the desk. He grabbed them and unlocked the cell, then turned and pulled the marshal's gun from his holster. "Come on, let's go," he said to the bounty hunter. Puzzled, the man stepped to the cell door. Jessup tossed him his gun and shot him at the same time. He shot him again, then shot the marshal and dropped him on the floor and shot him again. He dropped the marshal's gun on the floor next to him and dashed out the back door. He ran down the alley and almost tripped over the town drunk, who was passed out behind the jail. Voices were already coming from the front of the jail. He trotted behind the buildings, until he came to the alley by the general store. Easing out to the boardwalk, he looked both ways. It was clear. He stepped out onto the boardwalk and ran toward the marshal's office.

"What happened?" he yelled as he came up to the crowd in front of the jail. "Let me through."

He looked for just a moment and asked the man next to him, "Has anyone sent for the doctor?"

The man looked up at him. "Looks like they shot each other. They did a danged good job of it too. Ain't no doctor needed. This'll be for an undertaker."

Jessup walked out of the marshal's office and took a deep breath. He stood there for a moment, then walked back to the hotel. He called the waitress and ordered another whiskey. The warmth of the fire chased the chill from his body.

Occasionally life tosses you some bumps, and you've just got to ride over them until the road smooths out. His mind shifted to Naomi, her gold, and then pictured Callum Logan dead. He smiled and took another sip of his whiskey.

13

The scream echoed through the valley. Floyd lowered his axe, smiled, and nodded to Jeb. "Reckon our visitor came back. I'll go take a look."

"Is that the surprise you were talking about?" Callum said.

"Yep," Floyd answered. He had made his way to the corral and was saddling his horse. "Looks like I've got just about enough day left to make it up there and back before dark."

Jimmy had gravitated to his ma, and Sarah was standing with her arm around her son. "It sounded like someone is in a great deal of pain."

Floyd chuckled. "Imagine he is, ma'am. Pain brought on by trying to backshoot folks." Floyd stepped into the stirrup and swung his long leg over the saddle, his Henry and reins gripped in his left hand. He rode slowly up the narrowing valley, leaning slightly forward as the incline steepened.

Callum spoke to Jeb, "Guess we better keep a sharp eye out. This could mean another attack."

Jeb had replaced his axe with his Sharps. "Could. But I'm thinkin' Mr. Backshooter was sent to check on us, and maybe to lower the odds, if he felt a mind to. Whichever way it goes, we'll be ready for 'em."

Callum checked the loads in his new Remingtons, then called over to Sarah. "Ma'am, could I impose on you to bring me a cup of that fine coffee, and your Henry out of the wagon?"

"Jimmy," Sarah said, "get the Henry out of the wagon for Mr. Logan, and bring an extra box of ammunition, please."

"Yes, ma'am," Jimmy said as he dashed to the wagon. He disappeared for a moment but was soon out with the Henry and the box of ammunition, dashing back to Callum.

"Whoa, Son." Callum said. "Careful where you point that muzzle. If you fell, you could end up shooting someone."

Jimmy, a sheepish look on his face, slowed to a walk and controlled the muzzle of the Henry. "Sorry, Mr. Logan. I forgot."

Callum took the rifle, worked the action, and a round came flying out. "Could you pick that up for me, Jimmy?"

Jimmy picked up the cartridge and handed it to Callum, who wiped it off and slipped it back into the Henry. Callum reached over and squeezed Jimmy's shoulder. "You're a big help, boy. We all have to learn."

Callum looked up and caught Sarah watching the exchange. Her eyes glistened, and a single tear escaped down her cheek. At Callum's glance, she quickly turned back to the fire.

Jeb leaned his Sharps against a log, picked up his axe, and went back to cutting a notch near the end of the lodgepole pine. "Callum, let me know if you see something. I'm gonna get back to work."

"Will do." Callum sat in his chair with the Henry across his lap. He much preferred his Spencer. Though the Spencer only had seven rounds where the Henry had sixteen, Callum felt the Henry was extremely underpowered. He liked the big hunk of lead the Spencer tossed out, plus the accuracy at a longer range. Yes, he had to cock the hammer every time, to fire, but he knew the odds were that when he hit something, it would go down and stay down. But you work with what you have.

The sun was just slipping behind the Sangre de Cristo range, burnishing the Greenhorn Mountains with the last rays for the day. Callum sat admiring the beauty of this small canyon, where they were building Ma and Pa's homeplace, and longing to get back into the saddle to explore the mountains and their big valley. *I wonder where the young couple is that the storekeeper mentioned. I've got to find them and see if we can work something out. This valley is bigger than I thought, and there's room for all of us in here. Hopefully they'll work with us. It'd be good for Ma to have some neighbors.*

Callum was pulled from his reverie by the sound of horses coming down the mountain from behind him. He turned to see Floyd riding in, leading a horse. The horse had a body draped over the saddle.

Floyd pulled up and dismounted. Jeb had walked over and was examining the body.

"Reckon they did the job, Floyd," Jeb said.

"They did," Floyd said, as he pulled the body off the saddle and let it drop to the ground.

Sarah gasped when she saw it. Jimmy walked up to the body, staring at the man's hands, or hand. "Ma, his hand is missing."

"Jimmy," Sarah said, "get away from that man's body. Go fetch some water."

Jimmy walked over to the bucket, muttering, and headed for the stream.

"James Patrick Radcliff, don't you backtalk me."

Jimmy kept walking, but said, "Yes, ma'am."

The men were silent for a moment, then Floyd glanced over at Sarah. "Sorry for bringing this into camp, ma'am, but I wanted to see if anyone recognized him."

From his seated position, Callum couldn't see the man's face. "Floyd, would you turn him this way so that I can see him?"

Jeb was closest. He grabbed the man by the collar and tossed him over. The man's face was turned to Callum.

"Nope, don't recognize him."

Jeb looked him over. "I ain't seen him before, but I reckon if he got upwind to me I'd sure smell him."

"So what happened to him?" Callum asked.

"You remember I mentioned I left him some presents?"

Callum nodded.

"Well, Ole Jeb here likes to trap bear. I just borrowed three of his bear traps and laid those rascals out along where that back-shooter came crawling up to his log."

Floyd grinned at Jeb. Jeb shook his head, laughed, and said, "Them traps have caught a passel of bear, but that's the first back-shooter they can claim."

Floyd continued. "It looked like he crawled up to his log, missing the first trap. But he put his left knee slap-dab in the middle of that second trap." Floyd pointed to the man's left leg. "You can see where the jaws slammed shut around about the middle of his lower leg and just above his knee. Darned near took his leg off. You could see where he tussled around. The ground was some chewed up. But he made his big mistake when he fell forward. He musta stuck his hand on the jaws of the third trap. He set it off, and those jagged jaws hit him just above the wrist. It cut that hand clean off." Floyd stood there shaking his head. "I figger that's when he screamed."

A picture of the man in the two bear traps raced through Callum's mind. As much as he hated the man for killing James and backshooting him, he had no wish for any man to die like that.

Floyd had more to say. "When I got there, the young feller had about bled to death. Had a chance to ask him some questions. He told me where the gang's holed up. Seems there's a cabin farther up the valley and back in the Sangre de Cristos below Purgatory Peak. It had been built by a younger man and woman. They killed the man and abused the woman till she died." Floyd stopped and looked at Sarah. "Sorry, ma'am. Ain't no other way to say it."

"I've seen the worst in men, Mr. Logan. You don't need to apologize. I just feel sorry for the woman."

"Yes, ma'am. So do I. Callum, I imagine that's the couple that the storekeeper was talking about."

"Reckon you're right, Floyd. Go ahead with your story."

Floyd took a deep breath. "Well, I got more bad news. Seems this here boy knew he was dying and wanted to get everything off'n his chest. He said that about three or four weeks back, they attacked a Mex wagon train, down south of here."

Callum looked over at Floyd. "You think that was the Lopez party?"

"I reckon. He said they killed everyone. Left no witnesses, and took a bunch of gold off the coach."

Callum could feel his anger rising. This Wister Gang had to be stopped. These men were brutal killers, who would kill anyone, man, woman, or child. "Floyd, we've got to stop 'em. That kind needs to be put away like a rabid dog."

Floyd's square, weather-beaten face reflected Callum's anger. His blue eyes seemed to spark with rage. "Son, I'm way ahead of you. Josh ought to be gettin' here before too long. When he does, we'll hunt that vermin down and exterminate it."

Callum looked off in the distance, watching the darkening shadows in the valley. "I can't believe that whole family is dead."

"That's what this backshooter said—everyone. I been thinkin'. It had to happen shortly after we left 'em. All those folks have been dead for over a month, and us not knowin' it. Mighty sad."

"I've seen him," Sarah said.

"Ma'am?" Floyd replied.

All the men looked at Sarah.

"Yes. Just a few days before you arrived." She indicated Blue.

"I came down the stairs of the hotel. Mr. Jessup, the banker, was talking to a big man, even bigger than him. The man had a full dirty beard, brown hair, and frightening hazel eyes. I quickly took my eyes from them and walked outside. Several men were standing around outside the hotel. One of them was this man. I remember him because of the blue mark on his face."

Callum said, so low it was hard to hear him, "Jessup's up to his hip bones in this dirty business." He realized he had been thinking out loud. He looked over to Floyd and Jeb. "This explains a lot. He sold this valley to the couple that was murdered. Floyd, you may remember how calm he was when Mr. Lopez said he was withdrawing all of his money from the bank and wanted it in gold? Right then, he figured he'd be gettin' that gold back. Jessup is as bad as Wister."

Floyd nodded. "But, Callum, we'll have to go easy where Jessup is concerned. The man has banks in Denver City, Colorado City, and Pueblo. In most circles, he's thought well of."

"I agree," Callum said. "But he's goin' down, just like Wister and his gang."

Jeb piped up, "You can count me in. But there's still only three of us, and you're not walking yet. You mentioned you counted fourteen when they rode up here. We're going to need more people."

"We'll have to wait until you're better," Floyd said to Callum, "and Josh gets here. As much as I can't stand him, Asa will join us. He's a fighter. That'll give us five. In the meantime, we need to stay alert, and probably get Mrs. Radcliff and the boy back to Pueblo."

"Now wait just a minute," Sarah said. "We can take care of ourselves. I can shoot a rifle just as well as a man, and Jimmy is useful around here. We'll not be leaving. That is, unless we're fired." The last comment was directed to Callum.

"Mrs. Radcliff, I—"

"I wish everyone would stop being so polite! My name is Sarah, please."

The men looked at each other, then Callum said, "Sarah, that's fine. We'll start doing that, and no, you're not fired. We just want you and Jimmy to be safe. In fact, Jessup knows you saw him with a member of the gang, probably Wister, so town might not be safe either. I think you and Jimmy are just as safe here as in Pueblo."

Floyd and Jeb nodded their agreement.

"One more thing, before I haul this body off. Look what he was shooting." Floyd pulled out a rifle from the left scabbard, walked around to the other side of the horse, and pulled out another.

"Haven't seen one of those since the war," Callum said. "Those Whitworth rifles are so unwieldy, I can't imagine anyone using them out west."

"True," Floyd said, "but your snipers used 'em pretty effectively during the war. I understand they could reach out over a thousand yards. He had two of them."

"Seven or eight hundred was about the max. Although I've heard of them hitting at a longer range. Don't know how much of that is pure exaggeration and how much is true. Only problem is, since they're muzzle loaders, it takes a while to reload. Reckon that's why he has two. I guess he must have been a sniper during the war. Never met him, and a face like that I'd remember."

Jeb looked through the man's saddlebags. "Well, thanks to him, we've got some more powder and lead. Plus a couple of handguns, a couple of rifles, and a horse. Why don't we load him back on his saddle? I'll take him up the hill a ways and bury him."

Floyd helped Jeb tie the body across the saddle. Jeb picked up a shovel and led the horse back up the sloping mountainside.

Jeb disappeared into the thick pines.

"Mr. Logan, there's a rider coming up the canyon," Jimmy called. Both Callum and Floyd turned to watch the mouth of the canyon, which was hard to see in the dim light. A lone rider loped his horse toward them.

Callum watched the rider drawing nearer. Then his face broke into a wide grin. "Look how erect he sits the saddle. I'd recognize that rider anywhere. How about you, Uncle?"

"Yep, if that ain't Josh, I'll eat that chair you're sitting on."

The men watched the tall rider and the big horse, until he pulled up in front of them.

Josh tipped his hat to Sarah, a big grin on his face. "Ma'am, I'm Josh Logan, and I have to say, you sure keep some sorry company."

Floyd looked up at the big man. "Boy, get yourself down and shake your uncle's hand."

As Josh was dismounting, Callum said, "You still riding that old gray nag?"

Josh rubbed Chancy's neck. "This old gray nag has got me out of a lot of trouble." He dropped the reins to the ground and walked to his uncle. The two men shook hands, their left hands resting on the other's shoulder.

"You're a welcome sight, boy. A welcome sight."

Callum looked over his brother. The saber scar that Josh had received near the end of the war was still evident but fading. Surprisingly, it contributed to Josh's rough good looks. The man stood six two in his stocking feet. *He could have been a Yankee recruiting poster.*

When Callum didn't rise from his chair, a look of concern crossed Josh's face, and his gray eyes examined Callum more closely. He strode over and extended his hand. "It's good to see you, Cal. But I have to say, you don't look quite as good as you did when I left you in Nashville."

Callum grabbed the rope hanging from the tree with his left hand and pulled himself up, his legs giving more assistance each time he tried. "I've been a little feeble here of late." He stood there gripping his brother's hand. "It's good to have you here." He turned his body slightly. "This is Mrs. Sarah Radcliff and her son, Jimmy. Sarah, as you've probably gathered, this is my brother, Josh."

Callum sat back down, and Josh strode over to Sarah, extending his right hand and removing his hat with his left. "Ma'am, it's nice to meet you." He glanced at the coffee.

"Mr. Logan, would you care for a cup of coffee?" Sarah asked.

"Ma'am, you have no idea how badly I could use a good cup of coffee right now."

"Good, let me pour you one. Now, Josh, I have just explained to your uncle and brother about calling me neither ma'am nor Mrs. Radcliff. My name is Sarah, and I expect you to call me that. If it's all right, I'll call you Josh."

Josh took the cup of coffee and said, "Sarah, that sounds most agreeable to me." He took a sip. "Mighty fine coffee."

Jimmy stepped up to Josh and stuck out his hand. "I'm Jimmy Radcliff, Mr. Logan."

"Nice to meet you, Jimmy. With three Logans around here, I think you better call me Josh. Can you do that?"

Jimmy beamed in the firelight. "Yes, sir, I sure can."

"Good. Now, if you'll excuse me." Josh took his coffee and moved back to his brother and uncle. On the way, he noticed the bloodstain in the shadows. He knelt, looked, and touched the blood. He checked his fingers and wiped them on the grass. Standing, he turned to his brother and uncle. "That's fresh."

Floyd said, "Long story. Not ours."

"Uncle, if you could move me by the fire?" Callum asked.

Josh stepped over to the chair and helped Floyd lift. The two men carried Callum near the fire.

"Supper will be ready in a few minutes," Sarah called.

The two men sat on a big pine log that had been pulled up next to the fire, across from Callum.

"Looks like you've gotten a lot done around here," Josh said as he looked at the barn and corral. "Let me drink my coffee, then I need to get Chancy to water and a good rubdown. He's earned it."

"Josh," Jimmy said, "I'd be pleased to do it."

Josh looked at Sarah, and she gave him a slight nod.

"Well, Jimmy, that's a big horse. You think you can handle him and get that saddle off of him?"

"Yes, sir. I've handled our team horses quite a bit. I can do it."

"Fine. There's a brush in the saddlebags. Just stack the rest of the gear out of the way, and be careful of the rifle. There's one in the barrel."

"I sure will, Josh."

Jimmy walked slowly up to Chancy and let him smell him. He had slipped a little sugar from his ma's stash. He held it out to Chancy on his palm with his hand flat. The horse smelled it and then licked it from his hand. Then Jimmy picked up the reins, rubbed the horse's cheek, and led him back to the corral and water.

Josh had been watching the drama play out. "Smart boy. Chancy doesn't usually make friends easily. That sugar really helped."

Sarah had watched the whole proceeding. Now, with one eyebrow raised and her hands on her hips, she said, "I noticed. Looks like I'm going to have to watch my sugar."

The men chuckled. Then Josh looked across the fire to his brother. "I've waited long enough. Tell me what happened to you."

Callum leaned back in his chair, and with Floyd supplementing, he told his story. About halfway through, Jeb came back from burying Blue. Introductions were made, and everyone ate the supper that Sarah had prepared. Later, Jeb stepped away to keep a lookout, and Callum continued. Through the years, Callum had learned to read his brother. He watched Josh as he told the story, and, in the reflected firelight, he could see the cold fury behind the steel-gray eyes.

When Callum was finished, Josh stood and stretched. "I don't know how you've been running your night watch, but add me in. I can't be first. I'm asleep on my feet right now, but give me a couple of hours and I'll be fine."

Floyd said, "I'll take the first one. If it's all right with you, Callum, you take the next, then Jeb, followed by Josh."

"Fine with me," Callum responded.

Josh nodded. "Wake me when it's my turn. We'll talk in the morning." He then dug out his bedroll, stretched it out with his saddle for a pillow and was fast asleep.

Callum had a bed made in the lean-to, where all he had to do was prop himself up against the wall and see down the valley. Using the arms of his chair, he pushed himself upright. With everyone watching, he used one of the Whitworth rifles as a cane, and shuffled over to his bed. Because it was dark, no one could see the beads of sweat on his forehead. His legs were more responsive, but they hurt like the dickens. While Sarah and Jimmy went to the wagon, Callum stretched out on his pine-bough bed. He was elated, both with his improvement and to have Josh here. Tomorrow would be the beginning of retribution.

14

Josh came wide awake when Jeb tapped his leg with the muzzle of his rifle. He nodded in the moonlight, and watched Jeb walk over to his bed, under the trees, and stretch out. Josh put his hat on, shook out his boots, and slipped them on. He stretched his long arms, then picked up his gunbelt and swung it around his waist. He slipped his heavy coat on and pulled it tight. Fall mornings in the Colorado mountains were cold. With his 1866 .44 Winchester in his left hand, he slipped away from camp toward the mouth of their little valley.

The waning moon, slowly disappearing behind the western mountains, cast the valley with an eerie light. He found a fallen tree lying in front of a lodgepole pine and took a seat, leaning his back against the pine.

He had to start making plans. He knew that wasn't his brother's strong suit. Callum was truly a man of action. When they were young and threatened by other boys, Callum would be in the middle of them swinging, while Josh was determining which one to take on first. Now, they were up against a ruthless gang. They couldn't afford to make any mistakes. When the gang figured out their backshooter wasn't going to show up again, they would probably decide to attack. The question was, how long would they wait? He knew it was only a matter of time. But how much time?

He didn't like the idea of bringing his new wife Fianna, into this fight. However, like it or not, the fight was coming. *It might be over before she got here*, he thought. He heard a leaf rustle behind him. His hand drifted down to his Colt.

"Josh, it's me, Floyd."

He relaxed. "Come on up, Uncle."

Floyd sat next to him on the log.

"Callum looks pretty bad," Josh said.

"You should've seen him when we showed up. Your brother's lucky to be alive. Either one of those wounds could've gotten infected, but they didn't. He had the gumption to crawl into the creek. I think that fast, cold water helped slow the bleeding and wash a lot of the debris out. It's a question how that bullet got through his chest without killing him. Never been much on religion, but when I saw that chest wound, and him still alive, I surely had second thoughts. He should be dead, but he's still got a lot of healing to do."

"There's some folks that have tallied up a big debt," Josh said, "and I'm aiming to collect. We've got to go easy about it, though. I figure that we have maybe a week before this gang attacks. They've got to decide the backshooter isn't returning. Then they have to plan. Having the back door closed with Jeb's bear traps, all we need to worry about is the front. That being the case, I think we can cut them down to size when they come up our valley. By the way, is all of the big valley yours?"

Floyd smiled in the dark. "It's ours, boy. There's room to grow a big ranch, and it's all deeded, nice and legal. All we have to do is stay alive."

"I couldn't see the north end. How far does it go?"

"From end to end maybe twenty-five miles or so, and seven or eight wide. I think your ma and pa are really gonna like it here."

Josh nodded. "Our job is to hold it. I'm thinking the best thing we can do is fortify our position, and continue to build. With me here, we can move along a little faster with building the house. We ought to do that and add a couple more shooting positions on each side of the approach. We build them so that we can't get flanked. Our guests will be in for a big surprise."

The two men were quiet. They sat side by side on the log. Two big men, one older, one younger, but both having seen more than their share of death and destruction. Both committed to taming this land.

Daylight slipped silently into the valley. Puffy clouds, racing across the heavens, turned pink, then golden, then white. A herd of antelope fed slowly across the entrance of the homeplace, ignorant of the two men, each wrapped in his own thoughts, watching.

"We oughta be gettin' back to camp," Floyd said. They could hear the camp coming to life. The smell of bacon and coffee drifted down the valley toward them.

Josh stood slowly, stretching his back. "Good idea. That bacon's smelling mighty good. Let's head back."

JOSH AND FLOYD walked into camp as everyone was sitting up to breakfast. Sarah turned to them. "Coffee's by the fire, bacon's in the skillet, and biscuits on the table. It's not much, but it'll have to do."

"She makes some mighty fine biscuits," Callum said. He was standing, with one hand against the lean-to frame.

"How are your legs doing?" Josh asked.

"Fine. They're getting better every day. I'm thinking about taking a little ride today."

"Best not push it, Callum," Floyd said. "That chest wound's gonna take a while to heal. It don't need no bouncing on a horse. Also, while we're talking about it, you can probably handle a revolver fine, but no shoulder guns. The recoil's liable to break somethin' loose. Then you'll be down again."

"Thanks, Uncle. We'll see."

Callum turned to Sarah. "If it's all right with you, I'd like to get Jimmy fed and get him on the lookout for a while. We've still got some jawing we need to do. Could you handle that, Jimmy?"

"Yes, sir." Jimmy looked to his ma. "Is that all right, Ma?"

"That's fine, Son. Just stay awake. If you feel yourself getting sleepy, come right back. You understand?"

"Yes'm," he said, headed for the corral.

Callum sat in his chair and pointed at Josh. "Okay, Brother. I spilled my guts last night, now sit yourself down and bring us up to date."

Josh grinned. *Get ready for a big surprise*, he thought. He sat on the log, on the opposite side of the fire. He took a big bite of biscuit and bacon, while everyone moved around, getting their breakfast and finding a place to sit. Sarah pulled up her rocker. He finished chewing his biscuit, took a sip of coffee, and began. "I'm married."

"What?" Callum exclaimed. "Are you kidding us?"

"Nope, met a really nice girl in Fort Griffin. Her name is Fianna Caitlin O'Reilly. Of course, it's Logan, now."

Floyd looked over at Josh. "Your ma is gonna be right happy."

"I hope so. Anyway, Cal, you might remember me talking about First Sergeant O'Reilly? She's his sister. He's also on his way here. I was gettin' so concerned about you, worrying about me, that they finally told me to get up here and let you know I was still alive."

"You mean, you left them alone to make their way here? I can't believe you'd do that," Callum said.

"Well, there's more to tell. We'd left Fort Griffin and were about a week out, when one of Mr. Nance's riders caught up with us. He said that Mr. Nance had a herd headed over to Fort Sumner in New Mexico, up the Goodnight-Loving trail. They were driving a thousand head. He said that he'd make me a real good deal on five hundred of them if I wanted them. Of course, I did. So, about a week behind me, five hundred head of longhorn are being driven up to our valley. When they get here, at least for a while, we'll have three more men to help. Counting Pat, that means we'll have an additional four good men. They all know their way around cattle and firearms."

Floyd leaned back, shook his head, and said, "Well, I'll be. Who would've thought it? If we can hold out till they get here, we can put those killers in the ground." He thought of what he said and immediately looked at Sarah. "Sorry, ma'am. Sometimes I speak before I think."

She smiled at him. "Floyd, no need to apologize. I couldn't have put it better."

Josh laughed. "One more thing I need to mention."

Everyone looked at him expectantly. Then Callum said, "Well, spit it out, Josh."

"We think Fianna's pregnant."

The men laughed and offered their congratulations.

Sarah clapped and said, "That is so exciting. Congratulations, Josh. I just can't wait to meet Fianna."

They were all laughing and talking when Jimmy came racing up on his horse. "I tried to get your attention, but no one looked my way!"

"Tell us, Son, quickly," Josh stood and said.

Jimmy turned and pointed down the valley. "Indians!"

Callum checked the Remingtons on his hip and tossed the Henry to Sarah. "Into the barn."

"Don't run," Floyd said. "Just walk nice and easy."

She picked up the box of .44s and, with Jimmy pressed to her side, moved to the barn.

"Shoshone," Jeb said. "Looks like four riding in. More at the mouth, but they ain't wearing paint."

Josh watched Callum push himself to his feet. He looked steadier than he was yesterday.

"Be best if we leave our rifles," Jeb said. "They may not be friendly, but they ain't looking for a fight—right now."

The other men followed Jeb's suggestion. The four of them moved out in front of the camp, facing the oncoming riders.

When they drew close enough to be recognized, the Indians let out a whoop and loped their horses forward, pulling up in front of the men and leaping from their horses' backs. Floyd and Jeb laughed and stepped forward to greet the riders.

"Friends," Floyd said to Callum and Josh.

The two older men grasped the arms of each of the four Indians and spoke in a tongue neither Callum nor Josh could understand.

Floyd turned to the barn and called, "Sarah, you and Jimmy come on out. Brew up some fresh coffee and some more bacon and biscuits."

Sarah came out of the barn and went directly to the cooking fire, setting the rifle against the lean-to. Jimmy walked up to the group of men and stood quietly, watching the animated conversations.

The Indians' excitement was contagious. Jeb held the younger Indian, a man in his early twenties, at arm's length and looked him up and down, then spoke to him in the Shoshone tongue. The younger man beamed with pride.

The leader of the group said something to Floyd. Floyd nodded to Callum and Josh. "This here is my Shoshone brother and great chief, Kajika." He grasped the older Indian's shoulder and gave it an affectionate squeeze. "Kajika, these are my brother's sons, Callum and Josh."

Kajika stepped forward and shook hands with first Callum and then Josh, by grasping the forearm of each man, while they simultaneously grasped his. He was a tall man, able to look

Callum, all of six feet, in the eyes. "Is good to meet family of Igasho." He turned to Floyd and spoke quickly in Shoshone.

Floyd laughed and said to Callum and Josh, "Kajika said my brother fed you well, especially you, Josh."

Callum and Josh grinned. "Reckon that's true," Callum said.

Floyd continued, "Let me introduce Dyami, and Lonato. Both good friends." He said something in Shoshone to the two men. They stepped forward and shook hands with Callum and Josh.

"I'll let Jeb do the honors, now," Floyd said.

Jeb, with his big hand placed affectionately on the younger man's neck, said, "This here is Mingan. His name means Gray Wolf. He was named that because, as a boy, he slipped through the forest like a wolf. He is my son. I'm sorry to say, his ma died in childbirth."

Mingan stepped up to Callum and Josh. "I am proud to meet you."

"You speak good English," Callum said.

Mingan looked at Jeb. "My father taught me well. He is named Netis, because he is a friend of the Shoshone."

Callum said, "He is my friend, too, because he saved my life."

Mingan spoke quickly to the others in Shoshone. Kajika responded, "My chief says, you must tell us the story."

Floyd said, "It's a good one. Let's all sit down, have some coffee, and we'll tell you. But first, this here is Jimmy, and that lady at the campfire is Sarah, his mother."

The four Indians looked down at the boy. Then Kajika reached for Jimmy's hand and shook it, followed by each of the other men. They turned to Sarah and nodded.

In Shoshone, Kajika asked, "Who's woman?"

Jeb responded in Shoshone, explaining that her husband had been killed and she was helping them. The Indians nodded.

Jimmy said to Floyd, "Mr. Logan, I'd be pleased to take their horses to water."

Kajika nodded and gave the reins of his mustang to Jimmy.

The other three men followed his lead. Jimmy led the horses to the water trough at the corral, while the men gathered around and sat by the fire. Sarah brought each a cup of coffee. Their faces lit up when they tasted it.

Floyd and Jeb carried most of the conversation. Finally, the conversation turned to Sarah and James. Floyd explained how Callum had saved them, only to have James killed here by some of the same men. Then he told about Callum being shot and where.

Kajika looked over the fire to Callum and said, "Show me."

Floyd nodded. "Go ahead, Son."

Callum stood to remove his coat, his vest, and his shirt. Then he pulled his long johns down around his waist. All four of the Shoshone stood and walked around the fire to Callum. Talking among themselves, they looked at the entry wound in his back and the exit in the middle of his chest. Then each man touched the exit wound. Kajika said something, and they all returned to where they had been sitting, and Callum pulled up his long johns and finished dressing.

They spoke softly, their tones almost reverent. When the conversation was ended, Floyd turned to Callum.

"I told them everything, even about the wolf. They're mystified how you could have survived and be walking around. Kajika would like for you to come to their village and see the medicine man. This is important, Son. They believe the Great Spirit stepped in and saved your life. They want to help him and complete your healing quickly. Kajika says their medicine man is a man of great power. He gets his power from the Great Spirit. I think you should do it."

"Well, Uncle, you know we grew up around the Cherokee, back in Tennessee. I've got nothing against their beliefs. Sure, I'd welcome gettin' better quicker."

Sarah stepped in. "You can do whatever you want, but if you

want these biscuits and bacon, you'd better eat it now, while it's hot."

Mingan translated, and the four Shoshone moved to the little table, where she had the biscuits set out. Each man picked up a hot biscuit and some bacon and returned to their seats.

Kajika tasted his first, then took a big bite. He chewed for a moment and turned to Sarah. "Very good, Lady."

She beamed at the compliment. "Thank you."

While the Indians ate and drank their coffee, Floyd explained that they were moving south. Every year, when they made their move, they came through this valley because of the buffalo that wintered here. They usually made their camp west of where the north ridge tapers into the big valley. That gave them protection so that they could set up their teepees out of the northwest wind. So that would put them just a short distance from the homeplace.

Josh thought for a moment. "If they're family to you two, they're family to us."

Callum looked at Kajika. "It is mighty important to understand that we could be attacked by the men that shot me. I wouldn't want your people to be harmed."

Kajika smiled, but there was no humor in it. "Scalps are always welcome."

15

Three days had passed. Light was growing dim as evening approached. The house was taking shape. Some of the Shoshone men and women had helped with the building. The roof would be added the next day.

The night the Shoshone had arrived, it started snowing. The next morning they awoke to a wilderness of white. The storm had left almost a foot of snow, but the day had turned off clear. Where the rays of the sun could warm the ground, the snow melted quickly. White still remained in the shadows. Winter was closing in.

There had been a big celebration the night before, for the return of Floyd and Jeb. Dancing went long into the night. Callum had met the Shaman, and the man examined his wounds. There would be another ceremony tonight and, with Mingan interpreting, the Shaman had said he would chase all of the evil spirits from Callum's body.

Callum walked over to where Floyd was notching a log for the side of the house. "Got a minute?"

Floyd stopped, leaned on the axe, and pushed his hat back. "Surely. What can I do you for?"

Callum looked across the valley. "I'm feelin' better. The legs are workin' like they should, and most of the pain in them has gone."

"Glad to hear it. You had us some worried."

"I know, but I was wonderin'. You think I should let this Shaman work on me?"

"Callum, that's up to you. Like we discussed earlier, you and Josh spent a lot of time with the Cherokee back in Tennessee. You know an Injun can get insulted mighty easy. This ain't gonna do you no harm, but it could surely strengthen yours and the family's ties to the Shoshone. Ain't much chance of you makin' friendly with the Comanche, Apache, or the Utes, but you got a chance with the Shoshone. That's somethin' to think about.

"Another thing. You got more than a hundred braves in this bunch. Wister ain't tryin' nothin' till they're gone. Make friends. Keep 'em here as long as possible. Ain't nothin' wrong with that. Anyway, seems like you and Dyami have hit it off. He's in line for chief, after Kajika. That could set the family up for years to come."

"What you're saying makes sense. Yeah, reckon you're right. Guess I'd best be getting ready."

Floyd looked at the sky. "Reckon that goes for all of us. It's about time to call it a day."

They had all been invited to the temporary Indian village for supper and the Shaman's ceremony. Sarah had cleaned up and was ready for the short trek to the village. She rounded up Jimmy and, with a bucket of water, managed to wash most of the grime from his young body. The men all washed up, slipped on their best clothes, and were ready.

"Reckon we can all walk down," Josh said. "I'm looking forward to this. It's time Cal got healed up enough to get back to work. He's been lazing around too long."

Callum laughed. "You can say that again. I don't know if I can stand to sit around another day."

Large ceremonial fires could be seen burning in the village. The flames reflected off the remaining aspen leaves, giving them a blood-red appearance. The fires gave off sufficient light for the group to make their way to the village. As they neared, Kajika, Dyami, and Howakan, the Shaman, met them at the edge of the encampment. The Indians were dressed in ceremonial clothing. Each man wore a breechcloth with deerskin leggings. Kajika and Dyami had multicolored beads adorning their soft, yellow leggings. The two men's deerskin, pullover shirts had wide sections of the colored beads flowing down the front, with quills interspersed in the beads. Their moccasins were the same soft yellow, outlined with beads. Kajika, tall for a Shoshone, wore a headdress that extended to his waist. It was made of eagle feathers and decorated with quills and shells.

Howakan was dressed in beautiful white deerskin, with many of the multicolored beads and quills. In his hand, he held a stick that was decorated with feathers and shells, and attached to the end was the foot of an eagle.

"Welcome," Kajika said to the group. "Come join us at the fire. We will eat, all except Callum." Kajika pointed at Callum. "You will go with Howakan."

The Shaman motioned with his arm for Callum to go into a nearby teepee. Callum stepped forward, leaving the others. He bent to enter the teepee entrance. When inside, he straightened and looked around. The first things he noticed was the small fire in the middle of the teepee and the large black kettle of liquid heating at the side of the fire. Inside the teepee was warm. On further inspection, he saw Mingan and three Shoshone women waiting to Mingan's left.

Immediately upon entering, the Shaman spoke in a commanding tone. Callum looked to Mingan.

"The Shaman says you will now be washed."

Callum looked at him with a start. "You mean all over?"

Mingan smiled. "Yes, the women will remove your clothes

and wash you with the cleansing water. Then you will be clothed in sacred garments."

"I reckon no woman is going to wash me, Shoshone or otherwise."

A frown drifted across Mingan's face. "You must allow this. This is a great honor for these women. They have been personally chosen by the Shaman. This will bring you good health and protect you. But if you refuse, it will be a great insult to these women, our Shaman, and the tribe."

Callum nodded to the Shaman. Then he looked over to Mingan. "Tell him I am deeply honored."

Mingan spoke to the Shaman. The man nodded to the women. They approached Callum and began undressing him, respectfully laying his clothing on the side of a bearskin rug. The other side was occupied with clothing he assumed he would be wearing when they were finished.

It went quickly. They had him sit on the rug while his boots were removed. Then his clothing rapidly disappeared.

Each woman had a deerskin cloth that she soaked in the concoction in the kettle and then scrubbed his body with. Standing on the rug, with not a stitch of clothing on, he had to admit that the scrubbing felt good. Whatever was in the water was soothing to his body. When the women came to the wounds in his chest, they stopped. The Shaman said something and stepped forward. He took a pouch from around his neck and spoke to the older woman. She wrung out the cloth, put it into the kettle, soaking up fresh warm water, and then held it out to the Shaman. He sprinkled the powder from the pouch onto the cloth.

The woman turned to Callum and motioned for him to turn around. Then she gently pressed the cloth to each of the entry wounds. She turned him back around, the Shaman sprinkled more of the powder on the cloth, and she washed around the wounds, then again pressed the cloth to the wounds.

Callum could swear he felt a tingling in the wounds, not only at the surface, but following the track of the bullets through his body. He mentally scoffed at the possibility, but before he had time to think about it, the women were back, drying his body with soft rabbit fur. Once they were finished, the women fastened a breechcloth on him, and then deerskin leggings individually on each leg. He marveled at the softness of the deerskin. They then picked up the deerskin shirt, almost as white as the one the Shaman was wearing, had him bend over so that they could slip his long arms in, and slid the shirt down, covering his upper torso. The shirt reached to just below his hips. It was followed by a beaded mantle that hung in front of his chest and down his back. Lastly, the older woman knelt and slipped the white deerskin moccasins on his feet. He was amazed that everything fit so well. The older woman moved away to a small pot that sat near the fire. She dipped a carved wooden cup into the liquid in the pot and brought the cup back to the Shaman. The Shaman held the cup in front of him and spoke soft words over it.

"He is blessing the magic water," Mingan said.

There was silence in the teepee, while, with gnarled hands, the Shaman gave the cup to the woman, who in turn lifted it up to Callum.

I've got to be as respectful to these folks as they have been to me. He took the cup, and bowed slightly to the woman, then turned to the Shaman and bowed deeper. He stretched his body to his full height and slowly swallowed the drink. He felt it almost immediately. It was like a wave of well-being swept over him. He turned to the Shaman and smiled. The Shaman said something to Mingan. Mingan moved the flap and spoke to the brave outside of the teepee. The drums started immediately.

Mingan said to Callum, "We go outside now. One woman will lead. You will take the hand of each of the other two, and they will take you to a bed, near the fire and inside the circle of stone. You will lay down on the bed."

The woman led off, followed by Callum and the other two women, then the Shaman and then Mingan. The women helped Callum lie down on the bed. He was feeling a little light-headed. The warmth of the fire and the bed felt good. The Shaman walked up to the bed, shook a rattle that he was holding in his left hand, and began singing and moving the eagle claw up and down Callum's body.

This part of the ceremony was short. It ended when the Shaman stopped singing. Dyami stepped up to Callum's side and extended his hand. Callum took it, and Dyami helped him sit up and then stand. He guided him over to a place of honor next to Kajika. *I'm glad to sit. I feel mighty weak.*

Floyd broke away from the group, and, with great dignity, presented the Shaman with a bowie knife resting in a beautifully trimmed scabbard. The Shaman took it, looked to Callum, and spoke.

Floyd translated for Callum and the group. "Tonight, you have been cleansed. You are now a member of the Shoshone tribe. You are healed. You have survived a bullet that no man should survive. Now, I make this promise to you, no other bullet will ever again be strong enough to break your skin. This you can trust. This you can believe."

Callum inclined his head and asked Floyd to translate. He looked at the Shaman and then Kajika. "I thank you. It is a great honor for me to be a member of the Shoshone. I will hold this sacred."

Floyd then leaned over and patted Callum on the shoulder. "You did good, Son. I reckon for however long the Logan family lives in this valley they will always be friends of the Shoshone."

Callum was brought food to eat, and the festivities continued. He glanced over at Jimmy. The boy was watching with rapt attention. He had made friends with several of the Shoshone boys, and they were sitting together.

Kajika finally stood and called the gathering to an end. He

spoke to Dyami. Dyami walked behind the chief's teepee and led a big roan and white spotted appaloosa. Kajika motioned for Callum to stand. He took the reins of the appaloosa from Dyami and began to talk in Shoshone. Floyd translated. "We have come to this valley for many years. This time, we were reunited with our good friends." He nodded to Floyd and Jeb. "But we also met Callum. He who has survived a bullet to the heart. No man lives from this, but Callum has. He is a great warrior who fought in the big war of the white men. He and his brother have come here to this valley to make life for his family.

"Our Shaman tells us he is a special man—a spirit warrior. He will be a friend of our people. For this reason, we make him our brother and give him a new name—Cheveyo—by which he will forever be known to the Shoshone. A spirit warrior should ride a spirit horse. We, as a tribe, give this horse, which was taken from the dead Nez Perce chief, to Cheveyo."

Kajika handed the reins to Callum.

Floyd said, "You've got to say something."

Callum bowed to the chief and then turned to the people. "First, I am honored to have been welcomed into the Shoshone Nation by such a well-known and honorable chief as Kajika. I hope to be strong and worthy of your trust. I must thank you for this special horse. I will always think of the Shoshone people when I ride him."

Floyd finished translating, and there was much nodding in agreement among the tribe.

Kajika continued to talk. "We have found many buffalo in this big valley. Tomorrow, we will hunt." He turned again to Callum. "You, along with all of your men, are invited to hunt with us."

Floyd translated this, and he said to Callum, "You can't go. You ain't healed up."

"Floyd, you know I've got to go. Tell them, tomorrow, with my spirit horse, I will ride, with the Shoshone, to take many buffalo."

. . .

DAWN HAD NOT YET BROKEN when Callum, Josh, Floyd, and Jeb rode into the Shoshone camp. The camp was active with men and women packing horses and preparing for the hunt.

Callum felt good. This morning was the first morning since he had been shot that his chest had not hurt. His legs felt like they were back to normal, and he was looking forward to finding out what his new horse could do. His only concern was leaving Sarah and Jimmy. But his fears were allayed with half of the warriors remaining behind. That would leave over fifty warriors in the camp. He felt sure Wister wouldn't attempt anything with the Shoshone here.

Mingan and Dyami rode with Callum and his group as they trotted out of camp. Callum felt the excitement, surrounded by fifty Shoshone braves. Mingan explained a herd of about five hundred buffalo were grazing on the east side of the valley five miles north of the camp. Their plan was to ride slowly toward the buffalo until they spooked, then they would race alongside and take as many as they could. Most of the Shoshone had rifles, but still preferred the rapid fire of their bows. Callum had elected to use his new .44 New Model Remingtons with a maximum powder load.

Mingan explained to Callum and Josh that Dyami was in charge. It would be up to Dyami to begin and end the hunt. He also told them to ride almost against the buffalo and then fire down behind and between the shoulders.

The morning sun, not yet risen, but reflecting off the scattered clouds, cast light across the big valley. Callum felt his heartbeat increase when they rode over a swell in the valley. There, no more than a half mile away, a herd of the wooly beasts fed peacefully. The women stayed behind, and the men started spreading out. As they moved closer, Callum picked a big cow feeding near the edge of the herd. It was a cold morning, and steam rose from the backs of the shaggy beasts. Several were now standing with their heads lifted, watching the riders. The herd started moving out at a walk. The moment they moved, the Indians let out a bloodcurdling whoop and raced toward the animals.

Callum, keeping his eyes on his chosen cow, kicked the appaloosa in the flanks and swung him in near the buffalo. The herd was running hard now. Callum caught a glimpse of Floyd as he dropped a big bull, then disappeared in the dust. Drawing his .44, the appaloosa pulling in next to the cow, Callum aimed the revolver between the shoulder blades and squeezed the trigger. The sound of the revolver's discharge was lost in the noise of the stampeding herd. The cow didn't flinch. Callum eared the hammer back and fired again. This time the cow stumbled, carried on for a few yards, and fell. It rolled almost under the feet of the nimble appaloosa, but the horse dodged and pressed on. Callum rode to the next in line and fired again, resulting in a one-shot kill—another buffalo down.

The mayhem continued for another five minutes, and then Dyami was calling the braves off the hunt. The buffalo continued to race north as Callum slowed the appaloosa. "Good boy," he said, and patted the horse's neck. The bay had been an excellent horse, but this one was unique, much like Josh's Chancy. He pulled the horse to a walk to let him cool. Looking around, he saw Josh and then Floyd. He could see Jeb over with his son, Mingan.

Floyd rode up first. "How you feelin'?"

Callum laughed. "I hadn't even thought about it. I feel great."

"Good," Floyd said. They looked back, along the path of the buffalo stampede. It looked like there were over sixty buffalo on the ground. "This was a good hunt for the Shoshone. They will have plenty of meat going into the winter. I hate to tell you, but there will be a big celebration in camp tonight."

Callum groaned in mock despair. "Not again. Are we ever goin' to get any sleep?"

It was Floyd's turn to laugh. "You can sleep when you're dead. Enjoy their success."

Josh rode up. "What are you two laughing about over here?"

"I was just telling Callum there would be a big party in the Indian camp tonight."

Josh grinned and then said, "Whoever said that Indians were stoic didn't know what he was talking about."

The three men watched as the women moved in and started dressing out the buffalo. They were experts at it. Slicing through the thick hides with knives so sharp a man could shave with them, they made quick work of the huge animals. Nothing was wasted. The animals meant survival for their tribe. The extra horses were now being packed with over three hundred pounds of meat each. The dead buffalo had been strung over a quarter of a mile.

Callum had put down four and felt good that he was contributing to the tribe. They rode to the nearest buffalo and started dressing it out. With everyone pitching in, the work was done in three hours, and the successful hunters headed back to the camp.

When they rode in, there was great celebration. Immediately, hides were stretched and scraped, meat was cut into strips and hung for drying, bones were broken and the priceless marrow was drawn out. Choice cuts of meat were set aside for the evening feast.

Callum sought out Chief Kajika and Dyami. When he found them, he asked Floyd to translate. "Thank you, my friends. I have ridden today with the great Shoshone warriors. I have ridden like the wind on my spirit horse. My soul is light, and my body is strong, thanks to the friendship of my brothers and the medicine of Howakan, the Shaman. In the ride of the buffalo, a name for my spirit horse came to my mind." Now he spoke directly to Kajika. "If this pleases you, he will be known forever as Shoshone, for my brothers and sisters."

Many of the tribe stood near, silent, listening. Kajika thought for a moment. Then he stood to his full height and placed his hand upon Callum's shoulder. "Let it so be."

There were yells and whoops of celebration. Floyd turned to Callum and, before he stopped to think, slapped him on the back. "Son, you missed your calling. You shoulda been a politician."

Callum winced, coughed, and said, "Reckon I'll pass on that, Uncle. Now let's head back to camp."

16

Callum woke to the mournful sound of the wind coursing through the pines. His chest and shoulder were sore from the previous day's riding. He threw back his blankets, turned his boots upside down and beat them out, then pulled the cold leather over his feet. After getting dressed, which consisted of putting his hat, his gunbelt, and his coat on, he walked out to the fire. Callum laid kindling across the live coals and then added a few sticks. They smoldered for a moment, then burst into flames. After adding a couple of larger limbs, he crossed several logs across the top, then grabbed the coffeepot and got the water heating.

"You're up early," Sarah said as she came walking out of the barn.

Callum glanced up. "Mornin'."

"You know, that's my job you're doing."

"Sarah, I'm glad you're up. I'd rather be drinkin' your coffee than mine."

"I'll second that," Josh said as he came walking out of the lean-to. "How are you feelin', Cal?"

Callum watched Sarah making the coffee. "Good. Still a little sore, but I'm feelin' a lot better."

Floyd and Jeb joined them at the fire.

Callum looked through the early morning darkness at the house. Then he spoke to Sarah. "Reckon you ought to be able to move in today. You and Jimmy can take the bedroom toward the front of the house. Rest of us will be next to the big fireplace. It'll be a little crowded for a while, but we'll make do."

Sarah walked around to the back of the wagon and brought out the cups. "That will be nice." She started pouring coffee, and the men moved to her side to accept a hot cup.

Jimmy came bouncing out of the back of the wagon.

Sarah looked up and smiled. "Good morning, Son. Would you take the bucket and get us some water, please?"

The boy rubbed the sleep from his eyes, looked at everyone, and said, "Morning. Yes, ma'am." He grabbed the bucket and raced to the stream.

Josh watched him for a moment, then turned to Callum. "I'll be heading out after breakfast. I want to be sure I catch the herd before it gets too far north. We ought to be back in three, maybe four, days."

Callum took a sip of the hot coffee. "Keep your eyes open. I don't have any idea what Wister and his gang are up to. We'll be fine as long as the Shoshone are here."

Floyd spoke up. "They'll be leaving as soon as they get the buffalo meat dried and the hides ready for travel. I'm thinkin' two days at the most."

Callum looked over at Josh. "Hurry back. We've got a score to settle with the Wister Gang. I'd rather it be sooner than later."

Callum watched Josh disappear down the canyon. He could feel the white-hot anger burning inside him. He needed action. That's how he was made. The Wister Gang had murdered too many people. His mind drifted to the Lopez family. Those were good people, building a home for their posterity. Now their lives were ended.

Thanks to the backshooter, he knew that Jessup was involved. That whole family and their vaqueros gunned down. Alex. He would have grown to be much of a man, but now he would never get that chance, his life ended for no reason other than greed.

The couple that Jessup had sold land to in this valley, dead. His chest was feeling better, and his legs back to normal. Wister's time was drawing to a close.

Callum took a deep breath and turned back to the camp. *First things first.*

"WHERE THE HELL IS BLUE?" Wister shouted at his men. "He's been gone for four days. I'll have that boy's hide when he gets back."

"Boss," Milam said, "what if he ain't coming back?"

Wister cut his eyes toward Milam. "You think he's dead?"

"Maybe. The people we're dealing with may not be greenhorns. If they found his spot, they could have laid for him and killed him. Even worse, though, they could have caught him. You know Blue would have squealed like a stuck pig. What if they caught him, and he told them where we are? They could be on their way here right now. They could even be bringin' those Injuns."

"If they caught him. Blue's pretty slick. He's been doing this kind of thing since the war. Nobody ever caught him."

"Always a first time."

Wister stood and walked over to the fireplace, where the coffeepot was hanging. He picked up the rag that was hanging on the fireplace hook. Using the rag to protect his hand, he grasped the handle of the pot and poured himself a cup. Then he tossed the rag back on the hook and turned to Milam. "We've got a good deal here. We can ride out of the mountains, hit a traveler now and then, and do fine. I don't want this messed up.

"In fact, I'm thinkin' we might make this a permanent place for us. I'm gettin' tired of always staying a jump ahead of the law. We can become legitimate. Why, we could even start a ranch in this valley, but we've got to find out what happened to Blue, and who else has moved in."

A tall, gangly man sat with his arms across the back of his chair. "Boss, we cain't do nothin' till them Injuns move out. There must be two hundred, all camped right where those two were killed."

Wister gave the man a deadly look. "You think I don't know about 'em? Why do you think we're still sittin' here? As soon as those Injuns move out, we'll move in. I want to see what's going on down there. If those yahoos are still there, we'll take care of 'em the same way we've taken care of everyone else. You understand?"

The tall man gave a couple of quick nods. "Sure, Boss. I was just sayin'. I meant nothin'."

Wister slammed his fist on the table. "I wanna know what's goin' on! Milam, send one of the boys out that knows Blue's lookout. Give him your binoculars. Find out if those Injuns are still there and what's going on up that canyon. I'm tired of waitin'."

"Elwood, that's the only pair we have."

Wister gave him a withering look. "Ben, I said give it to him. Just make sure he's one that'll make it back."

Another one of the gang, a medium-sized man, leaning against the wall, leered and then said, "What about Jessup's woman? Ain't we gonna check on her?"

"No, we ain't gonna check on her." Wister glared around the room. "We need everybody we got, but I swear, the next idiot that asks me a stupid question, I'm gonna hang him up by his ears until they come off. Does everyone understand me?"

NAOMI HAD NEVER BEEN SO cold. Her hands were freezing, and her feet felt like blocks of ice. The wind came out of the western peaks, snow-capped now, coursing around the cliffs and straight down the little canyon they were in. The stream they were working washed down the western slope of the canyon. Unfortunately, the canyon was narrow, and the eastern ridge of the canyon blocked the afternoon sun. The area where Shorty had found the gold saw the sun only between eleven and one, not nearly long enough to warm the slopes and melt the snow.

Snow. It hadn't snowed much, for the mountains, but what had fallen stayed. They were now living and working in over a foot of snow. The first day, Asa had built a lean-to precariously located on the flattest area near the claim. The back sheltered them from the direct onslaught of the wind and snow, but it still swirled around the top and sides. Fortunately, the second day, they had found a cave that provided them with much better shelter. It was a large opening in the side of the hill, with a wide, level entrance. Asa had explored it, half expecting to find a bear or mountain lion claiming it as home. But they were in luck.

They explored the cave and found that it remained wide and high for almost fifty feet back, before it turned and disappeared into the mountain. With this much room, they brought the horses in out of the wind and snow at night. They weren't the first to make this a temporary home. They had found a rocked fire pit, with a few dry logs remaining stacked against the wall.

The cave provided for excellent shelter, but there was one problem. It was almost a hundred yards up the western slope from Shorty's vein of gold. So during the day, while working the claim, they would use the lean-to for protection and storage of their gear, and in the evening, when they were finished, they would take their flakes, nuggets, and quartz rocks with embedded gold, and climb back to the cave. Here, they would sit in the light of the fire and break the quartz, peeling out the soft gold.

Uncle Dave had been right this time. After all of his dreams and false finds, he had struck it rich, only to die by the hands of the Utes. She was sorry she had lost her uncle, but grateful for honest men, like the Logans. They could have kept the find to themselves, or demanded a large percentage of the claim, but they went out of their way to make sure she received the claim.

"Don't get too excited, Missy," Asa said. "This vein could play out or go deep anytime. It'll still make you wealthy, but it may not be a bonanza like it appears right now."

She glanced up at Asa. He had pulled a portion of a fallen pine into the cave, and they were using it as a chair. Between his feet, he had a pile of quartz that he was patiently breaking with his rock pick. He would hammer it with the flat end until the quartz broke apart. Then he worked the gold in the quartz with the pick end, if necessary going to his rock chisel to gradually separate the gold from the quartz.

"How much do you think we've collected, Asa?"

He glanced over at the five large bags of gold leaning against the wall. "Ma'am, to be honest, I cain't even imagine how much that gold is worth. If we could stay longer, I reckon we'd need several mules to haul it out of here. I'll just say, you ain't gonna have to worry about money for a long time to come. If you're smart, like I think you are, just the gold we have here should set you up for the rest of your life."

Naomi thought back to Asa's explanation of the vein. He had said that he'd never seen a vein occurring so close to the surface. He told her that most of the time, you found the gold in the streams, where, due to the wearing of the water, small pieces, some as small as flour, flaked off and washed downstream. Then,finally, because of its weight, it would settle to the bottom where the stream turned or lost its force. But this vein, at least ten inches wide, was only a couple of feet from the surface. It would have never been found if it wasn't for the stream.

The stream hit the quartz and turned to run across the slope. The constant wearing on the quartz had gradually exposed the gold vein. The more time passed, the more of the vein was exposed. By standing on the opposite side of the stream, four vertical feet of the vein was exposed, for anyone who might be walking or riding by to see.

From what Asa could make out from Shorty's tracks, her uncle had discovered gold while he was panning downstream and gradually worked his way up the stream, looking for the source. She could only imagine the excitement he must have felt when he first saw the quartz and the gold vein. He had searched for so many years. Even as a little girl, she remembered him telling her that he was going to bring her back a big gold nugget. It never happened, until now, and he had brought her not only a nugget, but an entire vein of gold.

Tears leaped to her eyes as she thought of her uncle. He had always been so caring toward her. Uncle Dave was one of the kindest men she knew.

She had sold the farm and come west, to join her parents, shortly after her husband was killed in the war. It was a sorrowful event when her parents were both taken by pneumonia only months after her arrival. She had been devastated, with no idea what she would do, with few finances remaining. Fortunately, Uncle Dave came into town within a week of their burials. He had stayed with her and helped her get through her grief. He was good friends with the Spiveys who owned the general store. He introduced her to them. They liked her and offered her the job. With what he brought in from the sale of hides and occasionally a little dust, she did quite well. He always said, all he needed was enough to fund another stake to keep him going.

She was jerked out of her reverie by Asa.

"Missy, we're gonna need to be gettin' out of these here mountains pretty soon. Up high here, we could get snowed in, and nobody'd find us until next year's thaw. We also got to be thinkin' about where we want to head. I know you got your home in Denver City, but it ought to be a mite easier to make it to Pueblo. We can go down the valley, spend a couple of nights with Floyd, and then head on over to Pueblo. Once we're on the east side of the mountains, we'll be in a lot better shape, far as the snow goes."

"Asa, we didn't leave on such good terms. Do you think they would welcome us back?"

"Oh, shaw, ma'am. That weren't nothin'. I know Floyd and Jeb are cranky ole goats, but they're good people. We've had way worse arguments over morning coffee. They'll be glad to see us." Asa chuckled and then said, "'Specially that Callum Logan. I reckon he's just a mite sweet on you."

Naomi felt her cheeks burning in the firelight of the cave. "Mr. Collins, I think no such thing. He showed no interest. In fact, when we left, he was just plain rude. Anyway, I'm seeing Mr. Jessup."

At the mention of Jessup's name, Naomi saw a frown drift across Asa's face. "Ma'am, I ain't no gossip, but that Jessup is bad mean, clear through. I just wish you could see it."

"Mr. Collins, I'll not have you speak of Mr. Jessup in that manner. He is a gentleman that I admire. I just think you and the Logans have made a grave error."

"Be that as it may, that there Callum Logan was way more concerned about you than your Mr. Jessup. I reckon if Callum hadn't been laid up like he was he would've just grabbed you right off your horse and wouldn't have let you leave. It seemed your Mr. Jessup was too busy to do anything but put your gold in his bank."

Naomi, now completely upset, decided to change the subject. "How much time do you think we have before we must leave?"

"Well, ma'am, to be on the safe side, I'd give us another two days, then we best get ourselves out of these mountains. With both of us workin', I think we could fill us up another two, maybe three bags. But then we have to start worrying about the weight. So I'd say two days, if'n we're going to follow the Arkansas and then head up to Denver City. If we decide to go down the valley and stop in at the Logan camp, we can stay another day."

She thought for a moment. It would be good to see Floyd again. If they went south down the valley, the Logans would know she and Asa were out of the mountains for the winter, and they wouldn't have to worry or try to search for them. She decided. "Asa, why don't we go south and stop at the Logans' place."

He nodded and went back to working on the quartz.

17

Several days had slipped by since Josh rode out. Callum took another bite of the buffalo tongue. Sarah had cooked enough for the camp, using her spices and the wild onions that Jimmy had found along the stream. "Mighty good, Sarah."

She smiled at the group as they all joined in bragging on her cooking. Callum knew it had been hard for her and Jimmy, losing James. Here she was, stuck in the wilderness with her son, with a group of men she didn't really know. *She's taking it mighty well.*

Yesterday, Jeb's bear traps had caught another killer. They could hear the man yelling for help. This time both the man's legs had been caught. Jeb had gone up to check on him, but by the time he'd gotten there, the man had bled to death. They also picked up another Henry, a couple of .44 Colts, ammunition, a pair of Lemaire binoculars, and the killer's horse. After bringing the man's horse over the ridge, Jeb had started a landslide down the path, blocking passage and closing off access. They wouldn't have to worry about any sharpshooters from up the canyon.

Earlier this morning, Chief Kajika had shown up to tell them the Shoshone were moving south. He had brought buffalo meat and several hides to thank them for joining in the hunt. By noon, the tribe was gone. Except for the beaten-down grass, there was little sign they had been there.

As soon as the Indians pulled out, Callum placed a watch on the valley entrance, which they would have to maintain until the threat of Wister's gang was gone. Wister was now down two men. If the fourteen he had shown up with when they had killed James had been all of his men, his gang now numbered twelve. He'd have a nasty surprise if he attacked again. The man was a killer and a bully. Callum fully expected him to make another frontal attack, believing he was dealing with a bunch of settlers. This time, the results would be different. Callum was using the dead guy's Henry. He much preferred his Spencer, but the Henry would have to do.

Floyd and Jeb were finishing up the roof when Jimmy came galloping in from the canyon mouth. Callum had allowed him to take the Lemaire binoculars.

"Mr. Logan," Jimmy said, "Mrs. Gwendiver and Mr. Collins are coming down the big valley, but—"

Callum heard shots. "Go ahead, Jimmy."

Jimmy was out of breath. He paused a moment and continued, "They're being chased by a bunch of men."

"Floyd, Jeb!" Callum called. "That's Asa and Naomi, coming in. Wister's gang is after them."

The three men dashed to the corral and saddled their horses. Floyd and Jeb took off for the point where the canyon joined the big valley. Callum paused for a moment. "Sarah, you and Jimmy get barricaded up in the house. You've got your Henry. Be ready, but don't shoot us when we come back."

Callum raced down the canyon. Shoshone was built for this. His ears were back, and his neck stretched as his long legs drove after the other two men. Callum could see the gap closing quickly. "Over the top of the ridge," he called. "That'll give us cover."

Now they could hear multiple gunshots. He knew it was almost impossible to be accurate from the back of a moving horse, but if you put enough lead in the air, it was bound to hit something.

They weaved their way between the pines. Just below the crest, they bailed out of their saddles, took a moment to tie their horses, then raced the remaining few feet to the crest, Jeb carrying his Sharps and the two Whitworth rifles. What they saw sent chills down Callum's back. The gang was closing on the woman and man. It was obvious that Asa had been hit, but he was game. Though he slumped in the saddle, he was still riding. So far, Naomi looked to be in good shape.

"Why don't we even the score a bit?" Jeb said. The three men lay down, their bodies just below the crest, their rifles resting on the ridge. Jeb took a careful sight, took a deep breath, let out just a little, held it, and squeezed off a shot from his 1859, .52 caliber Sharps. A moment later, the closest rider to Naomi and Asa rolled out of his saddle and hit the ground like a sack of oats. At the same time, Callum and Floyd opened up with their Henrys. It was a long ways for the Henrys, but with the two of them firing, a wall of lead met the oncoming riders. One fell from his saddle, and two slumped over, grabbing their saddle horns. The remaining men pulled up and stopped.

Jeb was watching the rider chasing the mules. He switched the Sharps for a Whitworth, adjusted the sight, took aim, and fired, sending a .45-caliber chunk of lead into the rider's chest. The man jerked, then slowly leaned to his left, dropping from the saddle. Now Wister's gang was in full flight, heading back up the valley.

"I'm gettin' those mules," Callum said. He dashed back to Shoshone, untied him, and leaped into the saddle. Racing down the shallow slope, he turned around the end of the ridge as Naomi and Asa pounded toward him. "Get up to the camp," he yelled as he streaked by them. Once around the point, he turned straight for the mules.

The shooting had stopped. Wister's gang had disappeared below a swell in the valley. He felt Shoshone's muscles working like a machine as he drove toward the mules. He pulled up to them, grabbed their lead ropes, and headed back the way he had come. The mules were tired and, though there had been a lot of shooting, had decided not to run. Callum tossed their lead ropes over their withers and turned behind them. He untied his rope and slapped both of them across the rump. Immediately, they changed their minds and raced after Naomi and Asa.

Callum breathed easier when he had the ridge between him and Wister's gang. The mules continued to race toward the camp, following Naomi and Asa. *I hope Sarah doesn't shoot them when they ride into camp.* He slowed and walked the appaloosa up the shallow ridge to Floyd and Jeb. "See anything?"

"Nary a sight. Looks like they've plumb changed their mind. Reckon they'll lick their wounds for a while and try to figger out what their next move might be," Floyd said.

"I'm gonna head back to camp," Callum said. "Might be a good idea for one of you to stay here for a while to discourage them should they try to slip back."

"I'll hang around," Jeb said. "This is a lot easier than finishing up that roof."

"One of us will spell you, in a while," Callum said.

"Jeb, we hear a shot, we'll come a floggin'," Floyd added.

"I'll be lookin' for you."

Floyd and Callum mounted up and headed back to the homeplace.

. . .

Sarah and Naomi already had Asa in the house and stretched out on the bed that Callum had helped Sarah move in just this morning. They had stripped him down to his long johns, which were unbuttoned and pulled down to his hips. Asa's wiry old body carried several scars from previous altercations. Blood was running from a wound in his lower right side, just above his hip. It looked nasty, but low enough to have missed anything vital and high enough to stay away from his hip bone. The old codger was lucky. Now if they could ensure no infection set in. "How you doin', Asa?" Callum said.

"How's it look like I'm doin'? I've got a durned bullet in my side, and it hurts like the dickens. Other than that, I'm doin' just fine."

Floyd laughed. But before he could say anything, Asa jumped in.

"That's it. Laugh at a dying man. If I could get up from this bed, I'd give you somethin' to laugh about."

Floyd turned to walk outside.

"Floyd." There was a twinkle in the old man's eyes. "We found it. I swear, in all my years, I ain't never seen anything that rich. It beats that puny 1859 strike. This is a pure, flaky vein of gold. I reckon I'll buy my own beer from now on." He cackled like a hen over her eggs.

Floyd laughed with him. "I'm right proud of you, Asa. You sure earned it."

Asa looked up at the tall man. "Floyd, I thank you. If'n you hadn't mentioned me to Miss Naomi, I wouldn't be here. You're a good man. But, thinkin' about it, if'n you hadn't told her, I wouldn't be laying here with a durned bullet in me. You got me in a whale of a pickle."

Callum stepped up to Naomi. "Are you all right?"

"Yes, Mr. Logan, thank you. I don't know what we would have done if you hadn't shown up. Those men were trying to kill us.

When we first saw them, we were riding down the valley and they were coming out of the mountains. They tried to wave us down, but Asa said don't stop. I took his word, and we continued down the valley. They were maintaining our pace for a while. Then they sped up and tried to catch us. When they were closer, they started shooting. I really thought we were dead or worse. When Asa was hit, I truly felt the end was near. But when you fired that first shot, I knew we were saved."

"That was actually Jeb. He's deadly with that Sharps."

"Well, whichever of you it was, I am eternally thankful.

"I must apologize for the way we left. That was completely ungrateful, after all you and Floyd had done for me. I am truly sorry."

"Not a worry, ma'am. Asa was the one that got that ball rolling, and it just got worse."

"Well, thank you anyway."

"You're mighty welcome. I'll go out and take care of your animals. When you get finished up with Asa, there's something I need to talk to you about." Callum turned and walked out of the house.

Jimmy had already led all of the animals over to the water trough, and each of their noses was buried muzzle deep in the cold water. Shoshone looked up at Callum and shook his head.

"That's a fine horse, Mr. Logan," Jimmy said.

Callum ran his hand over the appaloosa, feeling his muscles quiver. "He is, Jimmy, he surely is. Now let me give you a hand with these saddles and packs, especially the packs. I expect they'll be pretty heavy."

He was right. He slid each pack out of its frame and carried it into the barn. "We'll put all of Mrs. Gwendiver's and Mr. Collins's gear here in the corner. That way, it'll all be together."

"Yes, sir," Jimmy said, carrying in Naomi's saddle and blanket. The boy and man worked steadily unloading the animals. Once they had everything in the barn, Callum grabbed a brush and tossed one to Jimmy, and they started brushing the horses and mules. After each animal had been taken care of they led it into the corral.

"Mr. Logan," Jimmy said, "when your brother gets here with his wife and the herd, are you going to stay?"

The question caught Callum by surprise. Floyd had talked about going to New Mexico, or over to the White Mountains in Arizona. He had figured on going with him. He wasn't ready to settle down, and there was plenty left to see of this Western country. But someone would probably have to go back to Tennessee to fetch Ma and Pa, his brothers, and his sister. He wouldn't mind that trip. He'd made it once. It would be easier the second time. But then there was Sarah and Jimmy. They would need to travel to Salt Lake. He hadn't mentioned it to Floyd, but he had thought about riding with them to make sure they made it safely.

"Jimmy, I rightly don't know. There's a lot of options coming up when spring comes around. You and your mom need to get to Salt Lake. Your uncle'll be worried about you."

"I like it here," Jimmy said. He was quiet for a moment. "Pa's buried here. I don't want to leave him."

Callum thought for a moment, then said, "I know that's important to you, Son, being close to your pa. But no matter where you go, he'll be lookin' out for you. He'd want the best for you, where you could get an education and grow up to be a good man. I just imagine, if your uncle is anything like your pa, he'll help you along the way."

"Don't you like me, Mr. Logan?"

Logan stopped brushing the appaloosa, and looked straight at Jimmy. "Son, I surely do like you. I figure you for a good friend, but even the best of friends eventually go their separate ways. They always remember each other. But life takes everyone down their own special trail. I've got mine, and you've got yours. Does that make sense to you?"

"Yes, sir. But I'll miss you."

"And I'll miss you too, Jimmy, but you never know, we could run into each other anywhere. I've always wanted to see that big salt lake. Maybe I'll see you there." Then Callum laughed. "Why, shoot, you could be almighty tired of me, 'fore this winter is up."

Jimmy grinned. "Maybe."

Callum finished the appaloosa and led him to the corral. He glanced back at the house as Naomi stepped out, looking around for him. When she spotted him, she nodded and headed his way. "How 'bout you finishing up these mules and get 'em some feed? I've got to talk to Mrs. Gwendiver."

"Yes, sir."

"You wanted to talk to me?" Naomi asked of Callum.

"Yes. Why don't we walk over to the creek?"

The day was growing late. Shadows drifted among the pines. Callum and Naomi stood near the creek as it gurgled around the rocks.

"It's nice here," she said.

"Yeah, I think Floyd outdid himself finding this valley. It'll make a good home."

"For you?"

"No. Reckon I'll be moving on when winter's done. Still a lot to see out there." Callum motioned west, toward the peaks of the Sangre de Cristos.

Naomi followed his hand with her eyes, taking in the snow-capped peaks. "Do you think you will ever settle down?"

"Don't know. Look at Floyd, he's still going, but maybe one of these days. How 'bout you?"

She turned her head from the mountains to Callum. Her soft brown eyes took in the chiseled face and dimpled chin gazing back at her. "Yes, I'd like to, someday, if I meet the right man."

Callum was uncomfortable with the subject he needed to bring up to Naomi, but the drift of the conversation, with this lovely woman, made him even more uncomfortable. He cleared his throat. "What about your gold?" *That came out wrong*, he thought.

Her face stiffened. "I know you and Floyd could have elected to never tell me about the strike. I'll be glad to give you a share."

"No," Callum said, shaking his head. "That's not what I was gettin' at. Winter's comin' on fast. I was just wonderin' what you were plannin' on doing until you can get back up into the mountains next spring?"

"Oh." Naomi blushed at her mistake. "I'm so sorry. I thought you were hinting for a piece of the strike. Of course, it depends on what Asa wants to do, but I imagine we'll be back as soon as the thaw starts. I will go back to Pueblo or Denver City and wait out the winter."

"What do you plan on doing about your banker, Jessup?"

Naomi flushed. "He is not my banker. Well, he is, but not the way you said it, and frankly, I don't think it is any of your business."

"Ma'am, I understand. Normally, it ain't any of my business, but I consider you a friend and I'd hate to see anything bad happen to you. You've gotten yourself mixed up with a dangerous man, and he's mixed up with this Wister Gang."

"That's impossible," Naomi said. "Richard will likely be governor of this state in a few years, and he'll make a good one."

"No, ma'am, he won't. Not if I have anything to do about it. Now, let me tell you what I know about your banker friend, and you can make up your own mind."

"Mr. Logan, Floyd told me about the altercation you had with Richard. He even tried to persuade me to have nothing to do with him. However, I can make up my own mind, and what I see here, is that you are just being vindictive. I know you don't like him, and I will not listen to any more of your vitriol. I appreciate you providing us a place to stay while Asa recuperates, but as soon as he is well enough to travel, we will be on our way."

With her last word, Naomi spun around, her back stiff and

chin up, and marched back to the ranch house. Callum shook his head in disgust. *How do I ever get through to this hard-headed woman?* He walked to the woodpile, picked up an axe, and slashed it into a waiting log. Pain coursed through his wounded shoulder and chest. *Smart*, he thought, and laid the axe back against the woodpile.

18

Wister yanked the horse to a stop. He threw one leg out of the stirrup, jumped to the ground, and tossed the reins to the rider next to him. "Take care of my horse," he commanded, then stomped into the cabin.

The moment Milam, followed by the other members of the gang, came through the door, Wister yelled, "What the hell happened? Who was shooting at us? I thought it was just a bunch of nesters that moved in there. Can anybody tell me anything?"

Everyone was silent. Finally, Milam spoke up. "Elwood, it's obvious those aren't nesters, not shooting like that. I'm beginning to wonder if Logan really died. Someone may have found him. Shot like he was, I don't see how he could've survived, but crazier things have happened."

Wister shook his head. "Logan's dead. You saw how he was shot. I'm surprised he didn't die while we were watching. There ain't no way he could be alive!" Then he went off on another tirade. After several minutes, he cooled down some. "Who fired the shots at the girl and the old man?" He glared at the men.

A voice came from the back of the room. "Boss, you said stop 'em."

"Who said that?" Wister had calmed down. His voice was cold and dangerous. No one answered. "I meant catch 'em, not kill 'em." He turned to Milam. "How many men did we lose?"

Milam shook his head. "Three were killed outright. We have two wounded. I don't think one will make it. Whoever was shooting knew what they were doing." Milam had a touch of admiration in his voice when he said, "Those were long shots at moving targets. We're looking at some mighty salty men."

Wister moved over to the table and sat. Immediately, one of the gang brought him a cup of coffee. He took a quick sip and said, "We're down almost to half-strength. I was planning on wintering here, since we have plenty of grub and ammunition. But with these new settlers coming into this valley, we could be in trouble. I'm thinkin' we ought to pack up and head for Pueblo. Tomorrow, we'll get all the grub and ammunition packed up and pull out early the next day. With the extra horses we have now, it'll be easy. Who knows, we might find another place better than this. If not, when spring rolls around, we'll recruit some more folks, come back, and finish off those nesters."

At the mention of pulling out of the mountains and heading to town, all of the gang nodded enthusiastically.

"Good," Wister said. "Then it's decided. Day after tomorrow, we'll head for Pueblo."

Milam turned to Wister. "Maybe we should divvy up the gold before we leave."

The only sound in the cabin was the crackling of the burning logs in the fireplace. All of the men in the cabin had one thing in common, greed. Milam had brought to the surface what had been simmering since the raid on the caravan. The men wanted their share.

Wister turned a cold eye on Milam. "You don't trust me?"

Milam set the chair on all fours and, with his elbows on the table, leaned toward Wister. His lips drew back in a smile, but it wasn't reflected in his cold eyes. "It isn't that. I just think the men need their share, so they'll have something to spend when we get to Pueblo."

Wister looked around. Blatant avarice was evident in the eyes of each man. All men liked gold. Some men worked for it, others stole it. Wister knew that even though he was the leader of this gang, they were like a bunch of coyotes. They wouldn't hesitate to tear him apart if it appeared he was trying to cheat them out of their portion of the gold.

Wister held Milam's eyes for a moment. He wanted him to know he was on to him. "Good idea. When we got this gold, there was fifteen of us. Today there's only ten. That means more for everybody. 'Course, if those two wounded fellers died, that'd mean even more for each of us."

Almost immediately, shots rang out.

Wister laughed. "I'll say one thing, you boys ain't slow. Why don't you bring that chest over here and set her on the table? Looks like there'll only be eight dividing up this here gold. We're gonna have a fine old time in Pueblo."

CALLUM HAD BEEN on watch for several hours. Daylight had come, and he figured everyone was eating. Soon, Jimmy would be riding down to relieve him. There had been a light dusting of snow again last night. Every day that passed brought them nearer to heavy snow. He was glad the house and barn had been completed. They now had protection through the winter for the people and the horses. There was not a lot of time left, but if they could get hay cut, that would carry the cattle through the really hard days of snow.

He had been watching north. When he turned back to the south, he saw some movement in the distance at the southern entrance to the big valley. He put the binoculars to his eyes, and a big smile spread across his face. Riders were driving cattle into the valley. Ma and Pa would have a ranch. He watched as the herd moved slowly into the valley. The rider on point raised his hat and waved. He could just make out Josh. He knew Josh couldn't see him, but it still felt good.

Once the cattle were settled, they could start planning their attack on the Wister Gang. He was tired of being on the receiving end. It was time to deliver quick and permanent justice. He was feeling much better, although he knew that he wasn't completely healed. That would take a while. He was just thankful he wasn't dead.

He stood and stretched his back. It felt good to stand and move around. His feet felt as cold as the snowcapped mountain peaks looked. He could see the rider on point ride over to the wagon that was to one side of the herd. The man leaned into the wagon momentarily, swung his horse around, and headed toward Callum. Callum moved over to the appaloosa, dusted the light snow off his saddle, and swung up. He looked up the canyon to the ranch house. Jimmy was on horseback, just leaving the corral. Callum waited until Jimmy arrived, then gave him the binoculars and pointed at the herd. Jimmy took a look and grinned.

"I'm goin' to meet 'em. Keep an eye out all around."

"Yes, sir," Jimmy said to Callum's back as he watched the appaloosa trot toward the arriving herd.

"You're a sight for sore eyes," Callum said, as he rode up to Josh. The two brothers shook hands.

"You're looking much better," Josh said.

"Feelin' better. Now, where is this bride of yours?"

Josh grinned. "Follow me." He turned his horse, Chancy, and rode toward the wagon, with Callum by his side.

When they rode up, Callum was pleased with what he saw. The young woman was handling the reins of the horses like a skinner. Brilliant red hair slipped out from under her bonnet as she pulled the horses to a stop. She reached up with a gloved right hand and pushed it back into place.

"Cal," Josh said, "it's my pleasure to introduce my wife, Fianna Caitlin Logan. Fianna, this is my brother Callum."

Her sparkling green eyes lit with pleasure. She extended her right hand. "It is nice to meet you, Callum. Josh has told me so much about you."

Callum took the small hand and swept his hat from his head. "It is my pleasure, Fianna. Welcome to your home. I must say, Josh didn't do near justice to your beauty."

Fianna's smile radiated happiness. "Thank you, although I fear you are filled with the same blarney as Josh."

The three of them were laughing as a wide-shouldered, thick-necked rider joined them, dressed in his Union pants and campaign hat, a sheepskin coat over his burly chest. "Callum," Josh said, "you've heard me speak of him, this is Patrick Devane O'Reilly. Pat, my brother, Callum."

Pat extended his hand. "Aye, 'tis a pleasure to be meeting you. Josh told us of your misfortune. It is glad, I am, to be seeing you up and about."

"Thanks," Callum said. "Nice to meet you. Thanks for looking after my brother."

Callum turned to Josh. "Let's get these cattle moved up near the mouth of the canyon. There's plenty of feed and water. Don't reckon they'll stray far."

The men rode back to the cattle and pushed them up the valley. Good grass and water had the herd slowing to eat and drink. They reluctantly kept moving. Upon reaching the mouth of the canyon into the homeplace, Floyd and Jeb rode out. They greeted Josh and were introduced to Pat and Fianna. The rest of the men were working the herd. Josh stood in the saddle and waved them in, and they all headed for the ranch house. With plenty of food and water, the cattle weren't going anywhere.

Fianna drove the wagon, and the rest of the hands rode up to the ranch house. Everyone dismounted, and introductions were made all around, including the three men Callum hadn't met,

Scott Penny, the ramrod, and Jimmy Leads and Jack Swindell. After everyone had met, the men got busy and moved the things from the wagon to the house. Callum said, "Josh, that room at the back is yours and Fianna's bedroom. Naomi, Sarah, and Jimmy are sleepin' in the bedroom at the other end of the house. The rest of us can pitch our bedrolls near the fireplace. It might get a little tight, but it'll work."

Scott Penny spoke up. "I noticed the lean-to with the fire in front of it. I've been sleeping under the stars for the past couple of months. That ought to do me fine."

Jimmy Leads and Jack Swindell chimed in. "Us too."

"Boys," Callum said, "you're more than welcome to sleep in here."

Scott replied, "If it gets too cold out there, we'll take you up on it. But for now, the lean-to ought to be fine."

"If it's all right with Miss Naomi," Asa said, "we'll be headin' for Pueblo tomorrow. I'm feelin' a heap better."

"I'm sure Naomi will agree, you need to rest up for a few more days before you get back in the saddle, Asa," Floyd said.

"Dang it, Floyd, don't be tellin' me what I need to do. I'm feelin' way better today."

"You won't be after a couple of miles on the back of a horse."

"Are you sure you feel up to it, Asa?" Naomi asked.

"Miss Naomi, why, that weren't nothin' but a graze. I could leave today, if'n you wanted to."

"Asa, are you sure?"

"Yes, ma'am, I ain't foolin'."

"Asa," Floyd said, "you ain't nowhere near fit to ride."

Asa swung out of the bed. "You stop your jawin' and get them horses and mules loaded up, and I'll show ya how fit I am. We're leavin' today, just as soon as you get us loaded up."

Naomi looked over at Floyd. "Please, Floyd. We do need to be getting back to Pueblo as soon as we can."

Floyd shook his head. "You won't make it to Pueblo in one

day. You'll have to camp. Who's gonna unload the pack mules or take care of the horses? Asa is in no shape to do any of that. You'll have to do all of the heavy liftin' and take care of him. You don't need to leave today—at least wait two days. That'll give him more time to heal, and maybe one of us could ride back with you."

Naomi turned a concerned look to Asa. "That makes sense. You can't handle those heavy packs, and even if I could get them off, I don't think I could get them back on the mules."

Asa did not accept his defeat graciously. "Fine, but we don't need no babysitters."

Josh watched the little melodrama play out. Then he turned to Callum. "Scott and the boys are going to head back to Texas as soon as possible, but they've told me they'd like to hang around until we get this Wister Gang taken care of."

Callum looked over at the Texas crew. "Thanks, men. Why don't we take today to rest up? Tomorrow, we'll ride over to where their cabin is supposed to be and see if we can't even up the score a little."

Callum turned back to Josh. "I'd like to get an early start in the morning. It'll take us all day to get there, hit 'em, and return. I figure you, me, and Floyd, plus three others. That'll make it six against eight to ten. Sounds like a fair fight to me."

"That's fine with me, but are you up to that long a ride?"

"I chased buffalo, and that was several days ago. We need to stop Wister, and do it before he kills someone else. You're darned straight I'm up to it."

19

Breaking daylight greeted the six riders as they rode out of the ranch. Turning north up the valley, Floyd, Callum, and Josh were in the lead. They were followed by Scott Penny, Jimmy Leads, and Jack Swindell. Pat O'Reilly and Jeb had remained at the ranch to protect the women.

Callum looked across the valley at the cattle, frost shining on their backs. "This valley's gonna make a fine ranch. Ma's never had a place like this. Floyd, she and Pa owe you a lot."

"I'm just plannin' ahead, Callum. If I live long enough to get tired of roaming around this country, I'll have a porch to sit on and rest my old bones."

Daylight came quickly. Once they could see the ground clearly, the men increased their horses' gaits from a walk to a distance-eating lope. They would hold the lope for a while, then drop back to a walk to rest the horses. Silence rode heavily on them. In a few hours there would be a battle resulting in dead men, probably from both sides. But all of these men had been in battles before, where men were killed and maimed. They knew what was coming and were ready to exterminate the vermin. Men like those who made up Wister's gang didn't deserve to live.

The miles fell away. Floyd slowed his horse to a walk, and the others followed. "According to the information the back-shooter gave us, that's the canyon we're looking for. When we turn up the canyon, the house should be only a couple more miles. It's a climb all the way, so we best keep the horses to a walk."

Almost in unison, they pulled their rifles, Henrys and Spencers, from the scabbards. The horses made little noise as they moved up the canyon. The lodgepole pine and occasional ponderosa had covered the ground with soft, sound-deadening pine needles. Along the sloping canyon walls, white and gray aspen stood as silent sentinels on watch as they passed.

When they had progressed some distance up the mountains, Callum signaled to stop and dismount. He spoke in a low voice, for sound carried in these mountains. "Don't know how much farther, but let's spread out a little and take it on foot from here. Lead your horses. We might need 'em."

They had gone only a short distance when the cabin came into view. Here, the men tied their horses, and slipped up to within fifty yards of the house. The previous owners had built a sturdy home. Besides their living quarters, they had a corral that was attached to a barn, protected by a thick stand of pines behind it.

There were no horses in the corral. Callum motioned for Josh and Scott to circle around the house and check the barn. Minutes ticked by slowly as the two men worked their way around the house. They disappeared into the barn, only to appear moments later, shaking their heads.

Callum and Floyd eased up to the front door and threw it open. Empty. Callum stepped back outside. "Looks like they're gone. Look around and see if you can find any sign."

Josh walked in as Callum looked over the strong box sitting on the table. Callum turned to Floyd. "Does this look familiar to you?"

Floyd examined it for only a moment. "Yep. That sure looks like the one that Señor Lopez's Segundo loaded into their coach."

Callum nodded. "I'm sure it's the same one. They must have split up the gold."

"Cal," Josh said as he walked over to the fireplace, "there's two dead bodies behind the barn. Looks like they've been dead for at least a couple of days."

"A pair of them boys," Floyd said, "that caught lead chasing Naomi and Asa."

Josh nodded in agreement and poked at the ashes with a rod that was leaning against the fireplace. "Still a few hot coals. They must have left around daylight. I'm surprised we didn't see fresh tracks as we came up here."

About that time, Jack Swindell stepped into the house. "I can explain it. Looks like eight riders took out five or six hours ago. They cut up and over that north ridge and turned east. I'd say they were headed down the canyon just to the north of this one."

Callum turned to Josh. "So, if they pulled out at daylight and were on their way to attack us, we should have met them in the valley. Since we didn't, odds are, they're leaving the valley."

Floyd pitched in. "They can exit the valley up here on the north side, but it's rough country. There's a gulch that cuts through the Greenhorns that'll put us on the east side of the mountains. If they decided to go that way, we would have never seen them or crossed their tracks, especially if they went out through the next canyon. I can guarantee, they're going east. Too much snow has fallen up high for them to try to cross the Sangre de Cristos."

"Let's get those two buried," Callum said, "and hit Wister's trail. I want this bunch out of business. They've killed too many good people."

"Cal," Josh said, "how far are we going to follow them? I'm with you, whatever you want to do, but the folks are expecting us back this evening."

Callum thought for a moment, then said, "You're right. We'll follow them until we determine they are definitely pulling out. Once we know that, you, me, and Floyd will stay on their trail. The rest of the boys can head back to camp. We've still gotta get hay cut and a bunkhouse built, and we need to keep an eye on the cattle."

Scott Penny had been quiet up to this point. Now he shook his head. "Callum, Josh and I have been through too much together in the past few months. I reckon Fianna would never forgive me if I let something happen to him. The other boys can go back, but I'm going with Josh."

Callum looked at Josh. Josh took his hat off, and thick, black hair fell around his ears. He looked down at the floor and rubbed the saber scar that ran across his forehead. Then he looked over at his brother and grinned. "If it's all right with you, I think Scott has a good point. He's already saved my life a couple of times. He might need to do that again. That'll make it four following Wister, and four men back at the ranch."

Callum laughed and said, "Well, I wouldn't want you to be without your compadre." He turned to Jimmy Leads and Jack Swindell. "If you boys don't mind burying these two stiffs before you head out, I'd appreciate it. We need to get on the trail, pronto."

"We hate to miss the fun, but I reckon we can do that," Jack Swindell said.

"Jack," Josh said, "would you tell Fianna that we'll be back in a few days?"

"Be glad to."

Callum was anxious to get on the trail. "All right. Let's get in the saddle. We're burning daylight."

The four men walked out to their horses and mounted up. Callum looked over at Floyd. "You know this country. Why don't you lead the way."

Floyd pointed down the way they had come. "We'll head back

down into the valley. Those boys are headed east. Instead of following up over that ridge, we'll pick up their trail in the valley."

They swung their horses down the mountain, determined to see the Wister Gang either dead in the dirt or hanging from a cottonwood limb.

Floyd found the tracks of the Wister Gang shortly after crossing Grape Creek. They stuck to the trail until darkness caught them in the gulch in the Greenhorn Mountains. There, they made a cold camp.

The next morning they were in the saddle as soon as they could see the gang's tracks, and by mid-morning they were riding out the eastern side of the mountains.

"How far behind them you reckon we are?" Callum asked Floyd. The men had pulled up at a small creek to let the horses water and to give them a breather. The men stepped down from their saddles.

Floyd placed his hands on his hips and leaned as far back as he could. His back popped in a couple of places. "I could be getting a little old for this." Then he looked out across the open plains. "No more than a couple of hours. From the looks of it, those fellers are headed for Pueblo. With the Lopezes' gold, I'm bettin' they're looking for a big time."

Josh, his eyes glinting like gun metal, said, "I'm looking forward to giving them a *big time*. They've had free rein far too long."

Callum rubbed Shoshone's head, scratching him between the ears. "I'm with you, Josh. Wister and Jessup are responsible for the death of too many good people. I find no pleasure in killing, but I might make an exception where this bunch is concerned."

After the horses had finished drinking, the men swung back into their saddles, and, following Floyd, headed east.

. . .

THEY WERE MAKING good time when they topped a rise. Off in the distance was a creek lined with cottonwood and willow trees. Floyd signaled a halt. "Gimme those spy glasses you got there," he said to Callum.

Callum reached back to his saddlebags, unstrapped the top flap from the left one, and pulled out the binoculars, handing them to Floyd.

Floyd adjusted them, while concentrating on a big cottonwood around seven hundred yards from them. He looked for a moment and handed them back to Callum. "Look in the shadows on the back side of that big tree."

Callum took the glasses, focused them for his eyes, and looked for only a moment. He then looked north, up the creek, and south. "Let's go." He rolled the strap around the binoculars, stuck them back in the saddlebags, and kicked Shoshone in the flanks. The horse leaped forward, taking off at a gallop.

Floyd, Josh, and Scott did likewise. As the men drew closer to the creek, they could see a man hanging in the big cottonwood. At the end of the rope, he was swaying in the afternoon breeze, his boots well off the ground. Drawing near enough for recognition, they saw the man was Asa.

"Damn," Floyd said. He rode straight up to Asa, lifted the old man's body, and slid the rope from around his neck. It had cut into the flesh, and the loop was bloody. "They moved his horse out from under him slowly. They didn't want his neck to break. They wanted him to choke to death. And look around at the tracks. They sat their horses and watched him die."

Josh had dismounted and took Asa's body from Floyd, gently laying it on the ground in the shade of the old cottonwood.

Floyd sat in the saddle, looking down on Asa. "For them to have gotten this far, they had to leave right after we did, and taken that shortcut through the mountains.

"Asa ain't never changed. He was just as stubborn and cranky when he was young. I told him not to leave the ranch. But no, he was dead-set on doing it his way—always was. It just ain't right for a good man who's seen and done what he has, to end his life hanging from a noose."

Callum nodded. "He was mighty happy about finding that gold. I reckon he planned to relax some and enjoy it."

Scott, still in the saddle, rested his hand on his six-gun. "I hate to mention it, but if they caught him, they must have Miss Naomi."

"He's right," Callum said. "We've got to be after them. I hate to think what they'll do to her."

"I figure she's all right for now," Josh said. "From what you told me, Cal, she and Jessup are pretty close. I don't think they'd hurt her and mess up their gravy train with Jessup. We're not far from Pueblo. Why don't we take Asa's body into town, so he can get him a fine burial."

"That's a good idea, Josh," Floyd said. "I know he'd like that. Swing him up here with me. He'll be fine."

The four horsemen mounted and continued to Pueblo. When they neared the little town, the brilliant noonday sun reflected in the buildings' windows, welcoming the body of Asa Collins. The debt kept mounting.

20

They rode four abreast, with Asa draped across Floyd's saddle. Dust exploded from under the horses' hooves, drifting away quickly in the afternoon breeze. The citizens of Pueblo stopped and stared at the rough-hewn riders and the dead man. A man stood on the boardwalk. The four men pulled up.

"Mister, can you tell me where we can bed our friend down?" Floyd asked.

The man pointed in the direction they were riding. "Just down the street on the left. He's got a big sign out front."

"Much obliged," Floyd said.

The riders continued down the street, pulling up in front of the undertaker's office. Floyd stayed in the saddle, while the other three stepped down. Josh moved over and took Asa's body in his big arms, and carried him into the dim office. Light came only from the front windows, and was dispersed by the dust in the air. There was a table, waist-high and roughly eight feet long.

"Just lay him on the table," came a man's high-pitched voice from the back of the building. "I'll be up there in just a second."

Josh laid Asa on the table. The man's arms splayed out on

each side of the table, and Josh, grasping Asa's hands, laid them across his chest.

A little fat man dressed in black, pale and bald-headed, stepped into the front office. "That's good. You put him in the right place." The man walked up to Asa and looked him over, touching his neck. "My, my." He looked up to Floyd. "Rustler, horse thief?"

Callum developed a quick dislike for the man. "Our friend."

The undertaker never missed a beat. "Oh, I'm so very sorry for your loss. How did it happen?"

Floyd looked down on the man. "He was murdered by the Wister Gang. You seen 'em?"

"The Wister Gang, you say? No, no, can't say as I have. Heard of them, though. Bad, bad folks. Now, tell me, what would you like for your poor departed friend? I'm sure he deserves the best."

Floyd responded. "We want him in the ground as soon as possible. How much?"

The little man rubbed his hands together. "Well, let me see, preparation, casket, mourners, preacher, music, and hearse." While looking down at Asa, he cut a side-glance up at Floyd. "I think I can give you a very nice funeral for twenty-five dollars."

"We're the mourners," Floyd said. "Don't need no music either. All he needs is a casket and a way to get him to the graveyard. Just tell us how much and when, so we can be there. I'll say words over him."

A frown crossed the little man's face. "My, my, no mourners, no preacher or music? Not a very good send-off for obviously such a good friend. Are you certain—"

Callum could take it no longer. "Mister, we don't have time to dicker with you. If you don't want the business, we'll take him to the graveyard and bury him ourselves. Now, how much?"

The little man stepped back from the hard tone of Callum's voice. He took a moment and looked at each of the grim-faced men. Making up his mind, he said, "It'll be eight dollars. Will ten in the morning be all right?"

Floyd took out a ten-dollar gold piece and handed it to the man. "We'll be here at ten sharp."

Callum spun around and, with the others following him, marched out of the undertaker's office. Once outside, he stopped on the boardwalk, while the others gathered around him. "That place ain't pleasant."

Josh nodded in agreement. "Where to now?"

"Any idea where we might find Wister and his bunch? We've got to get Naomi away from them," Callum said.

"Why don't we check the saloon across the street?" Floyd pointed at it. "If they're not in there, we can check around, but we best be careful. We don't want them surprising us."

The four men slipped the leather thongs that held their six-guns in their holsters. Josh stopped at Chancy and pulled his 1866 Winchester out of the scabbard. The wind had picked up, pushing dust and tumbleweeds down Pueblo's main street. The saloon sign, hanging from the building's false front, swung and creaked in the wind as the four men crossed the street.

Floyd entered the saloon first. Without looking at the clientele, he walked to the far end of the bar. Josh and Scott spread out along the bar. Josh laid his Winchester across the polished bar. Callum, since he was known to the gang, came in last. The front legs of a chair, in the back of the saloon, hit the floor hard.

"Can I help you fellers?" the bartender asked.

"A beer for those two," Callum said, indicating Floyd and Scott. "We'll have a couple of sarsaparillas and some information."

All four of them were examining the other men in the bar through the big mahogany-framed mirror that ran the full length of the bar. As the last to come in, Callum's eyes were the last to adjust to the darker interior. After they adjusted, he slowly looked at each man in the saloon. The table in the back of the room was occupied with two men. He recognized them both. One had been a rider with Wister when he and James were attacked. The other was Ben Milam. That table was where the chair had hit the floor. The man with Milam was trying to look disinterested, but the trapped look on his face was obvious. Milam sat, relaxed, drinking his whiskey with a faint smile on his face.

Callum finished examining the inside of the saloon and swung his eyes back to Milam. The bartender brought them their drinks. Keeping his eyes on Milam, he asked the bartender, "You seen the Wister Gang in town?"

The bartender's eyes cut to Milam's table and then back to Callum. "Don't reckon I know who you might be speaking about, Mister."

"In that case, Mr. Bartender, I'd be much obliged if you'd step out from behind that bar and have a seat at one of these tables while I deal with Mr. Milam."

"Now see here, Mister, this is my establishment, and I aim to stay right here."

Josh grasped the pistol grip of the Winchester, eared the hammer back, and moved the Winchester's muzzle to where it covered the bartender. The harsh rachet of the hammer, going to full cock, reverberated through the saloon. "My brother asked you nicely to step out front. This would be a good time to do it."

The bartender hurried around the bar and sat at the nearest table. Josh followed him with the rifle, now standing with his back to the bar. Floyd had been drinking his beer, along with Scott. The two of them turned around, standing clear of the bar.

Callum turned with them, his back now to the bar, facing Milam, who still sat at his table. "Milam, the last time I saw you, I was laying on my back with blood pumping out of my chest."

"If Wister hadn't stopped me, you wouldn't be standing here today. I wish I'd put a bullet right between your eyes."

"That's where you made a mistake, and now you'll pay for it. But first, I want to know where Wister is."

"Not very fair, the four of you against one," Milam said.

"It looks like it's four to two, but let me clear that up. Boys, Milam and I have a score to settle. I'd be much obliged if you'd stay out of it. If that other feller decides to deal himself in, then he's all yours."

At that statement from Callum, the other man slowly placed both hands flat on the table. Milam looked over at the man. "Well, thanks, Sneed. I'll remember that."

Sneed just looked at Milam, never uttered a word, but kept his hands flat on the table. When Milam slid his chair back, the three men at the table between Callum and Milam jumped to their feet, chairs falling to the floor, and dashed out of the line of fire. Milam stood and faced Callum, thirty feet away.

"Wister thinks you're dead," Milam said. "After we had two disappear, three killed, and two wounded, I suspected you might still be alive. Didn't count on you having all this help."

Callum watched Milam. The man stood, his right hand hovering over his six-gun. Time had slowed for Callum. He took in Milam's shined black boots and black pants. The revolver, tied down and low, rested on the man's right hip. He wore a black vest, lined in red, over a white shirt. Red garters stretched over his biceps, pulling his sleeves tight. A black, low-crowned hat, set level on his head.

"I asked you, where's Wister?" Callum could see the man's face tense. *He'll be going for his gun any moment*, he thought. Milam's hand started for his six-gun. Without any conscious thought, Callum's Remington leaped to his hand, the barrel coming level while Milam's was just clearing the holster. Callum could see the realization in Milam's eyes that, this time, he was too slow. Smoke and flame leaped from his Remington.

Milam took the lead in his chest. The man's revolver was starting to level when the second bullet hit him just above his vest pocket. He took a step back, surprise registering, but determination also. His hand kept coming up, and his finger squeezed the trigger. The bullet cut through the loose portion of Callum's coat.

Milam grasped the edge of the table with his left hand and pulled the hammer back on his Colt. Callum's third bullet hit Milam a high, lethal blow, striking just below his chin and exiting through his spine. The killer collapsed like a little girl's rag doll.

Sneed never moved. He remained seated with his hands on the table throughout the bedlam. He knew that if he even twitched, there were at least two guns that would find him and end his career.

Smoke filled the saloon. Callum walked over and stood above Milam, looking down at the dead man. Floyd, Scott, and Josh kept the other men in the bar covered. Callum calmly removed the cylinder from his six-gun, pulled a fully loaded one from his belt, locked it in the revolver, and dropped the Remington back into its holster. He turned his hard blue eyes to Sneed. "You feel like answering some questions?"

"What do you want to know?" Sneed answered. He owed no allegiance to Elwood Wister. Yes, he had ridden with him, but Wister was a loose cannon, capable of killing any member of his gang at any moment.

"Where's Wister?" Callum asked.

"Last I knowed, he's over at the hog ranch. They rent out some rooms, among other things, and that's where we usually stay when we come into town."

"Where's it located?"

"It's east of town on the river. Everyone was there when Milam and I came into town a couple of hours ago."

"How many?"

"There's six left, if they're still there."

"Where's Naomi?"

"You mean Jessup's woman?" Sneed went on without giving Callum time to answer. "They've got her gagged and tied up in the store room. She's been saying she's gonna see us all dead, after . . ."

"After what?" Callum said.

"You gotta understand, Mister. I ain't had nothin' to do with that hangin'. It was all Wister. He's almighty mean."

"Tell me about the hanging."

"Well, we come up on Mr. Jessup's woman and this old man. The old man was plumb tuckered out, lying on the ground next to their fire. Looked like he'd been shot before, but he still almost managed to get his six-shooter out from under his coat in time. Wister kicked it away, and then whomped on the old man something fierce. This Naomi lady tried to get to the old man's gun, but Wister hit her. Hit her with his fist, he did. Then he hung the old man, gentle like, so his neck wouldn't break, and let him just dangle there choking to death. It weren't pretty."

Callum continued to interrogate Sneed until he felt he had all the information he could get out of the man. He didn't think he was lying about Naomi and where she was located. The man was too scared that he would end up like Milam. Callum turned to one of the saloon's customers. "How about getting the marshal?"

The man shook his head. "The marshal was killed a few days ago by a bounty hunter. I mean, they shot it out right there in the jail."

"Where's your jail?"

"Just up the street, Mister. You can't miss it."

"Get on your feet," Callum said to Sneed, "and shuck that hogleg."

The man laid his holstered gun on the table, and Callum picked it up. He knelt down and took the gun and gunbelt from Milam's corpse. He stood and turned to Josh. "Let's take this one to jail, then we'll call on Mr. Wister."

"Mister," the man who had told Callum about the marshal and the jail said, "the jail's locked."

"Who's got the key?"

The man thought for a moment. “I’m thinking the head of our town council probably has it. His name is John Thatcher. He owns the general store, just down the street.”

“Much obliged,” Callum said. “We’ve met.

“Boys, let’s take a trip to the general store first. I imagine Mr. Thatcher won’t mind us using his jail for a while.”

They started out the door with Sneed in the lead. The bartender stood and said, “What about this body?”

Floyd tossed back over his shoulder, as he was the last one leaving the saloon, “He’s your friend. You take care of him.”

The men walked up the street to the general store. Callum pushed Sneed through the door and followed him in. Floyd, with Josh and Scott, came in behind. Thatcher looked up from the counter at Sneed and then at the men behind them. A younger man with an apron on and a broom in his hand stepped into the store from the back.

Callum looked at him for a moment. “Well, Jake, I see you didn’t take my advice.”

“Mr. Logan, I actually did. As soon as we got our horses from the army, I left that bunch. I know I did wrong by being with them and not doing anything to stop Bloody Tom. But that ain’t ever happening again. Mr. Thatcher was good enough to give me a job. I told him everything. I aim to stay in this country.”

Callum looked Jake over. “Good for you, boy. Looks like you’re taking the right trail. Good luck to you.

“Mr. Thatcher,” Callum continued, “we need the key to your jail. This feller is one of the Wister Gang. He’ll only be in there for a while.”

“What was the shooting?” Thatcher asked.

Josh spoke up. “A fella by the name of Ben Milam thought he could beat my brother to the draw. Didn’t quite make it.”

“I recognize you, Mr. Logan,” Thatcher said to Callum. “And you also,” he said to Floyd. “I don’t believe I’ve had the pleasure of meeting you gentlemen.”

Floyd said, "This big galoot is the other nephew I mentioned to you when we were here last, Josh Logan, and his friend here is Scott Penny. They brought our cattle up from Texas."

Josh and Scott nodded to the man.

Thatcher looked at Josh for a moment. "You ever been to Fort Griffin?"

"I have."

Thatcher nodded. "A gunslinger was through here a while back headed for Montana. He had a funny name, Gizzard? No, it was more like Grizzard. That was it Grizzard Bankes. He said you were cleaning out some rustlers around Fort Griffin."

Scott spoke up. "He wasn't just cleaning, he cleaned. The place is a lot safer around there now."

"I had a lot of help, including Scott. A man doesn't do something like that by himself," Josh said.

"True," Thatcher said. He turned back to Callum. "You say you need the jail?"

"Yes, sir, we do. This man is a member of the murdering Wister Gang. He needs to sit in jail while we take care of the rest of that bunch. They've done a lot of awfully bad things, and we're about to end their success. But we need to stash him for a while."

"Just a moment." Thatcher had moved out in front of the counter, but now he walked back and reached under the counter shelf, pulling out several keys on a ring. "These are the keys to the jail. You can lock him up. I'd be obliged if you'd bring the keys back when you're finished."

"Be glad to," Callum said.

"If you don't mind my asking, what are you planning?"

Callum was impatient to get out of the store, get Sneed locked up, and rescue Naomi. "Mr. Thatcher, the remainder of the Wister Gang is down at the hog ranch. They've got a young woman by the name of Naomi Gwendiver."

"Why, I know her. She's the lady that Jessup is seeing. I believe she's from Denver City."

"That's right. She's in danger, and we need to get down there and get her away from that gang."

"If you can clean out the hog ranch, while you're at it, the town will owe you. That's a filthy place that Pueblo needs to be rid of."

"Not what we're concerned about right now," Callum said. He grabbed Sneed by the arm and shoved him through the door, followed by the others.

They locked the man in a jail cell, stepped outside of the marshal's office, and locked the door.

Callum looked at his uncle and brother and Scott. "Let's get it done."

The men checked their weapons again. Then the four of them walked to their horses, swung up into their saddles, and headed for the river.

21

The four men rode northeast, out of Pueblo toward the Arkansas. The sun was warm on their backs as it settled toward the mountains, turning the white, puffy clouds to gold medallions. In sight of the ranch, they spotted three women out front. It was plain that the women had seen them.

"Let's just act like customers," Callum said, "until we can get them clear. Floyd, you do the talking. Those boys can't see us from inside, but they might recognize my voice."

The women were sitting outside of the building on a long bench. Barefooted, they were dressed in dirty nightgowns. One of them had a nightcap on her head that looked like it hadn't seen water since it was purchased.

"Howdy, boys," the fat one said. "I bet you fellers are starved for some good fun. You jist git yoreself down off those horses and come on inside with us. You can have a drink, and we'll show you a good time."

The other two primped, pushing their hair back, in an attempt to look appealing. The one with the nightcap took it off and ran her fingers through her long, matted hair, in a caricature of seductiveness.

The men dismounted, tied their horses at the hitching rail, and checked their weapons. When they pulled their handguns, the fat woman said, "We ain't lookin' for no trouble, Mister. You won't need those guns."

"Is Wister inside?" Callum asked quietly, then motioned Josh and Floyd toward the front door.

"Elwood's inside. He's with Martha. He always liked her."

"Laugh," Callum said to the three women.

Their eyes were wide with fear. The fat woman threw back her head and roared with laughter, while the other two joined in half-heartedly.

"Good. Now, I want you to continue laughing and open the door. Then step aside. I'd recommend you put some distance between you and this ranch because I guarantee there's gonna be some shootin'."

Callum and Scott moved around the sod house to the back door. Just as Callum turned to say something to Scott, the door opened and a bleary-eyed, scruffy-looking redhead stood in the door, his eyes going to the Remington in Callum's hand. The redhead went for his gun. He was fast. He thrust it into Callum's stomach, and pulled the trigger. With Callum turning toward Scott just before the door opened, the muzzle of his Remington had drifted out of alignment with the door. Time seemed to stand still for Callum. He felt the pressure of the muzzle against his belly. In his peripheral vision, he could see the hammer falling. It seemed to fall so slowly. Then the hammer disappeared into the revolver, and the next moment, it made contact with the cap on the revolver cylinder.

Nothing happened. The revolver misfired. The man didn't have a chance to pull the trigger the second time. Callum's heavy Remington slammed into his temple, dropping him like a sack of rocks. Callum and Scott stepped quickly into the house, as shots rang out from the front. The shots were fired so quickly, they sounded like a continuous roar.

Callum moved out of the hall into the first room, Scott moving on to the next one. Facing Callum was a tall, lanky man with his red long johns down to his waist. He was pulling his six-gun from the holster hanging on the iron headboard. "Drop it!" Callum yelled.

The man continued to swing the muzzle around toward Callum. Callum's bullet tore out the man's elbow. He screamed, dropped the six-gun, and fell across the screaming woman in the bed. Blood poured from his mangled arm, covering the woman from the waist down. Continuing to scream, she pushed the man away from her, leaped out of the bed, and dashed out the back door. Callum picked up the loose revolver and moved back into the hallway.

Several gunshots came from across the hall, followed by a bloody bandit staggering into the hallway. He held the doorframe a moment before he collapsed to the floor. Scott followed him out of the room. He led the way into the large sitting room. Two men lay on the floor. Callum took only a moment to examine them. They were both dead. Josh held Wister at gunpoint on the settee, but the one who caught Callum's eye was the person Floyd was leading from the storeroom. It was Naomi. Her left cheek was black and purple.

"Are you all right?" Callum asked her.

She nodded, but at that moment saw Wister. She charged him and slapped him with all of her strength. "You animal, you killer. How could you hang an old man like you did?" She looked around as if she were looking for a weapon. She saw one of the dead men's guns lying on the floor and reached to pick it up.

Floyd grabbed her. "Now, ma'am, it's over. He'll be taken care of."

Wister laughed. "She's a mite upset, ain't she? If I'd had a little more time I woulda calmed her down." Then he looked at Callum, and hate leaped from his eyes. "Milam said you were still alive, but I didn't believe him. No man could've lived the way you were hit. I shoulda let him go ahead and plug you between the eyes."

"He won't be pluggin' anybody again," Callum said. "And, Wister, your pluggin' days are over too."

The fat woman stuck her head in the door.

"Come on in," Josh said. "You ladies best get your stuff. We'll be burning this place down as soon as we're finished. Don't be taking anything that isn't yours, or we'll come after you."

He turned to Callum. "Is that all right with you? I thought we might do the town a favor."

"Good idea. What happened in here?"

"Well," Josh said, "those two boys on the floor were sitting talking with Wister. I told them to sit still, and they decided they'd rather test me. Mighty bad thinking when a man's already got a gun on you."

"I didn't get a chance to fire a shot," Floyd said. "I've never seen a man shoot as fast as Josh. When those boys made their play, they didn't have a chance."

Callum gave a quick nod. "Pa always said Josh was the fastest of the boys." He turned back to Wister. "You killed all of the Lopez family?"

Wister grinned. "One of the best ambushes I've ever set up. They never knew we were there. Jessup wanted no witnesses left. He wanted us to kill everyone, including you, but you'd left before we hit the caravan."

"You shot the women and boy?"

"That's what Jessup wanted. But there weren't no boy. Just the vaqueros, the old man and old lady, and the girl. I sure hated to do the girl. She was right pretty." Then Wister grinned again.

Callum had a hard time holding himself back. He had killed men before, but those were in moments of hot blood and in fair fights. He didn't like this side of himself. He knew it would be so easy to blow the grin off Wister's face. He saw Wister watching him, grinning, knowing what he wanted to do.

He turned to Josh. "Would you check the barn? Make sure all the animals are there, and check for Naomi's gold. I doubt they've had time to do anything with it. Floyd, there's a man with a headache at the back door, and one with a broken elbow in one of the back bedrooms. Would you mind bringing them around front?"

Josh and Floyd left, leaving him and Scott with Naomi and Wister. He turned back to Wister. "You didn't see a boy?"

"Weren't no boy, I tell you. I checked all the bodies."

"What did you do with their gold?"

"Just before we came to town, I split it with the boys. Reckon it's scattered around here."

"One last question. Where's Jessup?"

Wister scratched his full, dirty beard. "Last I saw him, he was headed for his bank. He were none too happy. He'd set his cap for this here gal." He motioned to Naomi. "But he figgered she was done with him now."

Naomi was sitting in a chair, pale from hearing the ordeal, her hands folded in her lap. She looked up at Callum. "You and Floyd tried to tell me. But I just couldn't believe that Richard could be that kind of man. When he came in to meet with this animal, I was completely appalled. He was always such a gentleman. He could have been governor!"

"When we have feelings for someone," Callum said, "we can become blinded. You can't blame yourself. You just have to put this behind you and move on."

Josh stepped back into the house and spoke to Naomi. "The packs haven't even been opened. I loaded them back on the mules. We'll be able to take them to whatever bank you like."

"Thank you," she said. Her voice was small.

Callum could hear Floyd bringing the two men to the front of the house. One was moaning, the other cussing a blue streak. "Uncle, could you persuade that feller to shut his mouth?"

"Reckon I can do that, Nephew," Floyd called. They could

hear him outside. "Did I ever show you my pig sticker? This is one of the best danged knives made. Got it back in Tennessee. It holds an edge forever. Notice how sharp it is? If I let it slip just a little farther, you might not be able to say another word. So you think you could close that filthy mouth?"

The only thing that could be heard from outside was the moaning of the man with the shattered elbow.

THEY HAD SEARCHED the ranch and the bodies. The Lopez gold had been gathered. Hopefully most of it was there. Josh had ridden back to Pueblo, and at Callum's request, stopped by the general store and told Jake to join him. Then he got Sneed, put him on a horse, and brought him down to the river near the ranch. Callum had wanted to send Naomi back into town, but she insisted on staying. The women from the ranch had loaded up a wagon and were headed for Colorado City.

The four outlaws, now on horseback, were lined up under an old cottonwood tree, a rope from each one thrown over the big limb and tied off at the trunk. The tree had been standing along the Arkansas for over a hundred years. It had almost been trampled by buffalo, as a sapling. But it continued to grow. Young Indian couples had sat under its shade and gazed across the buffalo-covered Colorado plains. It had stood tall and strong when the first white man came to this country. When it grew bigger and its limbs became strong, it had been used for the dark duty that it would again provide today.

Callum sat on Shoshone, watching, Jake at his side. Then he nodded to Josh.

"You boys have anything to say?" Josh asked.

Sneed said, "I'm from south Texas, down Refugio way. Grew up on a farm there. Swore I'd never amount to nothing as a dirt farmer. Reckon I'd sure like to be farming there right now. That's it."

"Anybody else?"

The other three men were silent.

Callum nodded at Josh. Josh swung his reins against the rumps of the three horses, and they leaped out from under their riders. The audible snap of three necks breaking carried out across the plains.

Wister watched his men swinging, then he turned his malevolent gaze to Callum. "You can go straight to hell."

"Reckon I probably will, but you'll be roasting a long time afore I get there, " Callum said and nodded to Josh.

Josh slapped the rump of Wister's horse with his reins, causing it to leap forward, leaving Wister hanging. The man was strong. His shoulders and neck were heavily muscled. For that reason, his neck didn't break, and like Asa, he slowly died of strangulation, his feet dancing above the Colorado prairie.

Josh rode over next to Callum. "You had it to do."

Callum nodded and patted his coat pocket, where the signed confession from Wister, implicating Jessup, safely rested. Then he turned to Jake. "You made the right decision when you left that bunch. You could just as easily be hanging with them."

Jake swallowed audibly. "Yes, sir. Thank you. The owlhoot trail ain't for me."

Callum looked over to Josh. "You're gonna be needin' some cowhands, aren't you?"

"Yep, several."

"Well, I can recommend this young feller."

"That's good enough for me. You looking for a cow nurse job, Jake? Thirty a month, and work from can to cain't."

"Mr. Logan, I'd be right pleasured."

"Good. Let's get these boys buried, and find Jessup."

Callum sat a moment longer. "All except Wister. Leave him hangin'." He produced a board with two holes punched through it and a rope tied on one end. He rode next to Wister, leaned over, and put one end of the rope around the dead man's neck and tied the loose end to the other end of the board. The board lay across Wister's chest. Only four words were written on it. *Murderer and Woman Killer.*

THE RIDE back to Pueblo was short. They rode straight to the bank. Callum led the group in, followed by Naomi. The teller, Tom Jenkins, was sitting at a small desk behind the barred bank counter. He turned at their entrance. When he saw Naomi, his gaze went to the bruises on her face. His mouth fell open.

"My goodness, Mrs. Gwendiver. What happened to you? Are you all right?"

She smiled at the man. "I'm just fine, Tom. Is Mr. Jessup in?"

Tom couldn't take his eyes off her bruised face. "No, ma'am. He sure isn't. He left in a big hurry." The man frowned and looked at Callum. "In fact, it was right after the gunshots at the saloon."

"Tom," Naomi said, "I left some bags of gold in the bank, a few weeks back—"

"Yes, ma'am. I remember."

"Yes, thank you. I would like to pick them up."

Tom turned back to his desk and removed a key. "It'll be a moment." He walked over to Jessup's office and opened the door. When he stepped inside, he stopped. "That's odd. Mr. Jessup left the safe open. He is usually very adamant about keeping the safe locked. He must have been in a hurry."

He disappeared inside Jessup's office. "Oh, no! All of the cash is gone." He stepped back to the door and addressed Naomi. "Mrs. Gwendiver, do you suppose Mr. Jessup could have taken it with him?"

"Yes, Tom. I think he did. Now, could you bring out those three bags, please?"

The cashier disappeared into the office. A few moments later, he returned with the three bags and brought them around the counter. "I'm afraid I must close the bank until Mr. Jessup returns. I only have the funds in my cash drawer. I don't know what's going to happen."

Callum spoke up. "Your Mr. Jessup is now a fugitive. I'd start looking for another job, were I you."

The man looked at Callum and then to Naomi. She smiled sadly. "I'm sorry, Tom. Unless someone buys it, this bank will close. Callum's right. You should start looking for another job. With your experience, you should have no trouble."

With Callum and Josh carrying the bags of gold, the group left the bank. They could still see smoke rising from the burning hog ranch northeast of town. A few folks stood in the street, talking and watching the smoke.

"What now?" Floyd asked.

"Jessup has a big head start on us, and it'll be getting dark soon. I'm thinkin' he's headed to his banks, to get as much out of them as he can. He couldn't carry the gold because it's too heavy, but he'll raid the cash. If I take a couple of fresh horses, I might catch him before he reaches Colorado City. If not, I'll catch him there."

Naomi spoke up. "I'm going with you."

"No, ma'am, you ain't."

Naomi's back stiffened, and she started to say something.

Callum spoke up again before she could speak. "I don't have time to argue."

She frowned, but kept silent.

"Floyd," Callum continued, "you bring her along in the morning, after Asa's funeral. I hate to miss it, but this has to be done. You can rest up the horses tonight and get a fresh start in the morning. Bring Shoshone with you. Josh, you need to get back to your wife, and Scott and his boys need to get headed back to Texas before the weather catches 'em. Scott, thanks for the help."

Josh shook his head. "I hate to leave you to do this by yourself, when we have plenty of men."

"No," Callum said. "This is the best way. If I catch him in Colorado City, I'll wait for Floyd and Naomi there." He turned to Naomi. "Are you planning on spending the winter in Denver City?"

"Yes. I can put the gold in another bank there. That'll give me the winter to decide what I want to do in the spring."

"I've got to get movin'." Callum shook hands all around.

When he came to Naomi, she grasped his hand in both of hers. "You've done so much for me. Please be careful."

He looked into her soft brown eyes, and saw her concern for him. It'd been a long time since a woman had looked at him like that. He held the handshake for a moment, then released her hands and said, "I'll see you in a day or two." It came out short and gruff, not the way he meant it. He could see the hurt in her eyes, before she turned away and headed for the hotel.

22

Jessup rode, cursing, into Colorado City just before daylight. Nothing had gone right. He had been in the bank in Pueblo City when the gunshots rang out from the saloon. At first, he thought that Wister's men had gotten into a gunfight, but a few minutes later he saw Callum Logan with a bunch of other men, and Sneed in tow.

He was shocked to see Logan still alive. Wister had assured him the man was dead. He watched the men go into Thatcher's store, then, a few minutes later, they came out of the store and headed for the marshal's office. He continued to watch through the bank's front window. Shortly, they came out of the bank, mounted up, and headed toward the hog ranch.

"Mr. Jessup, what do you suppose is going on?"

Jessup jumped at the voice and turned on Jenkins. He had totally forgotten anyone else was in the bank. "How should I know?" he snapped. "I'll be in my office. I'm not to be disturbed."

Tom Jenkins, used to Jessup's overbearing manner, shrugged and went back to work.

Jessup closed his door, took out his handkerchief, and wiped his face. This was bad, real bad. He knew that Wister or one of his men would spill the beans. It wouldn't be long before the horsemen would be pulling up in front of his bank. His mind raced. I've got to get out of here. He opened his office door and yelled at Jenkins, "Bring me my saddlebags."

The saddlebags were hanging on a peg next to Jenkins's desk. Mr. Jessup used them to transport money and important documents between the banks. He grabbed them off the peg and hurried over to Jessup's office. Without another word, Jessup jerked them from Jenkin's hand and closed his office door.

He had to get out of here, fast. He had opened the safe earlier, and now he swung the heavy door wide. Naomi's three bags of gold caught his eyes first. He hated to leave them, but they were too heavy. They would just slow him down. On the shelf above the gold, sat the cash and change. He would take only the cash.

His fingers closed around the bills, and he thrust them into his bag. Once the safe was empty of cash, he slammed the safe door. It banged hard and then slowly swung open. He looked around the office. This had been such a good deal. *I wish Logan was dead*, he thought. *He's cost me this whole operation*. He spun around and yanked the door open, striding out of his office. Without a word to Jenkins, he moved to the front door, jerked it open, and stepped out into the cool Colorado afternoon.

He tied the saddlebags on behind his saddle, and swung up onto his horse. As his right leg was going over the saddle, he heard multiple gunshots from the direction of the hog ranch. His right leg froze momentarily, and then continued over the saddle. He had no plans, other than getting the money from the banks in Colorado City and Denver City. He turned the big buckskin toward Colorado City and walked it out of town. Once clear of town, he kicked the horse in the flanks. The animal responded by breaking into a gallop, and Pueblo slowly disappeared behind him.

Jessup had ridden no more than ten miles. The sun had disappeared behind the tall mountains, and nighttime was falling across the land. Suddenly, the buckskin stumbled on some loose rocks and almost went down. Jessup reared back on the reins and kept the horse's head up, averting a fall, but immediately, the animal began to limp.

Jessup stopped the horse, stepped down, and checked the animal's left front leg. It was already beginning to swell. Compassion for his horse was not in Jessup. Concern for his own well-being permeated every cell of his body. He checked the buckskin's left front leg again. In that short time, the swelling had increased. He could save the horse by walking, but he didn't have time if he was going to save his own hide. He swung back into the saddle and urged the injured animal forward. The best he could get was a shuffling fast walk. He kept looking over his shoulder, riding on into the night.

As Jessup rode into Colorado City, the buckskin was hardly able to put his front left hoof on the ground. Every time it touched the ground, it left a bloody track. Jessup pulled the ruined animal up in front of his bank. The buckskin stood gazing at the water trough just a few feet from where Jessup tied him up.

After stepping from the saddle, Jessup pulled out his keys, dropped them, cursed, and picked them back up, finally finding the correct key in the dim light. He'd have to get another horse, he thought. I just hope that worthless stable owner is up.

He quickly walked through the bank to his office door, opened it, and marched in. He was tired. But he knew that if he stopped, Logan would catch him. In his haste, he bent the safe key. He looked at the key as if it were his worst enemy. He placed it on the floor, put his boot heel on it, and then, with one huge arm against the wall, he leveraged all of his weight on the key. Picking it up, he examined it, inserted it into the lock, and turned the key. The safe unlocked.

Jessup emptied the cash from the safe into his saddlebags. He relocked the safe and walked to the door. He opened the door only a little and looked up and down the street. The town was starting to come to life. Maggie's Kitchen was open for breakfast, and several horses were already tied in front. He could see no rider coming from the direction of Pueblo. He thought about riding to the stable, but after looking at the buckskin, he knew that wouldn't work. After grabbing the reins, he led the injured horse to the stable.

"Anybody here?" Jessup yelled as he hammered on the big, closed, swinging doors of the stable. He was about to yell again when one side swung slowly open.

"Not necessary to yell," the owner said. He stood in the door, his galluses pulled up over his red long johns, scratching at his graying beard. "How can I help you, Mr. Jessup?"

"I need another horse."

The man looked at the buckskin's leg. "Danged if you don't." He took the reins from Jessup and ran his hand down the horse's injured leg. "What'd you do to this animal?"

Jessup looked down the street impatiently. "He stumbled and hurt his leg."

"And you went ahead and rode him hard after that happened?"

"I had to. I'm running late for a meeting in Denver City. Now, get me a horse."

The man spat, wiped his mouth on his sleeve, and said, "Reckon not. You already ruined one horse. He's gonna have to be put down."

Jessup's face flushed, and his eyes drew tight. "You'll get me a horse, and now."

"You think I'm gonna rent you one of my horses so you can stove it up like this buckskin? No, sir. You ain't gettin' no horse here today."

Jessup looked first one way, then the other. The street was clear. He dropped the saddlebags, and, using his body as leverage, he swung his huge right fist into the man's temple. The man dropped like he'd been poleaxed. Jessup dragged him inside the stable and tossed him into a stall. He kicked hay over the man and turned to look at the horses. He spotted a big bay gelding and quickly transferred his saddle and gear to the horse. He had been so focused on what he was doing, he didn't hear a horse walk up to the barn door. He turned the bay toward the open door, swung into the saddle, and walked him outside.

"Going somewhere?" Callum asked, his right hand hanging down by the .44 Remington on his hip.

CALLUM HAD FOLLOWED the tracks of the injured horse to the bank. Blood had pooled under the buckskin's hoof, and then the bloody track continued to the stable. Just as he started toward the stable, he saw the buckskin limp out to the water trough. He bumped his horse in the flanks and walked him to the stable. About to step down, he heard a horse coming out. He slipped the leather thong from his Remington and waited.

He watched the stunned look on Jessup's face change to anger.

"Get out of my way. I'm a law-abiding citizen."

"Jessup, the only law you abide is the law of Jessup. Now fork that bay on over to the marshal's office. If that's too hard for you, then you're welcome to join Wister and his bunch. We left him hanging on a big cottonwood tree, and there's a nice, strong beam just above your head."

"You wouldn't dare. The people here would stop you. I'm their banker and their friend."

Callum tilted his hat to the back of his head. "You may be their banker, but I'm willing to bet you ain't their friend. I just imagine, that after I let them read the signed confession from Wister, the fine folks of this here town will want to help string you up."

There was a chill in the air, but Callum could see the beads of sweat dotting Jessup's forehead.

The town of Colorado City was wide awake. Callum and Jessup were starting to attract attention. Callum saw the marshal step out of his office, hitch his six-gun to a more comfortable position, and stroll toward them.

The marshal, looking first at Callum and then at Jessup, said, "Mr. Jessup, what's this all about?"

"I'll tell you what's goin' on," came a yell from inside the stable. Moments later, holding his head with his left hand, the stable owner staggered into the street, stopping in front of the marshal. He pointed to Jessup. "That there banker is a horse thief. He come in here on that fine-lookin' buckskin he'd rode to death and stole the finest horse in this here stable. He done topped it off by slugging me."

"Marshal, I can explain," Jessup said.

"Well, Mr. Jessup, you're sitting on a stolen horse. I'd say you've got a lot to explain."

Callum had been watching the exchange. "I think I can clear this up, Marshal."

The marshal looked up at Callum. "And who are you?"

"Name's Callum Jeremiah Logan."

"You any kin to Floyd Logan?"

"He's my uncle."

The marshal nodded and, with his left hand, pulled lightly on his well-trimmed goatee. He looked around at the gathering crowd. "Why don't we move this into my office? Mr. Jessup, you climb down off that bay and walk with me."

Callum watched Jessup climb down and look at his saddlebags.

"Marshal," Callum said, "you might want to bring those saddlebags with you." He watched the distressed look on Jessup's face as the marshal stepped over, untied the bags, and flung them over his left shoulder.

Callum stepped down from his horse and handed the reins of both of his horses to the stableman. "Mister, you mind taking care of these for me? They'll need water and a good rubdown. They've been rode hard."

The man took the reins. "Glad to do it."

Callum joined the marshal and Jessup. The crowd parted, as the three men headed for the marshal's office.

"Marshal," Jessup began, "I can explain. This man has been chasing me. I believe he intends to kill me."

Callum looked around the room. A gun rack sat behind the marshal's desk, with two Spencers and two Henrys ready for business. The jail was small, about the size of the one in Pueblo. The marshal's desk faced two chairs with a bench under the front window. After the marshal sat behind his desk, Callum took a seat on the bench.

"Is that true, Logan?"

"Partly. I intended on catching him. If he'd put up a fight, I woulda killed him. You might want to read this, and then take a look inside his saddlebags."

"That's money inside the saddlebags, Marshal," Jessup said. "I was moving money back to the Denver City bank. You know I do that on occasion."

Callum handed Wister's signed confession to the marshal. The man read it, handed it back to Callum, and opened the saddlebags. They were bulging with money. The marshal looked up from the money. "Jessup, I need your gun."

The big man stood to take off his gunbelt. He unfastened it, rolled the belt around the holster, and handed it to the marshal, muzzle first. The marshal saw, too late, what Jessup was doing. His chair slammed against the wall as he leaped to his feet. The roar of the six-gun filled the office, and the marshal stumbled back against the wall. Jessup spun, yanking the gun from the holster, and looking for Callum. But he wasn't on the bench.

Callum saw the move with the holster that Jessup made. He

stood, stepped to his left, and drew his Remington. When Jessup turned, the bench was empty, but Callum's hand was full. His first shot hit Jessup in the right side of his chest, driving him back against the desk. Jessup's eyes were wide with surprise. He turned farther to his right to bring his gun to bear, and Callum shot him again. This time he didn't stop. There was a continuous roar as Callum pumped round after round into Jessup's dying body. Five bullet holes appeared across the big man's chest. He slumped to the floor, his back against the desk.

Blood ran from Jessup's mouth, back, and chest. He gasped and said, "You were supposed to be dead."

Callum looked down on the dying man. He had replaced the empty revolver with the loaded one from his left holster, and had it trained on Jessup. "I'm not, but you are."

Jessup's eyes lost their focus, and he slowly slid over, sprawling across the floor. Callum watched him for a few moments to make sure he was dead. He holstered his Remington and moved behind the desk to check the marshal. The man was lucky. Jessup's bullet had taken him high in the left shoulder. "You're lucky, Marshal. Looks like you ought to make it."

The door burst open. The first man through was the marshal's deputy. He was waving his revolver around the room, not sure where to point it. Then, it settled on Callum.

"Get the doctor," Callum said to the deputy. "The marshal's been shot."

The doctor pushed through behind the deputy. "I heard the shooting. Move out of my way," he said to Callum as he rushed to check on the marshal. He glanced at Jessup, as he passed, and pronounced, "He's dead." He looked the marshal over and turned to the deputy. "Get some men in here to get this man to my office. And be careful, he's got a busted shoulder."

The doctor moved out of the way to let the men get to the marshal. He took a moment to look at Jessup, then turned to Callum. "You do that?"

"I did."

"Looks like you wanted him dead."

"Doc, that man deserved to be dead, long before this. Because of his scheming there's a lot of good folks in the ground."

The doctor nodded. "Never liked the man." He followed the men carrying the marshal out of the office.

Callum picked up Wister's confession and handed it to the deputy. "Read this, Deputy."

The deputy read the confession and looked over at Jessup's body. "Reckon you saved the town some money, Mister."

"Am I free to go?" Callum asked.

"Yes, sir. No need for you to be here."

Callum started out the door, then stopped. "You have a hotel in town?"

"We do. Just down the street like you're headed for Denver City. You can't miss it."

"Thanks, Deputy. I've got some folks following me. A young woman and older man. When they come through, would you tell them I'm at the hotel?"

The deputy nodded. Callum stepped out into the cold wind coming out of the high mountains, untied his horses, and headed for the hotel. *I might just sleep for a week.*

23

Callum stepped outside of the bunkhouse. The warm spring sunshine felt good. He looked over the working ranch. They had managed to get the bunkhouse built before the heavy winter snows moved in. It was a good thing too. They needed to enlarge the ranch house before the family arrived from Tennessee. He, Jake, Pat, Floyd, Jimmy Leads, and Jeb had been sleeping in the bunkhouse. Josh and Fianna, and Sarah and Jimmy were sleeping in the big house, which was destined to get a lot bigger.

The creek was running bank to bank from the spring thaw. He watched a kingfisher dive into the water, disappear, and come out with a tiny trout. The bird flew back up to its perch, devouring the trout and watching the stream for more. A shadow passed over him. He looked up to see a red-tailed hawk sail by on its daily search for food. Spring was here. Flowers, in a blaze of colors, welcomed the early morning sunshine to the valley.

Callum chuckled at the sound coming from the ranch house. A demanding wail reverberated across the ranch yard, heard even through the thick pine walls. Matthew Conner Logan wanted his breakfast. Josh and Fianna had their hands full.

Josh stepped out into the ranch yard next to Callum. "You heard him?"

Callum laughed and then said, "I reckon they heard him in Pueblo."

The two men stood side by side. They gazed down to the mouth of the canyon, watching the cattle feed on the fresh grass. Fortunately, the winter had been mild. They had lost only a few cattle, and now the calving season was drawing to a close.

"Mighty pretty place," Josh said. "Uncle Floyd did mighty fine."

"Did I hear my name?" Floyd asked. He walked out of the barn and joined his two nephews. "Callum, you ready to leave?"

Callum nodded. "Yep. I want to get back to Tennessee and get the family loaded up and started back. Should put us here no later than the end of September." He looked over at the wagon, horses hitched and the cover rippling in the morning breeze. "Sarah and Jimmy loaded up?"

"Appears so," Floyd said. "I figger we'll travel with you to Pueblo. Then we'll turn north up to Denver and pick up a wagon train headed to Salt Lake."

Fianna walked out onto the porch carrying Matt. He was quiet now, taking in every new sight, sound, and smell. Josh put his arm around Fianna and reached his hand out to Matt, who grabbed his big finger in a tiny hand.

The woman he loved leaned against his chest. "It is wonderful country." She turned her head toward Floyd, her green eyes brilliant in the morning sun. "Thank you, Floyd. This is a lovely place."

He looked out across the valley to the Greenhorn Mountains. "I knew this valley had the Logan name on it from the first time I saw it."

"When do you think you'll be back?" Fianna said.

"Can't rightly say. After gettin' Sarah and Jimmy settled in Salt

Lake, I may mosey on down to Arizona. Been a while since I seen the White Mountains. Mighty pretty country. Much like this."

"We'll miss you," Fianna said.

Floyd picked up a big pine cone, looked at it for a moment, and tossed it farther out into the pasture. "Time passes fast, Missy. Before you know it, I'll be puttin' my big feet under your dinner table again."

Callum's thoughts drifted to Alex. After getting back from Denver, he had taken the gold to the Lopez ranch. He was relieved to see Alex and some of his vaqueros galloping out to meet him. Callum spent several days on the ranch. Come to find out, Alex had been trailing the caravan by several miles. When he heard the shots, he raced forward, but his horse stepped in a hole. He'd sailed over his mount's head and was knocked unconscious. By the time he reached the others, they were all dead. Alex hung on Callum's every word when he told about bringing the Wister Gang to justice.

From Alex, Callum's thoughts turned to Naomi. She was now living in Denver and doing quite well. She had insisted that Callum take Asa's share of the strike. He had refused, but she would not take no for an answer. Once they were legally partners, she sold the gold claim. With the rich ore that they had brought out, she got a price that guaranteed she would never have to worry about money again, and the Logan clan would have money to expand their cattle operation. Before they had parted, she elicited a promise from Callum that anytime he was in Denver, he would look her up. It wasn't hard for him to agree to that. Maybe someday . . .

Jeb rode in from down the canyon with Jake and Jimmy Leads. The three men rode their mounts to the water trough by the corral, dismounted, tied them, and walked back to the trio on the porch.

Josh had hired Jeb on full-time. He had said since Jeb was already working on the ranch he might as well get paid for it. It looked like Jeb had found a home. When Scott Penny and Jack Swindell headed back to Texas, Jimmy Leads had decided to stay on.

Sarah and little Jimmy, who was no longer little, walked out of the ranch house at the same time. "We're ready," Jimmy said.

Callum looked down at the boy. The now eleven-year-old looked much different than he had when Callum first met him on the plains. His shoulders were wider and he had put on more weight but hadn't lost his exuberance. Callum knew he would miss him. "Jimmy, would you get our horses and pack mules from the barn?"

"Yes, sir," Jimmy said, and dashed to the barn. A few moments later he came out leading Floyd's horse, Shoshone, and a loaded pack mule for each of them. He led them to the hitching rail in front of the house and looped the reins over the rail.

Callum turned to Josh. "We're burning daylight, Brother. We best be on our way. I'll see you in about six months."

"We'll be waiting," Josh said. The two men shook hands.

Callum leaned over and gave Fianna a hug. "Take care of that big galoot."

She smiled up at her brother-in-law. "You take care of yourself."

After shaking Josh's hand, Floyd stepped up to give Fianna a hug. "You don't have to worry about Callum. Just remember the Shoshone medicine man. He said no bullet would ever touch him. After all that shooting with the Wister Gang, durned if I'm not starting to believe it."

The men shook hands all around.

Sarah hugged Fianna. Through their smiles, tears ran down both women's cheeks. They spoke quietly for a moment. Sarah gave Josh a quick hug and rushed to the wagon.

Jimmy climbed up to the seat and waved as the wagon pulled out. Floyd and Callum swung up into their saddles. With the pack mules in tow, they rode alongside the wagon, toward the valley.

Before they turned south, out of the canyon and into the valley, Callum pulled Shoshone up. He looked back up the canyon at the people standing in the front yard of the ranch. His mind drifted. It had been almost a year since he and Josh had separated in Nashville. Good and bad men had died in that time, but life went on. He took one last look at his brother, sister-in-law, and nephew—a new Logan. In a few months, he would be back with all of the family. Callum waved his hat in one big sweep, spun Shoshone around, and galloped to catch up with Floyd, Sarah, and Jimmy.

Tennessee, here I come!

AUTHOR'S NOTE

Thank you for reading *The Savage Valley,* second in the Logan Family Series. If you enjoyed this book, check out the third book in the series, *Callum's Mission.*

I would love to hear your comments. You can reach me at: don@donaldlrobertson.com.

There will be no graphic sex scenes or offensive language in my books.

Join our readers' group to receive advance notices of new releases, short stories, or excerpts from new stories:

www.donaldlrobertson.com.

I'm sure you detest spam as much as I do. Your information will remain private and will not be shared.

ACKNOWLEDGEMENTS

Completed books are a team project. I'd like to take a moment and thank those involved in bringing this book to you.

First, in all of my writing projects, is my lovely wife, Paula. Yes, she is my cheerleader, but she is more. She is the first to read my book or short story and offer insightful suggestions and recommendations. She also, thank goodness, takes care of all of the marketing, for which my gratitude is boundless.

Huge thanks go to my editor, Melissa Gray. I can only say that she must have the patience of Job. She has an eye for errors, and my books provide her a fertile landscape.

I'm sure you're familiar with, "You can't judge a book by its cover." You may not be able to judge it, but I can assure you a striking cover attracts more readers. Thank you, Elizabeth Mackey for my great cover.

BOOKS

Logan Mountain Man Series

(Prequel to Logan Family Series)

SOUL OF A MOUNTAIN MAN

TRIALS OF A MOUNTAIN MAN

METTLE OF A MOUNTAIN MAN

Logan Family Series

LOGAN'S WORD

THE SAVAGE VALLEY

CALLUM'S MISSION

FORGOTTEN SEASON

Clay Barlow - Texas Ranger Justice Series

FORTY-FOUR CALIBER JUSTICE

LAW AND JUSTICE

LONESOME JUSTICE

NOVELLAS AND SHORT STORIES

RUSTLERS IN THE SAGE

BECAUSE OF A DOG

THE OLD RANGER

Made in the USA
Las Vegas, NV
06 March 2023